A Divided Kingdom

A wildly captivating book that invites you into a vivid, familiar, yet uniquely created world.

Akhil Rampersadh

The plot is tightly woven and seamless, devoid of any inconsistencies. Each character is given a solid background. This is a very good read!

Lavhelesani Mamphwe

Interestingly brilliant accounts of one's imagination, feels amazingly real.

Imran Fakir

A sublime exploration into African lore, "A Divided Kingdom" is a trailblazer within the fantasy genre and enchants within its intricately crafted narrative.

Michael Parker-Nance

A Divided Kingdom from the book series

The War of Rain and Thunder

Book one

To my family, friends and everyone who believed in this book,

thank you.

Emeka: Brother, thank you so much for your support. I am so blessed that our path crossed. May God continue to bless you and your family. Mulanga & Myself are so lucky to have met you. We truly love you and Steph so Much!

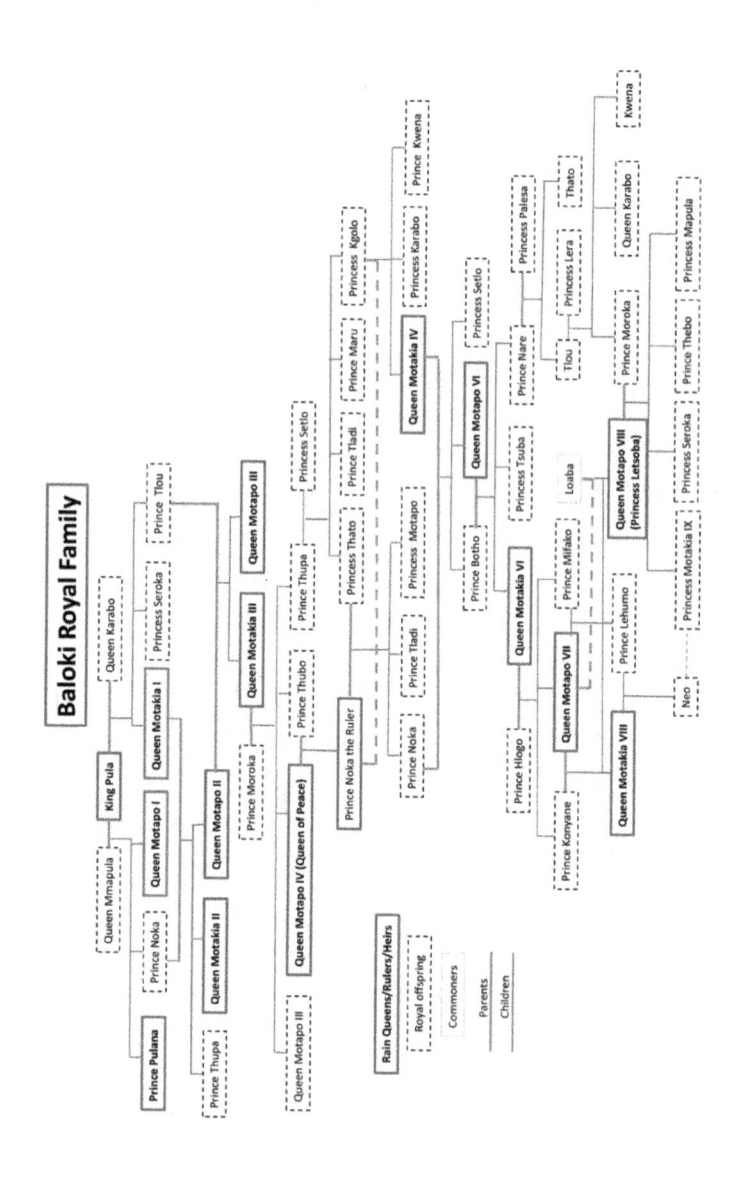

A Divided Kingdom

Baloki Royal Family

- Queen Mmapula
- King Pula — Queen Karabo
  - Queen Motapo I
  - Queen Motakia I — Prince Tlou / Princess Seroka
- Prince Noka
  - Queen Motakia II
  - Queen Motapo II — Prince Moroka
    - Queen Motakia III
    - Queen Motapo III — Princess Setlo / Prince Tlou
- Prince Pulana
  - Prince Thupa
  - Queen Motapo IV (Queen of Peace) — Prince Thubo / Prince Thupa / Princess Thato / Prince Tladi / Prince Maru / Princess Kgolo / Princess Karabo / Prince Kwena
    - Queen Motakia III
    - Prince Noka the Ruler
      - Prince Noka / Princess Motapo / Princess Tladi
      - Queen Motapo VI — Princess Tsuba / Princess Setlo / Princess Palesa / Prince Nare / Princess Lera / Tlou / Thato
        - Queen Motakia VI
        - Prince Botho
        - Prince Mifako
          - Queen Motakia VII — Loaba
            - Queen Motakia VIII
            - Prince Hlogo
            - Prince Konyane
            - Prince Lehumo
              - Princess Motakia IX / Queen Motapo VIII (Princess Letsoba) — Prince Moroka / Princess Seroka / Prince Thebo / Princess Mapula / Queen Karabo / Kwena
              - Neo

Rain Queens/Rulers/Heirs
- Royal offspring
- Commoners
- Parents
- Children

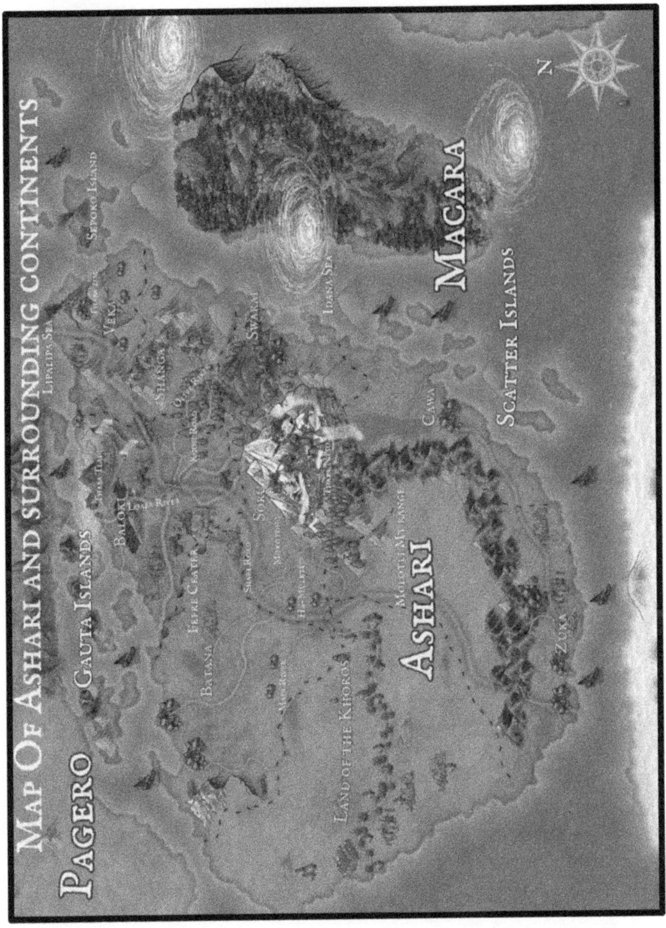
Map Of Ashari and Surrounding Continents
Pagero
Gauta Islands
Ashari
Macara
Scatter Islands
N

A Divided Kingdom

Prologue

The resonant beats of the ceremonial drums echoed for at least ten leagues in the hush of the night, while the dancers and villagers worshiped their Rain Queen. Lightning lit up the dark skies, shining with such radiance that it surpassed even the full moon, dimmed behind veiling clouds. The echoes of thunder, which were believed to be the drums of the rain gods, filled the entire village, a good omen to show that the rain gods were pleased with the ceremony.

"I told you we were going to be late," said Muse, one of the two maidens running up the relatively hilly Thaba Tladi to join the rest of the villagers in the rainmaking ceremony. Despite the chill, the two maidens were arrayed in their customary Baloki attire, consisting of reeds and grass painted in red, which did cover their heads and hindquarters, leaving their bosoms bare. These reeds were donned only for the rainmaking ceremony.

The villagers sang in unison, *"Motapo, wena metse, mmapula."* (Motapo, you are our water, mother of rain.)

"She is far to look upon. Can you see her?" said Pelo, the other maiden. Despite her tall and svelte stature, she could barely see past the crowd that was in front of them. She struggled to walk in the ill-fitting reeds and grass that draped her form, but her mother had insisted that she attend the ceremony in her traditional raiment. From where they stood, they could scarcely see the Rain Queen, who was wearing all white, suspended in the air, surrounded by a cloud of fog.

"Let us get closer," Pelo insisted.

The two maidens pushed their way through until they spotted a place among the crowd where they were able to join in the chanting. Pelo quipped, "My... my father told me that the queen's spirit lives in our land and is connected to all living creatures and streams in Baloki."

"And my mother told me that she draws her powers from her people, and the greater our faith in her, the mightier her power," Muse responded.

"Hush, and sing ye heart out, for your queen needs you," said one of the elder women in the crowd. The woman's face was long, with silvered hair and bloodshot eyes, which seemed to have frightened the maidens.

"Motapo, wena metse, mmapula," the chants continued in unison.

Queen Motapo was a member of a long lineage of rainmaking queens of the Baloki Tribe, which had endured for over ten generations. The ceremony of rainmaking was commonly conducted at night, during the full moon, and would often last until midnight.

"No matter how many times you witness this, it is always a wondrous sight to behold," said Prince Moroka, the queen's cousin, and father of her four offspring.

The queen was prohibited from marrying a man and could only "wed" those known as sister wives. The council chose these sister wives to look after the queen's every need. The selection of these maidens was primarily political, with the goal of strengthening the royal bond with the most influential noble houses in the kingdom.

Every year, the heads of these noble houses presented their daughters during the marriage ceremony, hoping that their daughter would be chosen to serve the queen. In Baloki, this was considered a most noble and high honour for a maiden. And lo, the noble houses desired the reward that came with their daughters being chosen as well.

Queen Motapo VIII, on the other hand, loved her cousin and, though not official, she considered Prince Moroka her husband in every way. According to the traditional laws, only a queen could rule the Baloki Kingdom. In addition, the laws made it impossible for a male heir or anyone not from the queen's bloodline to claim the throne or have any say in who would occupy it. In the rare occasions a clear heir was not found, the task was left to the royal council and the high priest to decide on who their next Rain Queen would be.

An ancient prophecy, which the common folk deemed to be olden lore, does forewarn that upon the day a king is crowned in Baloki, a great drought will ravage the land. However, apart from Prince Noka the Ruler, there has been no male heir in recent memory. Therefore, the truth of the prophecy has not been tested, but nevertheless, Baloki has not crowned a king since its founding father, King Pula.

Prince Moroka was a handsome man, who in his early forties was with partly grey hair, which he kept short, because his hairline had begun to recede. He was of towering stature, measuring just over six feet, and possessed a swarthy olive-brown complexion.

"Yes, Father, Mother looks fair today. I do wish I was more like her. She is very beautiful," said Princess Seroka, second in line to the matrilineal throne.

"Truly, both Mother and Motakia are fair," continued the princess with a doleful gaze. "I wish … I was like them."

Princess Seroka was a comely maid, albeit with an uncommon beauty that many might not perceive.

She was of a towering stature for a damsel, and her voice had a slightly deeper tone. From a young age, her training in the army had forged her with a brawny frame and distinct features that stood out on her sable skin tone.

Yet, despite all of these, Princess Seroka was very feminine and would occasionally wear flowers on her head, which gained her the nickname the 'Flower Thorn' amongst the common folks.

Prince Moroka grasped her palm with a firm grip.

"My beautiful daughter, we are all endowed with numerous talents. You've done things that surpass those of your sister and mother. You are the commander of our army."

In response, the princess gave a faint smile and grasped her father's hand, as she did when she was younger.

"I have seen you fight. Very few people could come out alive from one-on-one combat with you." Prince Moroka comforted his daughter with a reassuring smile on his face.

"When your sister shall ascend to the throne, her power to summon the rain shall be matched only by the reverence and devotion of her subjects. Just as your mother, grandmother, and great-grandmother were honoured before her."

"But Father, what use is my strength if I am not to inherit the mantle of the Rain Queen?" Princess Seroka enquired in a hushed tone, ensuring that no ears but her father's might catch her words.

"That is true, but do you know who will be there to protect your sister and make sure she keeps her throne?" the prince asked, pointing to Princess Seroka, and giving her a wink.

"Seroka, your hand shall hold the reins of this kingdom. A darkness is approaching, and you, my dearest, will play a substantial part in this coming war. I swear by my forefathers, history will sing the praises of your name," said the prince with sadness in his eyes.

With a troubled expression, Prince Moroka surveyed the crowd. "Please tell me, where are your brother and sister?" he asked.

"I don't know. Wherever they are, it is not good. They are probably setting someone's hut on fire," the princess remarked with a careless shrug.

As the prince surveyed his surroundings, a man in distress appeared before him, his face twisted with urgency. The man whispered something in Prince Moroka's ear, causing his face to appear puzzled.

Without a moment's hesitation, the prince and the messenger vanished from sight, leaving behind bewildered Seroka. "Find them," were his final words before disappearing into the crowd of people.

War Is Coming

Not too far from the rainmaking ceremony, Prince Thebo and Princess Mapula were embroiled in yet another heated argument. As always, the youngest member of the royal family was quick to place the blame on her brother.

"I told you we were going to get lost," she fumed, her voice rising with each passing word. "And now, thanks to you, we are late!"

"Catch me if you can!" The young prince sprinted ahead of the princess.

"Wait for me!" Mapula shouted as she tried to catch up to her brother.

Though her brother was a summer and two seasons her senior, the young princess held a higher rank in the succession line, a fact she often reminded her mischievous brother.

As she was about to hasten her steps, loud thunder and dazzling lightning struck, catching the princess off guard. She stumbled upon the path and slipped into a small trench beside the river.

"Ouch, I have broken my ankle!" wailed Princess Mapula, struggling to rise to her feet.

"Thebo, Thebo, help me," she called to no response.

Her brother had run off towards the crowd.

The ditch she had fallen into was most slippery, rendering it hard to climb back to the main road. Now all muddied in her white dress, she looked around and espied what seemed to be a small path, which would allow her to walk around back to join the road.

There was a big rock blocking the small path. The princess, who had sprained her ankle, tried to walk around this rock without slipping again.

As soon as she turned around the rock, she saw two figures who appeared to be in an argument.

"Help me," she called out, but there was no response.

She tried to call for the second time, but seeing how much these two figures were arguing, something inside of her told her to hide.

"Did you hear that?" a voice came out from the riverbank.

The princess moved closer towards a small bush she could hide behind and not draw attention.

"No, I heard nothing. It was probably the rumble of thunder," replied the second figure.

"I know the difference between thunder and a voice. I think I heard a voice calling for help," the first figure said.

The two figures, garbed in black hooded cloaks, spoke in hushed tones, rendering their conversation almost inaudible to Mapula.

"We can never be too careful. When do you plan on telling the queen about the death of the Prince Thubo?" the first figure asked hastily.

"The news shall be delivered on the morrow. My plan is for someone on the council to learn of it anon. I desire not to be too nigh to this affair.

In order for the plan to work, all those in the royal household must trust me without a shadow of a doubt," responded the second figure.

"What news could it be?" pondered Princess Mapula inwardly as she strived to draw even nearer to the whispers of the shadows. The tumult from the lightning and thunder did not ease her task. The rain also compromised her vision, making it hard to discern the identity of the figures. Yet, their comportment spoke volumes, informing her that their discourse was of great import. One of the many teachings the royal children received was that of body language and vigilance, a skill she found of use at this moment.

"Listen to me. We successfully killed Prince Thubo. If the queen does not surrender Baloki to King Shaza, we will have no choice but to remove her by force," said the first figure, in a tone above the rumble of rain and thunder.

"No, grant me more time to work on her. I have found a way to persuade her to surrender her throne without spilling the blood of our people, but I crave more time."

On hearing this, Princess Mapula emitted a gasp that would have carried afar had the night been still.

"Did you hear that? I think someone is watching us. Go quickly. We shall meet again before the meeting of the Keepers, but I promise you, both our heads are on the line if you do not have a plan to convince the queen to surrender the Baloki Kingdom to King Shaza."

"We are the keepers of men," declared the first figure with solemnity, as the second figure added, "The beacon of hope in the shadows of night," before they vanished into the obscurity.

Startled by their words, the princess was spurred to make haste and inform her father. Despite her now-muddied dress and throbbing ankle, she paid no heed to her discomforts and resolved to relay the grave news. *The queen is going to be so mad, but not as mad as Motakia,* she thought.

She shrugged and hoped they will forgive her when they learned what she had to tell them.

Back at the ceremony, Prince Thebo had just joined his sister and was looking around, trying to find Princess Mapula.

"Thebo, where is Mapula? I thought you were coming with her," Princess Seroka wondered.

However, the young prince merely shrugged, offering no explanation.

"She was behind me. Where is father?" Prince Thebo responded, also dressed in a white garment.

Prince Moroka emerged from the crowd and stood next to his children. Yet, before he could utter a word, a dishevelled Mapula appeared, clearly agitated.

"Father, they … they …" She gasped for air, struggling to relay her message.

"Mapula, your sister is not going to be happy at the sight of you in such a state. We shall discuss this further once we return home. At present, we must concentrate on the ceremony," Prince Moroka interjected, determined to maintain his composure amidst the disruption.

"But …"

"Young lady, I said we will talk later," Prince Moroka responded to a frowning Princess Mapula.

"Oh, Motakia is going to kill her." Princess Seroka laughed.

"Motapo, wena metse, mmapula," the chants continued.

This ceremony will make sure there is rain in Baloki for the next two moons. It is a ceremony the queen performs once every two full moons, upon the eve when the orb of night shines in its full glory.

The fog that shrouded the land began to dissipate, signalling the conclusion of the ceremony. All that remains is to offer a bull as a sacrifice to the gods of rain, as a token of gratitude for their benevolence. In ancient times, it was customary to offer a human life, but Queen Motapo IV, who was also known as the Queen of Peace, abolished this practice during her brief reign of a mere decade, before she succumbed during childbirth.

Even though the Rain Queen possesses the power to conjure rain, she is often accompanied by her heir, Princess Motakia, as well as *"moroka wa pula"* (the initiator of rain), a high priest who assists in conducting the rituals. The princess observes the ceremony, preparing herself for the day when she ascends the throne.

Six stout men brought forth a bull, which they struggled to contain. Amongst them was Folo, a portly man in charge of the royal animals and stables.

Folo handed the bull to Selo, the high priest. The bull brought forth was wild and fierce, spurred on by the beat of drums and the chanting of the people. Selo stepped forth to calm the beast.

Selo, a bald, skinny, tall old man, handed Princess Motakia IX a knife.

With grace and poise, the princess presented the queen with a blade known as *tladi* (lightning), a crystal-sharp rock said to have been gifted by the gods to the first Rain Queen. This blade was reserved solely for the sacred rite of rainmaking, its touch as cold as the clouds and its edge as keen as a serpent's tooth.

"Do not look away," the queen whispered to the Heir Princess.

With a swift thrust of his spear, Selo struck the bull at the base of its skull, sending the beast to the earth, lifeless. The queen then proceeded to slide the knife under the bull's head, and quick as lighting, she slit the bull's throat and blood gushed all over her beautiful white dress.

The sight of blood always made Princess Motakia uneasy, but she knew she could not show any sign of weakness if she was to lead her people one day.

She had to show strength and bravery.

Motakia handed a white cloth to her mother so that she could clean her hands.

The chants got louder. *"Motapo, wena metse, mmapula."*

As the chants grew louder still, Selo approached the queen and took the blade from her hand, reverently placing it in a box to be ritually washed and safeguarded until the next ceremony. All was done according to the ancient ways, and the people rejoiced, for they knew that the rains would quench their parched land.

Selo raised his hands, signalling to the crowd that the ceremony was finished.

"Motapo, wena metse, mmapula," he echoed the chants of the crowd.

"The gods have deemed to grant us rainfall till the next two moons. Rejoice and gather your crops, feed your animals, and let prosperity flourish in our land!" Selo addressed the villagers, who beat their drums and ululated in unbridled jubilation, making way for their queen to descend from the sacred hill, Thaba Tladi.

"Motakia, my daughter, I am getting old now. Soon it will be you performing these ceremonies," the queen said to the princess, who was still helping her wipe off the blood from her hands and face.

Queen Motapo was renowned for her beauty, tall and slender, with high cheekbones, a fair complexion, and long braided hair cascading down her back.

"Mother, you still have many summers ahead of you. I am grateful to stand by your side and learn from you."

The queen sighed. "I never desired this throne. The burden of this crown has weighed heavily upon me, but I am confident that you shall make a better queen than I have. You were born for this," Queen Motapo confided in her daughter.

Rain Queens would either be named Motapo or Motakia; the two names would alternate between the reigning queen and her successor.

Princess Motakia did not relish the thought of her mother abdicating the throne. She knew full well that such an event would signify her mother's passing, either of natural causes or by ritual suicide.

The latter was very common amongst the queens, when they were tired or just wanted an out in order to make way for the younger successor. The thought of becoming queen herself, and the means by which such an honour would come to her, weighed heavily upon the princess.

She shuddered to think of a world without her beloved mother. The crowd fell silent as the queen descended the ceremonial Thaba Tladi, whispers following her. "She is beautiful, she is elegant," the murmurs rose.

Even in her advanced years, the queen's beauty was a sight to behold. And her daughter, Motakia, was the very image of her mother's splendour.

The queen and her daughter made their way to the foot of Thaba Tladi, pausing a moment before proceeding to the queen's hut, located near the tranquil Loaba River.

Thaba Tladi stood tall on the royal grounds, soaring to a height of at least fifty meters whilst facing the mighty Loaba River. Upon the exposed cliff beneath the hill facing the river, ancient inscriptions were written in crimson.

Though the meaning of these inscriptions had been lost to the ages, legend had it that the words etched upon the hill read, "Drown to be reborn, die to live."

For many generations, these inscriptions remained, for as long as any soul could recall. It had also been whispered that the queen's power was at its apex whilst standing upon this hill, where she would have complete dominion over the rains and rivers.

Whilst the queen was often carried down the ceremonial Thaba Tladi by her sister wives, tonight she had insisted on descending the hill on foot.

"I have been having disturbing dreams of late," said the queen, coming to a halt far from the gathering throng. She felt safe from prying eyes now that she was near her hut. The royal huts were all beside the Loaba River's banks.

As the queen was about to continue explaining her dream to Motakia, they saw a limping Mapula running towards them, covered in mud, and visibly upset.

"Mother, I must speak with you at once!" the young princess shouted.

"What has happened to you?" Princess Motakia asked, as they entered the queen's hut.

The hut had a red thatched roof and black walls covered with ancient inscriptions in red around it. Inside it was draped in white and gold linen, with a fire that was kept alight in the middle.

"It is none of your concern," Mapula replied. "Father refused to listen to me. I had to come to you at once, Mother."

"Can this wait until the morrow?" the queen asked.

"How could you do this during the ceremony? I swear by the rain gods, I do not want you anywhere near me when I become queen. You always ruin everything," Princess Motakia scolded Mapula for her appearance. The two princesses were never in agreement.

Princess Motakia was a refined and poised lady, fit to be queen, whereas Mapula was adventurous, curious, and uninterested in rules. Whenever there was trouble in the royal house, Mapula always seemed to be involved, and her mischief often drew in the young prince.

"No, Mother, this is important," replied Princess Mapula with more urgency in her tone.

Princess Seroka, Prince Thebo, and Prince Moroka entered the queen's hut, just as Mapula was about to explain her story.

"How was the ceremony?" Prince Moroka, who was also the royal mage, asked.

Although the royal males did not have the ability to control rain, they still possessed some magical ability. Most of the young men would be trained to be royal mages, a responsibility that Prince Moroka had taken on when his cousin, Queen Motapo, was coronated.

The royal house descended from an ancient line of people who practiced magic. Most of the people in the royal line had magical ability of some sort; however, those abilities were poorly developed. Most people lived their entire lives without having manifested any magical potential. However, the firstborn son was trained in the highest level of sorcery to serve as a royal mage.

"So, no one here wants to hear what I have to say!" Princess Mapula shouted furiously.

"No need to shout, my dear child. We can all hear you. What is it that you want to tell us?" the queen asked.

"Mother, Father, I saw two men during the ceremony tonight. I could not make out their voices or faces, but they are conspiring to kill you, Mother. I heard them. I heard them with my own ears," Princess Mapula said, with a crack in her voice and almost sobbing.

Everyone in the room was shocked by this news.

"Are you certain of what you heard? Have you shared this news with anyone?" the prince enquired; his face fraught with concern.

"Do you know who said this? 'Tis a treacherous talk, and I shall have their heads on a spike!" Princess Seroka exclaimed.

"No, I wished to tell you earlier, but you did not listen. The men spoke of turning the queen, King Shaza, and death …" Mapula replied ere Prince Moroka interrupted her.

"Where did you hear this?"

"I fell into a ditch next to the river."

"Aye, that explains the mud," the queen remarked.

"You heard all this through the rain and thunder?

And these men did not see you? Sister, you love attention," Princess Motakia said, almost dismissing the young princess.

"Mother, Motakia thinks I am lying," the young princess protested. "I hate her."

"Children, stop it!" the queen ordered.

"I am not a child anymore. I am almost twelve," the young princess proudly declared.

"Oh, twelve! A grand age, indeed," Princess Motakia said mockingly.

"I swear, I hope on the day of your coronation, when you try to summon rain, it does not fall," the young princess retorted.

"Mother!" Princess Motakia exclaimed.

"Stop it, you two! What is wrong with you? I am tired of your bickering," said Princess Seroka, who always found herself as the peacemaker between Princess Motakia and Mapula.

Though Princess Mapula took the matter seriously, the rest of her family did not heed her concerns.

"My daughter, let us steer our talk in another direction," said Prince Moroka, his voice heavy with grief. "I have just spoken with Mamba, and he has told me that the heir prince of Soru has passed away in an accident. He has not shared the particulars, but I am certain that he will impart the news to the council on the morrow."

"What?" Princess Seroka cried out, taken aback, and bewildered by the news.

Upon realising the truth of her father's words, she could not hold back her tears. "Are you certain, Father?" she asked.

"Yes, child. I believe he fell from his horse. As I said before, Mamba and Morena Seriti will acquaint us with further details on the morrow."

The princess could not fathom that Thubo, who she knew to be the finest rider she had ever seen, could have met such a fate. She and the late prince had grown close during his two-summers apprenticeship at Baloki, and she had even been proposed to by him. But she knew that it could not be, as she was committed to leading the army and he was bound to ascend to his father's throne. Abdicating his rightful place was not an option.

"Are you certain?" Princess Seroka asked once more, tears streaming down her face.

"Your lover is dead," quipped Prince Thebo, known for his lack of tact and poor timing.

The young prince and Princess Seroka had never seen eye to eye.

"Thebo, stop your jesting! This is not the time nor place for such words," admonished the queen, while Princess Motakia did her best to comfort her grieving sister.

"Did he really fall from his horse?" Princess Motakia asked.

"We should have more information on the morrow, as this news spread like wildfire. In the meantime, remember, we are a family, and we should stick together, no matter what," Prince Moroka responded.

"This was no accident. The labour pains of what's to come have just begun, and I fear it comes for this family too. Remember, a house that is divided amongst itself cannot stand against its enemies. The seven of us in this room are blood, and we are to protect one another," the queen said.

"And I am talking to you too, Neo. You are as much part of the royal family as this lot," the queen said, looking at Neo, who as usual was standing in a corner, silently observing, and listening to what everyone was saying. "War is coming," she cautioned.

Justice Has Been Served

"My son, my heir, my own pride and joy has been slain! All who had a hand in this shall face a fate more dire than death!" said King Shadu to his council in wrath.

"Your Highness, we have captured all who worked on the prince's horse on the day he died. They shall face execution this very day," responded Sedi, the right-hand woman of the king.

Sedi was a tall, slender, cold, and emotionless woman, with high cheekbones and bronze skin tone, known to the common folk as the Black Widow - a name none dared utter in her presence. Her three husbands had all died under mysterious circumstances, and with each death, she had inherited a great fortune, making her one of the wealthiest persons in Soru.

During times that are now lost us, the Soru and the Baloki kingdoms, together with the Batana Kingdom were a single tribe, which migrated south of the Lipalipa Sea from the north. It is said that, in those times, the sea had not yet formed, and the continent was still one. Soon after they settled, the tribe grew too large for the available resources. As a result, the three noble houses agreed to split and formed three separate tribes: the Soru, who migrated south, the Baloki, who remained in the north, and the Batana, who chose the west. The Soru and Baloki tribes remained close allies, while the Batanas were often unreliable and were alienated from the other two tribes due to their practice of dark magic and cannibalism.

Sedi had one son, but very little was known about him or about Sedi's personal life; she lived very privately. Being of low birth, she did strive her way up to her current position, and even without the fortunes of her marriages, she would have reached it by some other means. She was full of ambition and great cunning, albeit at times too much so. She had served on the king's council for seven summers, taking the place of her late husband, who was the king's right-hand man.

"Well said, well said!" the king, seated upon his aqua-blue granite throne, said with a smirking countenance. "I bid you to set an example, that all may see what befalls those who dare to conspire against my family or the throne. I do not desire a swift demise for them, no, I wish them all to suffer."

The king had six wives and twenty-three children. The line of succession was through his first wife, who hailed from a royal bloodline.

With the exception of the Baloki Tribe, like all the other tribes south of the Lipalipa Sea, the monarchies were patriarchal and favoured males in the line of succession. Queen Karabo, the king's first wife, was of the Baloki Tribe, sister to Prince Moroka. It was not uncommon for inter-tribal marriages to take place, especially in royal families, to strengthen alliances between tribes.

The Soru and Baloki people considered each other cousins, with the latter dwelling in the lush greenery of the northern lands and the Sorus abiding in the high topographical lands of the southern regions.

The Sorus, also known as the horsemen, did reside atop craggy mountains that were bitterly cold and oft-times shrouded in snow.

Although they were not renowned for their prowess in battle, their mountainous abodes proved to be a formidable defence against any who dared intrude upon their lands. What they lacked in physical strength, they compensated for with their craftiness and tactical acumen.

Their ability to acclimate to the frigid heights did grant them the upper hand over any would-be aggressors, for they could defeat their enemies without ever engaging in direct combat. Soru people were generally of a pallid complexion, tall and lean of frame, as their diet was restricted to what meagre crops they could cultivate within their rocky terrain. The craggy mountains did make it challenging to grow anything, thus Soru Kingdom imported much of their sustenance from Baloki. Of the Molotli Mountain Range, Thaba Ntsu was deemed the most treacherous to traverse, for it was there the royal grounds did lay.

The royal grounds were situated in a prime location, on a flat terrain within Thaba Ntsu, affording a clear view of the kingdom in its entirety.

"Your Highness," said Sedi, "we have assigned two guards to watch over Prince Tlou, Princess Palesa, and Prince Maru. The council deems it necessary for you and your heirs to be guarded because you are still in danger," to which she received assent from the other members of the council.

King Shadu had borne three sons and two daughters from his first wife, Queen Karabo. However, the queen passed away whilst giving birth to her youngest son, Prince Maru. The king loved Queen Karabo so greatly that he could not recover from her passing. He often professed that she was the love of his life and that every subsequent wife he took was but for political gain. The king would oftentimes be discovered in a garden, wherein he had erected a statue of his beloved queen. To this very day, women and children sing songs of her beauty and grace.

During this period of sorrow, the king wished his dearest wife were still amongst the living. She always knew the right words to say and was a calming influence during his turbulent moments.

The queen and her brother were the sole individuals who truly comprehended the heart of King Shadu.

He yearned for his brother-in-law's company to aid him in his time of grieving. He had never truly confided in anyone, not even his five wives. The king was a stern man, fiercely proud, and barely communicated with some of his wives and children.

"Let them dare to try! Let them dare to come and try to finish the job. I shall be prepared," King Shadu bellowed in fury.

The cheers of the crowd echoed loudly, resounding from the throne room.

The throne room, which sat upon a cliff, was a thatched hut, adorned in the aqua blue colours of the Soru people, with a blood-red door.

"Your Highness, I do believe the people are ready to witness the judgement of the gods," Sedi said. "If it be your pleasure, follow me."

The council, led by Sedi, walked forth into the open courtyard, where all who were accused of the murder of the heir prince were held.

The king, garbed in mourning attire, took his seat under a heavily guarded thatched open hut, with a full view of where the accused men stood.

Sedi stood on the king's right hand, and the late prince's widow, Princess Palesa, sat upon his left, upon the seat formerly occupied by her late husband.

The princess was wearing *seana morena,* a thickly woven blanket of the deepest black, with a thin satin veil draped over her head. Above all others in the kingdom, Princess Palesa harboured an unquenchable desire for retribution against the one who had taken her husband's life. Though she was consumed with grief and anguish, her thirst for vengeance outmatched all else. Removing her veil, she gazed unflinchingly upon the accused men, hoping to impress upon them her fury and, more importantly, her utter lack of fear, as she hungered for their blood.

Then Sedi stepped forth.

"I believe we are all aware of the heinous charges levied against these men who now stand afore us. They have committed the gravest form of betrayal against our fair kingdom, and this shall not go unavenged," she said in a commanding voice.

"Let this serve as a reminder and example to all in Soru of the punishment that shall befall those who conspire against the throne.

By the blessing of the king, the council has decreed that their sentence shall be death without trial," she continued.

The crowd gasped.

"Your trial shall be *mudupa*, a fight to the death, and the victor shall be declared innocent before the eyes of the mountain gods," she declared in her resolute and daunting tone.

"*Modupa, modupa*" the crowd shouted over and over again.

The king lifted his hand, beckoning them to cease. "You," pointing at Kara, one of his guards, "pour me another ale," declared the king, who had imbibed too much.

"The drinking has worsened," Perega, one of the king's councillors whispered to Gasane, the royal mage.

"We can only hope it is not half as dire as when the queen passed," Gasane replied in his trembling old voice.

"You may choose any weapon you wish, but choose wisely, for it shall determine your fate in front of the gods, who will decide whether you are guilty or innocent," Sedi stated, devoid of any emotion.

Among those being sentenced were the slain prince's squire, spearman, groom, and cup bearer.

The cup bearer, a lad of twelve named Bohlale, had a father who had saved one of the king's daughters when she was attacked by a bull near a river. To express his gratitude, the king had enquired of Bohlale's father what he desired. He humbly asked the king to accept his son and make him an apprentice in the royal court.

The king thought it would be fitting for the boy to be a cupbearer, to express his heartfelt appreciation to Bohlale's father. Yet, on this day, the king saw not a youngling, but only one who may have slain his heir. The father of Bohlale did beseech the king's mercy for his only son and reminded him of how he had saved the king's daughter. The king's reply was that the gods are merciful and that if Bohlale were innocent, the gods would deliver him. Yet, the king was not a very religious man and had little faith in the gods.

"Our king is a merciful and munificent man," said Sedi, as she took her seat next to the king.

"He granted you three sunsets to produce the true culprit responsible for the death of the prince, and none of you are willing to speak. Your fate shall be determined by the gods, and so let the *modupa* begin."

Each man was given a choice of a spear, hammer, sword, and shield. With weapons in hand, the four men cast wary glances upon each other, uncertain of who should make the initial strike.

Lukobo took a step forward towards Bohlale, who was crippled with fear, even to the point of wetting himself. The young boy had ne'er before fought with a real sword, only a wooden sword when sparring with his peers.

Upon seeing this, Lukobo was reminded of his own son, who was of like age. He looked 'round and saw that the crowd was cheering loudly, almost drowning out the sound of the drums playing.

Then, at that very moment, when he looked at Bohlale, somehow the world stood still. All became silent, and he could hear naught but his own heart beating and feel every breath he took.

Suddenly, he heard screams coming towards him. It was Murule, the spearman of the late prince.

Murule was the most skilled warrior of all present, a man in his mid-twenties, lean but strong in build.

Murule tried to thrust his spear towards Lukobo, but alas, his attempt was futile. Though Lukobo was not a skilled warrior, tending to the horses had allowed him to be in the company of the late prince during his combat practice.

That was a close call, Lukobo thought to himself. As he was trying to collect himself, he could see from the corner of his eye that Bohlale stood motionless. Behind Murule stood Naka, the squire of the slain prince, who was in his late teens and was training to be one of the royal guards.

Lukobo thought of his son, his wife, and his little daughter. *I must live for them*, he contemplated. He regained his footing and assumed a defensive stance.

The crowd cheered on.

"My wager is on the squire," said Leko, the late prince's half-sister.

"I think the groom is innocent; the gods shall show him favour," answered Prince Tlou.

"Gasane has told me that all are guilty, and the gods must decide who they shall chasten the least," added Prince Maru.

"No one spoke to you, young prince," retorted Prince Tlou. The two princes bore enmity towards each other, so much so that they refrained from speaking for almost two summers at one point.

In truth, after the passing of Queen Karabo, Prince Tlou, who was four summers at the time, refused to lay eyes upon his newborn brother. He was angry that this child had taken his cherished mother away from him.

Prince Maru, the youngest offspring of Queen Karabo, had never beheld his mother, for she had breathed her last whilst giving birth to him. The young prince bore the burden of this dark cloud throughout his existence. Though his siblings never uttered it aloud, they blamed him for their mother's demise. The king also held his son accountable for his wife's death, but he never uttered a word. Nevertheless, Prince Maru could feel it; his father's gaze was sometimes icy towards him.

In the arena, Bohlale began to cry out with great sorrow.

"Be silent," Naka, who had a strong build for his age shouted, as he hurled his spear towards Bohlale. And with one single cast, the spear pierced through the side of Bohlale's head.

There was a moment of silence before the crowd erupted with cheers once more.

Lukobo took a deep breath, but then suddenly, both Murule and Naka charged at him.

A mere week ago, these three men were drinking together as friends, but now they sought to take each other's lives.

Lukobo stood his ground to face Murule and Naka. He dodged a spear that Murule nearly thrust into his stomach.

Lukobo glanced at the lifeless body of Bohlale and quickly went to take the sword that was still clutched in the young boy's hand.

The two men began to pace around Lukobo, to the delight of the crowd.

Lukobo stood firm and observed them with great care.

Naka charged again with his spear, but this time Lukobo manoeuvred himself in such a way that he was able to strike at Naka. Lukobo's sword made contact with Naka's chest, yet not enough to bring about fatal harm.

Naka smirked, "Old man, you believe that you shall emerge from this alive? Murule, let us put an end to this."

The three men clashed, with both Naka and Murule attacking Lukobo, who held his ground.

It was a fierce battle, metal clashing against metal. None of these men were skilled warriors, but they provided the audience with a magnificent spectacle.

Murule struck Lukobo with a mighty blow to the head, causing him to plummet to the ground. Naka then advanced with his spear to deliver the fatal strike, but Lukobo quickly regained his senses and deftly evaded the attack. He lifted his sword and plunged it into Naka's chest, to the great delight of the assembled crowd.

The crowd roared with approval, but Lukobo soon realised that his fall had left him with a broken ankle. Though he was in great agony, he seized Naka's spear, which lay just a few paces from Naka's body.

"I did not do it!" he cried out. "I did not slay the prince!"

The crowd jeered at his words.

"Nor did I," Murule replied. "We have been falsely accused, and there is no escape from this fate."

With that, the two men charged at each other, their weapons clashing in a shower of sparks.

Although Murule was smaller, he fought with great skill, and when he saw that he was losing ground, he grabbed a handful of soil from the ground and hurled it into Lukobo's eyes. Momentarily blinded, Lukobo was struck a fierce blow to the head, and before he could regain his footing, Murule thrust his spear into Lukobo's chest, ending the fight.

"I am truly sorry," Murule said, standing over Lukobo's lifeless body. "I swear to avenge your death, my brother."

The crowd fell silent for a few moments but then erupted in a joyous cheer. Masega, the high priestess standing high, raised her hand and spoke in a solemn voice. "I speak on behalf of the mountain gods," she said. "After a fierce modupa, the gods have found Murule innocent. He is now a free man."

Princess Palesa whispered something to the king's ear, and he nodded. She stood up fiercely and left. The crowd cheered even louder, shouting, "Murule, Murule!"

"Very anticlimactic," Prince Tlou whispered to Leko.

Bohlale's father ran into the battlefield and fell on his boy's body, crying uncontrollably. "He was just a boy; he did not do this."

"I hate it when the family cries, it is pathetic," Leko said to Prince Tlou.

The young Prince Maru, who was sitting next to them, was visibly sad. He had played on the royal grounds with Bohlale. He tried his best to not shed a tear.

"Well then, justice has been served," said Gasane, who was wearing a dark purple *seana morena*.

"Has it now?" Perega said, excusing himself and following after Princess Palesa.

The Mountains Are Calling

"We shall set forth for the funeral once all have partaken of their daybreak meal. If the rain gods favour us, we should arrive in three to four sunsets," Prince Moroka said to the queen.

He rose from his seat and moved carefully towards the fire, where flames danced in the heart of the hut. There, amidst the flickering light and crackling embers, he stood in solemn contemplation.

"I think 'tis wise for Motakia to accompany me to the funeral and present herself as our kingdom's future queen," he declared.

The queen appeared deeply troubled by the notion of Motakia leaving Baloki. "I think it is unwise for her to join you, for these are treacherous times.

Like flies, monarchs are falling. 'Tis the third royal funeral in the last few moons. She should stay here in Baloki, where I know she will be safe."

"She is the future queen, she will never be safe, you know this," the prince responded.

"I cannot have two of my most trusted people away from Baloki," the queen continued, unhappy with Prince Moroka. "I believe 'tis better for you to take Mapula with, as she is one for adventure. I am sure she will relish the expedition."

"But …"

"It was not a question."

"As you command," the prince responded and gave the queen a nod of respect. Queen Motapo and Prince Moroka had four children. The eldest, and heir to the throne, was Princess Motakia. She was followed by Princess Seroka, who was two summers younger. Princess Seroka was succeeded by Prince Thebo, who, though third born, was fourth in line to the throne, as he had a younger sister, Princess Mapula.

The line of succession favoured the female heirs o'er their male counterparts. But in rare cases wherein there were no direct female heirs, such as in the days of Prince Noka the Ruler, a male heir would become the custodian/guardian of the throne until such time as a female child would be born. Prince Noka's mother, Queen Motapo IV, was the sole daughter of her mother, Queen Motakia III, who had two other sons. Queen Motapo IV struggled with barrenness, until finally, at the age of thirty-nine, she gave birth to Prince Noka. Alas, when the young prince was a mere five summers old, his mother died during childbirth, along with the babe, after a wondrous pregnancy in her elder years, leaving Baloki without an obvious heir. The lack of an heir nearly incited a civil war between the young prince and his uncle, Prince Thupa.

After three summers of unrest, the council agreed to grant the young prince the status of Throne Custodian, until such time when he would have a daughter.

To put an end to future civil conflicts, the council proposed a union between Prince Noka and his cousins, the daughters of Prince Thupa, Thato and Kgolo.

Initially, Prince Noka only wanted to marry Kgolo, who was closer in age to him, however, it was not customary to marry the younger daughter before the older one was married.

To increase the likelihood of birthing a female heir, the council did advise Prince Noka to wed both his cousins, even Princess Thato, who was his elder by seven summers. When he was just fifteen summers old, he took Thato as his first wife, yet the first two of their three offspring were males. Then, three winters hence, when he took Kgolo to wife, she did bear him a female heir, who was born a short time before Thato's youngest child, who was a daughter.

A strife between the sisters erupted, for each did contend for the throne. This strife resulted in a civil war that split the kingdom in half. Echoes of those fractures are still felt to this day. However, after much contention, the high priest and the council did declare that the true heir was the eldest daughter of Prince Noka, who was the daughter of Kgolo.

Prince Noka and Kgolo were blessed with three children, and the firstborn, a daughter, became Queen Motakia IV, the youngest queen to ever rule in Baloki.

"I reckon you have already conferred with the council regarding your plans. It seems I am always the last person in Baloki to be informed of any matter around here," lamented the queen, her countenance downcast.

Queen Motapo had been crowned the Rain Queen and assumed the throne after her sister Queen Motakia VIII's demise. Only one Rain Queen may reign at a time, and the power to conjure rain is passed down solely to the eldest surviving female heir upon the reigning queen's passing.

Although the origin of the rainmaking ability was shrouded in mystery, one of the many tales told in the kingdom relates to how Queen Motapo I's father, King Pula, was a mighty mage. He had surrendered his beloved eldest son to the gods as a sacrifice after ten years of drought had ravaged the land. In exchange for his sacrifice, his eldest daughter was granted the power to communicate with the rain gods, who granted her the ability to summon rain at will.

However, depending on whom you ask, the tale differs, but this version is most beloved amongst the common folk in the villages.

"Your Highness, if it please you, I spoke with the seer last night. She spoke in riddles and parables, as usual. But her words were thus: 'The lion creeps in the shadows with the horse, watch the words you say when you leave the hills, and remember to trust no one, or you shall not return home.'"

"Seers! What is this supposed to mean?" enquired Prince Moroka.

"I asked her to be clearer, but she gave me no more than what I have told you," replied the queen's chief advisor, Black Mamba. With the exception of the royal children and the sister wives, only two of the seven council members were permitted to speak directly with the queen and allowed in her private chambers.

One was Prince Moroka and the other Black Mamba, who was the queen's most trusted confidant. The other members were able to discourse in the presence of the queen, yet they ne'er could address her directly, except she had instructed, most especially during her updates with the council and noble houses.

Black Mamba earned his name by always wearing black attire, being very cunning, quick of movement, and possessing knowledge of everyone's secrets.

Some even say that his tongue held enough secrets to destroy the entire kingdom. He was a man of middle age, slightly overweight, and possessed very dark skin. In his youth, he had lost one of his eyes, and thus wore a white patch over it. Though his face was not pleasant to look at, he had shown unwavering loyalty to the queen over many years, thus earning his position as chief advisor.

In contrast to other members of the council who hailed from noble houses, Black Mamba's origins were veiled by enigma. Whispers in the marketplace spoke of him appearing out of nowhere, with no one truly knowing when he came to Baloki or if he was born there. His dark skin, however, suggested that he may have hailed from the Gauta Islands or the Veka Tribe, or perhaps had some ancestry linkage to those area.

Black Mamba kept his private life private, such that even his marital status or whether he had children was unknown. Though he knew everything about everyone, no one knew anything about him.

Perhaps he had shared a few stories with the queen, but to what extent, no one knew. "Why else would she trust him so much? She must know something about him," people whispered in the corridors.

"Your Highness, it does seem to mine eyes that trouble may befall us on this journey," cautioned Black Mamba, unconsciously rubbing his belly with his left hand, as was his habit.

The queen arose from her chair and moved towards the window of her hut. "The seers' visions are not always accurate, but considering the dreams that have been haunting me of late, I fear there is cause for concern on this journey," the queen said, looking at Prince Moroka with worry.

"My queen, King Shadu is our closest ally. He is my brother by law, and the rain gods know that man loves me more than his own wives. I cannot leave him in his time of grief. We must show our support," Prince Moroka spoke sternly, and graciously took a step towards the queen.

Not wishing to intrude on this conversation, Mamba excused himself. "I will go join the others for the daybreak meal.

As he unlatched the door to depart, his gaze lingered on Prince Moroka,

"Shall I inform Princess Mapula that she is to accompany you to Soru?" the affirmative nod from Prince Moroka confirmed his task as he closed the door behind him.

"Please, do not go, send Morena Seriti to represent us," the queen pleaded with the prince.

He looked at her intently, conveying his decision without speaking a word. "I must also depart to complete my preparations. We leave shortly after the daybreak meal," Moroka responded as he left the queen's presence, just moments after Black Mamba.

The queen gave a nod of acknowledgement to the prince. "Summon the sister wives. I must ready myself for the day."

Just as Prince Moroka was walking towards his hut, he saw a figure running towards him.

"Father, Father, is it true that I am to accompany you?" Princess Mapula asked, almost out of breath with excitement.

"Mamba has informed me. You should have seen Motakia's face." The princess could not contain her excitement.

Prince Moroka gave a smile. "Princess, you cannot rejoice when your sister is sad. Always remember, she is going to be your queen one day, and might decide on who you marry, so best be nice her."

Princess Mapula, a maiden newly come of age, was of great wit and curiosity surpassing that of her sisters. Since it was unlikely that she would ever ascend to the throne, she had some freedom to do as she pleased, and none were overly concerned for her. Each had their own duties; the eldest sister, Motakia, was the heir; Seroka was the chief commander of the Baloki army; and Prince Thebo was about to start his training to be the royal mage and also to sit upon the royal council.

Everyone had some purpose or obligation, except Princess Mapula, who was happier to be left alone to her imagination and freedom.

"Who said I want to get married? Boys are stupid, just like Thebo," Mapula responded, rolling her eyes to her father's amusement.

"I am a boy. Am I stupid?" the prince jokingly asked.

"No, you are my father, the greatest father in the world," the young princess responded with a big smile on her face.

"Flattery will get you very far in life, Princess, not as far as that big brain of yours, but very far."

"So, it is true, then?" she asked again, waiting for her father's nod.

The young princess was considered the most beautiful of the three heir princesses. People would always make remarks such as, "Princess Mapula, if only you started dressing like a girl and present yourself like a royal lady, you will be the most beautiful girl in Baloki."

However, she was not having it. With the exception of royal ceremonies, she was always dressed in boys' clothes, quite the opposite of her sister, the heir, Princess Motakia. Princess Mapula was a slender maid, with light-brown eyes, golden-honey complexion, and long and beauteous coiled hair. She was renowned for always adorning the side of her hair with plait.

Although she was but a tender age, tales of her beauty had spread throughout the continent, and lords and kings journeyed from far and wide to present their heirs to her, with the hope of obtaining her hand in marriage.

Despite her exquisite beauty, she did not conduct herself as the other royal ladies did, and one might suppose that she was unaware of her own beauty.

The princess had a great interest in adventure and oftentimes was covered in filth, mistaken for a handsome lad. Princess Mapula abhorred the notion of being wedded and turned into a lady for some insolent nobleman. She was often caught in mischief, and when any such case was brought before the court, she was either already acquainted with it or was directly involved in it. Though her father did not approve, it was agreed that Princess Mapula must attend a school where noble maidens were taught how to comport themselves as befitting their station.

Typically, maidens from noble houses between the ages of eight and ten were sent to this school, but for the past four summers, Princess Mapula and Prince Moroka had opposed this matter. However, this year, the council overturned their opposition and decided that the princess must join the next cohort. Leboa, who was entrusted with the instruction, had made a pledge that when the princess returned, she would possess more feminine attributes and be considered more appropriate for a lord or king.

Among all his daughters, Princess Mapula was her father's most cherished child, and they often embarked on journeys together. However, unlike her sisters, the princess lacked any form of magical aptitude. Furthermore, she did not possess the famed white streak of hair that was a distinguishing feature of the royal lineage. This bothered her, but it was never broached in her presence except during altercations with Princess Motakia, who would mock her about it.

"Go forth and make yourself ready, for we shall depart shortly, and be sure not to forget to pack …" her father commanded, but before he could complete his sentence, the princess was already sprinting to her chambers.

"I will not forget to pack something warm," she called back as she disappeared around the riverbank.

The huts of the royal family were placed upon the bank of the Loaba River, set apart from the throne room. The chambers of the queen were the grandest, followed by the chambers of Prince Moroka on the left and Motakia on the right.

Surrounding the three dwellings were six huts allotted to the sister wives.

The rest of the royal offspring were placed somewhat farther away, yet still within the bounds of the royal grounds.

As soon as the daybreak meal had been taken, Princess Mapula awaited Prince Moroka at the royal grounds gate. The entire council, some high lords, as well as royal progeny were present to bid farewell to the prince and his retinue.

"Where is Father?" enquired Princess Mapula.

"The last I saw of him, he was conversing with the queen. I believe he was bidding her farewell. Have you bid her farewell?" Black Mamba asked.

"Aye, I have," responded Mapula, and as she gazed around, she caught sight of her father, who was mounted upon his white horse.

"Father, Father, I am here!" she exclaimed in great excitement.

"I can see you, my child. I was but bidding your mother farewell and asking her to bless the road. She did try to persuade me from my journey."

"My prince, perhaps you should heed the queen's counsel," Black Mamba interjected.

Before the prince could respond, the royal horn sounded, signalling that they were set to depart.

"May the rain gods keep you safe," proclaimed Morena Tlou. "Thank you for taking my son along. This is his first royal voyage as a royal guard. May he serve you well," he added.

The assemblage of Prince Moroka was composed of seven leaders of noble clans from the Baloki Tribe. Ever at the forefront marched two royal sentinels, bearing the emblems of lightning and rain that betokened the Baloki Tribe.

After them came the Tau noble house, leading the other tribes. The royal carriage was situated in the middle, well-guarded against assaults from both front and back.

In the company of Prince Moroka did ride his younger brother, Kwena. Kwena was a diminutive, plump, bald man, who, by all accounts, was not comely to behold. He was considered the opposite of his siblings, and many a jest was made that he had been exchanged at birth, though such quips did not bring him amusement. He served in the trade department on the royal council. Kwena possessed a sly and calculating air about him, his mind always at work scheming.

Despite frequently being half-inebriated and suffering from a hangover, he was quite intelligent and privy to all that took place across the continent, with Black Mamba being the sole individual who could outwit him and be informed of happenings before him. Kwena and Black Mamba harboured animosity towards each other, often quarrelling over who commanded the most spies and who could spy more effectively on the other. He was well read and knowledgeable in diverse subjects.

The sound of hooves echoed throughout the surrounding countryside as the procession began to move forward. Villagers gathered along the roadside, hoping to catch a glimpse of their beloved royals. They waved their hands and cheered, shouting blessings and prayers for their safe voyage.

Prince Moroka, Princess Mapula, and Kwena sat inside the royal carriage, taking in the sights and sounds of their subjects. The prince's face was expressionless, while Princess Mapula waved and grinned to the people passing. Kwena, on the other hand, had his eyes closed and appeared to be sleeping. They carried on their way through small villages and bustling communities, all of which had come to a halt to watch their passing.

"I do wish you had heeded the queen's advice. This journey is not worth risking our lives for," Kwena remarked, barely opening his eyes, with his balance almost forsaking him.

"Kwena, it is barely past daybreak, and you are already drunk? How many times have I told you about your behaviour around the kids?" Prince Moroka responded to Kwena.

"Also, if I recall, you volunteered to come along; no one forced you. We have not travelled far. It is not too late to go back," the prince added.

Prince Moroka and Kwena had a most interesting relationship. Although they did love and respect each other greatly, they were often quarrelling. Kwena knew how to perturb his brother's feathers, and Prince Moroka loathed how Kwena never took anything seriously.

"You know, dear brother, gods be kind sometimes. They give you good looks, first-born status, and not so much sense of fun and humour," said Kwena as he took a sip of his ale from his *kgabo*, (a drinking jar). "Have I offended my princely brother? These children have heard and seen far worse."

"Kwena, can you let me sleep? Can you please not talk to me until the Fefre Crater," said Prince Moroka.

"Well, you and I are trapped in this carriage for the next three sunsets. Least you can do is afford me some conversation. "If that be too much to ask for, I shall ride outside with those lowlife scums," said Kwena as he departed the carriage and slammed the door.

Kwena mounted his brown horse and rode forth, alongside a youth from the Tlou clan.

"You, there, young man!" he called. "If we shall ride together, we ought to know each other and become acquainted. What is your name?" he asked.

"My name is Tlounyana, Your Highness," answered the comely lad of no more than sixteen summers.

"Hah! Your Highness? Me? Your Highness? Do they teach you naught in that godforsaken dump you call a clan? I mean, truly, do I look like a royal highness to you? My brother is royal, not I. If we are to be companions on this journey, at the least pretend to possess wit," Kwena said.

"Forgive me, my lord," Tlounyana replied, perplexed.

Kwena rode ahead. "Keep up, young man, the mountains are calling."

And so, the entourage commenced their journey to the south along the open Shari Road.

Blood Will Be Shed

"Listen, you all! We shan't be victorious in this war if we are not of one accord," said a hooded man from the shadows of a cavern. The frigid and eerie cavern had pillars made of speleothem, both stalactites and stalagmites, created by a subterranean stream that ran through its depths. "We have devoted decades of resources and planning to this cause. We are in the midst of the fulfilment of a prophecy, wherein a king shall unite us," he continued.

The man slammed his hand upon the oaken table and spoke with a most grave and earnest tone, pointing his finger at those seated around it.

"You all agreed that the king who shall unite us is King Shaza, who has now proven himself a battle-hardened warrior, fit to preside over the eight kingdoms with just and prudent rule."

"Sorry I am late, my lords. The road was not too kind," a figure said as he took the last empty seat at the table.

The one who sat at the head of the table cast a disapproving gaze upon his fellow, with a contemptuous sneer etched upon his face. "As I was still saying, the great war does approach, and yet, only three of the eight kingdoms have pledged allegiance to King Shaza. The fate of our continent rests upon this unity. As the Keepers, you have failed in your duty to persuade your kings and queen to unite the continent," the man continued.

An old, trembling voice spoke from within the poorly lit shadows of the cavern. "My lords, King Shaza is indeed the king promised to unite us. My seers have all seen the same thing. He shall vanquish the darkness that looms over us."

"Your Eminence, if I may speak freely, my hesitation to motion this plan is due to the fact that my seer has interpreted the prophecy differently," a nervous voice interjected.

"For centuries, every generation thought that this war will come during their lifetime. What makes this generation any different? I am not convinced Shaza is the man to lead us, or if this war is even coming," the man continued in hesitation.

"It's King Shaza. Where is your respect," the man who was seated at the head of the long round table spoke, ere letting out a deep sigh.

"My lords, it be not needful to remind you that King Shaza was born during an eclipse, and his lineage boasts of strong warriors. No tribe has ever been victorious against him in open-field battle. King Shaza possesses the ancient blood of the Khoros and is a proven warrior. If we be not led by him, I fear that the world as we know it may cease to exist," the leader of the Keepers proclaimed, and he slapped his hand upon the table once more.

"But what of my seer's interpretation?" the nervous voice persisted.

"I do wonder, King Shaza does not meet all the traits of the alleged prophesied king who shall lead us. Perhaps we should have the best mage on Sepoko Islands re-examine the prophecy and provide us with an unbiased interpretation. But in the meantime, I'm inclined to lend mine ears to my seer's words."

The leader of the Keepers sighed. "The interpretation of a single seer should not outweigh the collective agreement of all the Keepers. We cannot let our doubts and fears jeopardise the survival of our continent. We must unite under King Shaza's leadership, for the sake of our people and our future."

The others murmured in agreement, echoing their leader's words.

Twice a year, usually in the beginning of the harvest season and at the end of winter, a group of sixteen carefully selected members from the eight tribes met secretly during the middle of the night, in a cavern located near the Fefre Crater to discuss the future and events of the continent.

The Keepers, as they call themselves, had been meeting for over ten decades to prepare for what seems like the inevitable doom of the continent.

The prophecies were as clear as day, for a great war was foretold to befall the kingdoms, which would necessitate their unity under a single ruler. Yet, the question of who that ruler would be had been a matter of great contention amongst the tribes, with each tribe claiming that the chosen one would be born from amongst their own people.

In response to this, a secret society was formed with the noble intention of preparing for the coming war and being able to identify the prophesied ruler. However, over the course of last five decades, corruption had seeped in, and the society had devolved into a tool for controlling the politics of the continent.

When the society was first formed, the first generation of members believed that the promised king would be born in their lifetime. When this did not come to pass, subsequent generations held on to the same hope, until people began to pursue their own personal agendas. At every meeting, the members donned long black robes with red lining, and their operations were shrouded in secrecy.

Only the sixteen members and four carefully selected guards knew of the society's existence, and membership was by invitation only.

Even after being recruited, one had to undergo rigorous testing and training to earn their place in the society. Most of the members recruited were people of great influence in their respective kingdoms, making it easier to carry out the society's agendas. Each kingdom had two representatives in the society, and once one became a member, the only way out was through death.

"King Shadu has made it clear that he does not support our efforts to unite the tribes. Our efforts to remove both him and his son have not been as successful as we hoped, nonetheless, we can still strike while the kingdom is in mourning," a voice resounded in the chamber.

"But my lord, it is not right to slay a man within his own house while he is still in mourning. It is not right, and the gods will surely curse us." A voice trembled with distress.

"We are not here to save one man, for the survival of the eight tribes far outweighs the survival of a single individual," declared the leader of the Keepers.

The Keepers sat around the table with blazing fire in the middle to keep the cavern warm, each member seated in their designated place.

"My lords, let us deliberate on this grave matter of utmost import. Who among you are in favour of carrying out our plan to have the king assassinated at the funeral of his son? Raise your hand, if ye be so inclined."

Fourteen hands were raised in favour, whilst two Keepers dissented.

"No, my good lords," said one of the Keepers who voted against the motion, "when I pledged my allegiance to this society, we were charged to unify the eight tribes, not to spill royal blood. I ought to have spoken out when we first caused the prince's demise. This is not right. Our duty as Keepers of this land is to unite and safeguard, not to murder."

As he was about to take his leave, another Keeper who also opposed the motion added his voice to the fray. "If this be the nature of our society, then count me out as well."

As they both stood up to make their exit, the leader of the Keepers made a signal with his hand, and arrows felled the two Keepers who sought to depart, killing them instantly. The cavern fell silent, with only the sound of nocturnal animals outside filling the air. Their lifeless bodies lay where they sat.

"Only three tribes have given us their assent!" exclaimed the leader," continuing on like he did not just have two people killed. "As Keepers, it is your task to persuade your respective kings and queen to unify the eight tribes under one ruler. If we cannot achieve this through this council, then we shall achieve it through blood. We will wage the greatest war these tribes have ever witnessed. Think about your wives, children, and kin. We have no time on our side, for darkness looms, and we must be prepared."

"My lord, if it may please you, perhaps we should consider poisoning the king during the funeral feast," ventured one of the Keepers.

"Poison, you say? 'Tis but a weapon for the frail womenfolk!" a voice exclaimed in disbelief.

"Death is death, no matter how it come to pass," replied the leader in a stern voice. "Do whatever needs to be done."

"Can I get everyone's consent?" he asked.

"Aye," everyone responded.

"Any news regarding the queen of Baloki?" he enquired; his eyes fixed upon the Keeper who sat next to one of the lifeless bodies.

"My lord, the plan has been set in motion," he replied with a nod to his leader.

"Did you instruct the queen to send her eldest daughter to Soru?" asked a feeble voice from the shadows.

"Plans were altered at the last moment, for the queen was hesitant to part with her heir. But fear not, my lord, for I have everything under control," reassured the Keeper with a hint of nervousness.

"What of King Gauta? Has anyone made progress with him?" demanded the leader.

"Aye, I did approach King Gauta with the proposal of uniting the kingdom under one ruler.

But he spoke ill words of King Shaza and claimed that he bows to no one.

However, his brother, who is his heir, may have a different opinion," replied the female Keeper who was seated at the immediate left-hand side of the leader.

"Time is of the essence. What of Veka and Shanga tribes?" the leader asked.

"They are allies of Queen Motapo and will not join our cause unless she joins first," reported the plump Keeper, who was seated at the opposite side of the table.

"I hear only of problems and not of solutions," said the leader with a frown.

"You have until the next council to sway your kingdoms to our side, else blood will be shed," declared the leader with a finality that brooked no argument.

A Kingdom Divided

"I have faced death countless times afore, yet I still draw breath. War does not scare me. However, I fear that death is drawing nigh, and I have nowhere to hide," Queen Motapo said, her voice heavy with foreboding.

"Mother, do not speak such. You are the strongest person I know, and the warriors of Baloki are the fiercest in all the land, who would die for you," Princess Motakia responded, holding her mother's hand close to her chest.

The slender-framed Princess Motakia was a comely maiden of olive complexion, with eyes of honey, and the trade royal birthmark of white hair in the middle of her head, much like her mother.

The Heir Princess possessed all the qualities befitting a true princess. Not only was she endowed with beauty, but she was also a wise and cunning warrior, feared by many men in single combat. Yet, she retained the grace and gentleness that endeared her to her people. When she walked, it was whispered that she glided as if on clouds. It was plain to see that Princess Motakia was born to reign, having spent her entire life preparing for her future role.

"If it came down to it," the princess said as she gave a big sigh and looked at her mother in the eyes, "I will die for you."

"No, never speak such words, my daughter. You are the future of Baloki. As your queen, I command that, if ever our lives are endangered, you shall always save yourself," the queen said with a commanding and stern voice.

"Mother, it will never come to that. Tell me what scared you so much in this dream."

The queen's eyes withdrew from her daughter and stared into the fire in the middle of her hut.

"I saw the sun and two moons shining down upon Thaba Tladi in the dead of night. But the first moon turned red and burst from within, and the sun burned so hot that it too exploded," said the queen. As she spoke of her dream to her daughter, she shivered, and her arms were covered in goosebumps.

In addition to her power to summon rain, the rain queen had the gift of foresight through dreams. However, this ability was less reliable, and difficult to interpret, so it was often left to the royal seers to tell the future.

"What happened to the second moon, Mother?" the princess asked.

"I have had this dream three times now. The second moon starts turning red, and I can see the cracks on it, and just before it explodes, I always wake up.."

"Be not troubled, Mother," Princess Motakia said. "You have been toiling hard of late. Rest well, for you have a long day ahead at the council of elders."

"You are right, maybe I am making something out of nothing. I will have a talk with the seer on the morrow," the queen said, trying to seem brave in front of her daughter.

"Mother, three sunsets have now past since Father and Mapula departed for Soru. Have you received any word from them?" enquired the Heir Princess with worry, seating herself dutifully on the edge of her mother's bed.

"We have not received any news from the south, but I have faith that they are in good health. You need not worry, my sweet child," reassured the queen, who loved all her children but favoured the Heir Princess above all else. Not only was she next in line for the throne, but the queen also tutored her daughter in the ways of governance, in preparation for her future reign.

The queen and Princess Motakia fell silent, their ears pricking up to the sound of foul language and bellowing coming from beyond the queen's chambers.

"Oh, your sister has arrived," the queen remarked.

"I swear, if you ever tell me I need an appointment to see mine own mother, I shall have you thrown into the river and revel as I watch you drown," an irate Princess Seroka exclaimed to one of the sister wives, barging into the hut and slamming the door behind her.

"By the rain gods, this place shows me no respect. I understand that I am not the next queen, but still, accord me some reverence," Princess Seroka continued.

The queen oft spoke of Seroka as a troublesome child, for the princess's birth had taken two sunsets of labour. Despite sharing the sable olive skin and white hair streak of her royal siblings, Princess Seroka was seldom spoken of as beautiful, which always bothered her.

The princess loved her family, and her loyalty to them was steadfast, but she oft chafed under the clear favouritism shown to her sister. Nevertheless, she would remind herself that it was the way of their people, the way of the rain gods, that Princess Motakia was the eldest and their future queen, and that it was her duty to support her.

"Mother," the princess exclaimed wrathfully, "did you send Mapula and Father to the slaughterhouse?"

"Perhaps you want to sit and tell me what troubles you, my child."

"I have just received a message from Soru," Seroka said, still standing. "Without a doubt, Prince Thubo's demise was not an accident; he was murdered."

"Murdered?" exclaimed Princess Motakia, taken aback by the news.

"Yes, the letter stated that the king is currently holding four men accountable, and they are to face mudupa."

The princess handed the letter to Princess Motakia, who studied it quickly.

"The letter says here that the men being charged are innocent and that the threat still looms."

"Continue reading," Princess Seroka urged.

"It also bore a warning to Prince Moroka, advising him not to travel to Soru, for there is a conspiracy afoot to do him harm," the princess added, her face struggling to apprehend the matter at hand.

"They intend to kill our father; who sent you this letter?" queried the Heir Princess.

Her gaze then fell upon her mother, who seemed unperturbed by the contents of the letter. Observing the expression on her mother's face, Princess Motakia instructed the sister wives present to withdraw from the queen's hut and give them some space.

"Aye, he was killed by his own people. His death was no accident at all, as I suspected," retorted Princess Seroka. "Morena Seriti bore this letter. He arrived this morning from his trip. When he handed it to me, the seal was still intact.

"Mother, a war looms on the horizon, and we must prepare," Princess Seroka continued.

"My daughter, I do not think an attack shall befall your father and Mapula; they will be safe in the company of King Shadu," responded the queen, as any mother would, seeking to shield her children from worry. She desired not to sow any unwarranted panic until all the facts had been corroborated.

"They would not dare to slay him and risk incurring the wrath of the north in retribution. As long as we have a queen, Baloki shall not falter," the queen said sternly, clasping Princess Seroka's hands.

Princess Motakia scrutinised her mother closely, uncertain if she truly believed her own words.

"Mother, I still ponder the conversation we shared earlier, when you confessed your fears of what is coming. You spoke of dreaming of the moon and the sun. When Seroka apprised us of this news, you scarcely flinched. What are you concealing from us?" enquired Princess Motakia.

The queen appeared hesitant, but the weight of her duty as a queen compelled her to speak.

Her daughters were not children anymore; they had a responsibility to the kingdom.

They can comprehend the truth, she thought. "My dear daughters, I received a letter directly from King Shadu, which arrived with the king's seal still intact, on the day your father departed. The message warns us to be vigilant, as the next royal death shall come from Baloki."

Princess Motakia, seeing the terror in her mother's eyes, took her hand firmly. "Mother, the seer foretold that this journey to the south would be fraught with danger. Father insisted on going to support our uncle. We have not heard from him since he journeyed south. I am worried."

Princess Seroka, moving away from her mother and sister, spoke out. "Why was I not informed of these dreams and the seer's warnings? Must I crawl through the streets to learn of my own family's troubles?"

The queen sought to reassure her daughter. "Seroka, we did not wish to worry you.

But we must stick together as a family. War is coming, and I fear for our safety. That is why I am training your sister to take over from me, and why I did not want her to travel to Soru. With a strong queen, Baloki will never fall. It is your duty to support your sister."

Seroka cast a doubtful gaze, but the queen pressed on. "My teachings have ever been of strength and solidarity. Now is the hour to put those teachings into practice and hope we weather the storms that befall us; we must remain as one, united and steadfast."

"Mother speaks true. The future of our kingdom and the legacy of our house depend on us," Motakia spoke with resolve.

The queen gave a nod, her face etched with concern.

"I am full of pride for you both. Our family and our people need us now more than ever. And Seroka, as the leader of our army, we need you."

"My duty is known to me. There be no need for reminders," Seroka bristled.

"Sweet child," the queen tried to placate her, "remember, a kingdom divided against itself cannot stand."

"What course of action should we take, then?" Motakia queried.

"Let us remain vigilant. Panic must not spread amongst the villagers. As yet, we know not all the facts. Seriti and Mamba have been charged with doubling their spies and to report all they learn, be it great or small," the queen spoke gravely.

"We need to send a message to Father immediately, warning him of what he is walking into," Princess Motakia suggested.

"I shall request Folo to send a messenger pigeon to Father without delay," Seroka offered.

"No," the queen replied. "A message of such import demands a hand-delivered letter. Our swiftest rider must be dispatched. I shall speak with the council on this."

Motakia spoke, her voice insistent. "Permit me to go, Mother. I trust not the council, nor anyone with this message."

"Indeed," Seroka chimed in. "I can make better time than you, sister. I will be in Soru within the day and a half if I make leave now."

"No," the queen stated firmly. "I require both of you here. I cannot have three royal people in Soru. Let the council see to this matter. Find Neo and your brother. We have a war to prepare for."

Condolences to the King

The journey to Soru lasted for three sunrises and three sunsets. Upon reaching the base of the Molotli Mountains in the early morning, they were forced to dismount from their carriages and proceed on horseback. The mountains were treacherous, with steep inclines and slippery slopes. Many travellers, unaccustomed to such terrain, have met with an untimely demise. Thus, it was deemed wise to commence the ascent after the rising of the sun, as Thaba Molotli was shrouded in an icy mist for the majority of the day. The view from atop the mountains was a sight to behold, and the snow that covered them for most of the year did little to detract from their grandeur.

Princess Mapula could scarcely contain her excitement, for this was her first visit to Soru. "Father," she enquired, "how far are the royal huts and the villages? Are we going to see them soon?"

"Soru people are a cowardly lot," replied Kwena, riding alongside the princess. "They like to hide in the mountains."

"Pay him no mind, Princess," interjected Prince Moroka. "The mountains are the primary defence of the Soru Kingdom."

"So, the people do indeed live in the mountains," said Mapula, smiling at her uncle.

"Aye, Princess," the prince replied. "This kingdom is strategically placed for battle and war, and their city gates have never been breached. None in living memory has dared to wage war against Soru and attack them in their own home."

"I have read that the Molotli Mountains are bitterly cold as well," added the princess.

"That is correct, if you do not die first from the cold, their many traps around the mountain will certainly kill you."

Soru people were known to be a peaceful folk, seldom engaging in wars, save for when their allies called upon them. And it was said that their land was one of great security, for the only way up the mountains was a narrow path that could barely accommodate three horses side by side, and definitely too narrow for a carriage. Thus, no matter how vast and mighty an army might have been, once they embarked upon this path, they were but easy targets, walking to their deaths.

"I have read that the highest point of habitation in Molotli is Thaba Ntsu, which is guarded by two massive gates leading to the royal grounds," the princess stated.

"Aye, that is so. Once we enter the kingdom grounds, you shall lay your eyes upon the gates, which have yet to be breached, and for good reason," replied Prince Moroka.

After many hours of riding, the Baloki retinue finally reached the kingdom gates. The princess, her eyes wide with wonder, gazed upon the gates in amazement, for she had never before seen such magnificence.

The grand gates were adorned with the gleaming metal of gold, and two giant figures, winged and mighty, stood on either side of the pathway. Their wings curved around their bodies, facing the road, and their spears jutted from the top.

Soru Kingdom had some of the most advanced and beautiful huts. The harsh and frigid climate had forced them to construct structures that were more adaptable to their environment. For most of the day, the mountain peaks were obscured by clouds, rendering habitation nigh impossible. Nonetheless, despite such challenges, the Soru people possessed some of the most wondrous architecture in all the eight kingdoms. Due to the inclement climate, they were clad in their *seana morena*, that afforded much-needed warmth.

The royal blankets were customarily of a regal gold and aqua blue hue, reserved solely for members of the royal house.

Prince Moroka and his retinue were greeted at the gates by the now second in line to the Soru Kingdom, Prince Maru.

Though just thirteen winters had passed over him, the lad towered nearly six feet, with a slender frame, fair countenance, and hair woven in braids that cascaded down to his shoulders. Unlike his late brother, he was not a man of the sword or a commander of armies; the young prince was rather a lover of ancient scrolls, blessed with wit and charisma. The people held him in great affection, and the women in the villages declared his smile reason enough to name their offspring after him.

"I would offer the customary salutations to welcome you to our resplendent kingdom, but I am certain your lordship is weary from the rigours of travel," greeted the young prince.

Outside of one's kingdom, it was proper to address other nobles as your lordship (morena) or ladyship, for only one king or queen could reign in each kingdom.

"By the gods, is this Prince Maru? The last time I beheld you, you were yet sucking your thumb. Now, you are a man grown. How many winters have you seen?" exclaimed Kwena.

"I have seen but thirteen winters, uncle," replied the prince.

"And you have not ceased to grow. What do they feed you on these mountains?" added Kwena.

The prince gave a subtle grin in reply.

"I pray you do not find the cold too harsh. However, as the rain people, you should quickly adjust to the mountains. Allow me to escort you to your chambers for the duration of your stay," offered the young prince.

"Why would anyone abide in these forsaken mountains? Who in their right mind would have thought 'I shall seek out the most inhospitable terrain and live there'?" Kwena, who had regained his senses after grappling with the high altitude, enquired with a grumble. The ascent had caused him to regurgitate all the ale he had consumed on the journey.

"Prince, is it true that Soru has never succumbed to invasion?" Mapula asked.

The youthful prince gazed upon her and bestowed a smile, for although they were cousins, they had not yet had the pleasure of meeting.

"You must be Her Ladyship Mapula, for tales of your beauty fall short of your magnificence," he remarked.

"Beware, young prince, this one thinks she's a boy and takes no pleasure in being praised for her beauty," Kwena mocked.

"I can speak for myself. Beauty is but one attribute that I possess, for I am also intelligent," retorted Mapula.

"Please forgive my foolishness. I shall come to learn of your wit in the days to come," responded the prince, giving a wink to Mapula.

"Flattery shall not earn you any favour with me, prince," Mapula cautioned with a frown.

His Lordship Moroka gave a faint grin. Although the kingdom was shrouded in mourning, with all attired in black garb, one could still glimpse the splendour of the terrain and the architectural marvels.

"Do you know that your father and I were raised together, before he married your mother?" Morena Moroka reminisced. "Growing up, we were like brothers."

"Are you the prince's uncle through our sister or his father? 'Tis a disturbing thought to confuse the two," said Kwena in a jocular tone.

"You understand what I mean, Kwena," replied Moroka.

"Truly? For I was under the impression that you already had a brother, brother," retorted Kwena, with a hint of wounded pride.

"Kwena, cease your prattling. You know well what I speak of," interjected Moroka, sensing his discomfort.

"Aye, indeed. My father has regaled me with tales of your youth, and he shall be most pleased to see you. You will have a chamber in the royal quarters, not far from our father's own. He has insisted that you be lodged near him. When you are rested, I shall escort you to the throne room to pay your respects."

"Your hospitality is most generous, nephew. Will there be any other noble guests lodging in the royal chambers?" asked Kwena, with a trace of sarcasm in his tone.

"No, only you, His Lordship, and Her Ladyship shall reside there. Your retinue will be lodged on the royal grounds, but not within the royal chambers," replied the prince, with a hint of annoyance.

"Are we the first to arrive?" enquired Moroka, seeking to change the subject.

"No, uncle, Morena Gauta arrived on the morrow of receiving the summons. He is presently in the company of his daughter, Princess Palesa," the prince responded.

"I hold no fondness for the Batanas, for their practice of dark magic, they scare me. I read that they even resort to cannibalism at times," Mapula said in a solemn tone.

"Though they may not be to your liking, they are still of kin to us, despite their inclination towards such sorcery," Moroka replied, his voice steady and composed.

"Throughout my years, Baloki has waged war five times, and on each occasion, Soru and Baloki have fought valiantly, side by side," he continued, recalling the battles he had fought. "Do you know how many times the Batanas came to our aid in battle? Once, they have aided us once, but arrived tardily to the battlefield," he said with a hint of humour in his voice.

Chuckles broke from Moroka and the young prince.

"Uncles, my father scarcely talks about my mother from when she was young. Can you please share stories that you remember from her childhood with me while you are still here?"

"Certainly, young prince," Moroka responded.

As they walked, one of the royal guards approached the young prince and whispered something into his ear.

"My lords, I humbly ask to be excused. My father summons me. I entrust you to the capable hands of my half-sister, Lera," he said before bowing and departing.

Lera was a woman of remarkable stature, standing tall at six feet with a complexion that radiated a dusky beauty. Despite being older than Prince Maru, she had no claim to the throne, for she was born to a commoner, although her father was the king. Her dark olive skin was an inheritance from her mother, Leshoba, whom the king met and impregnated during his visit to the Gauta Islands.

"Father, may I please venture forth into the royal grounds?" Mapula beseeched eagerly.

"No, not yet. Let us first cleanse ourselves and pay our respects to the king. You may explore the royal grounds thereafter," replied Moroka.

Kwena, however, was less prudent in his speech. "I shall make a visit to the nearest brothel," he declared, almost galloping away on his horse. "Call for me when it is time to go to our brother-in-law."

Moroka swiftly seized hold of Kwena's saddle and sternly chastised him. "Such conduct is unseemly, my dear brother. We must first cleanse ourselves and offer our condolences to the king in the throne room."

"Kwena, I asked you to conduct yourself with greater propriety. Do not make me rue the day I agreed for you to come along," he added, his tone severe.

Kwena yearned to speak, but the expression on his brother's face was enough to silence him.

Lera turned to Mapula. "Once you hast completed your ablutions and paid your respects, I vow to you this, I shall entreat my brother Maru to give you a tour of the royal grounds. He will take great pleasure in doing so."

Our Swords Are His

Queen Motapo delicately walked with grace and poise into the throne hut. Her fair gown, as white as snow, was adorned with precious diamonds, fashioned into the likeness of falling raindrops. A cape trailed behind her as she glided forth to her seat of power. On her right was the crown princess, Motakia, and on her left stood the enigmatic Black Mamba, dressed head to toe in black. Normally, Prince Moroka, would accompany her on her left, but in his absence, Black Mamba had taken his place. Following behind were Princess Seroka and Prince Thebo. Neo, the queen's nephew and adoptive son, trailed behind the royal children.

Upon every full moon, the queen would convene with the noble houses, and her council would apprise her of the matters that concerned the kingdom. This was the sole occasion in which the people were granted audience with the queen. She would always invite the royal children to attend, so they would also be informed of the kingdom's affairs. This ancient tradition had been upheld for generations so that if the queen were to fall, the heir would be able to take up the mantle and navigate the treacherous waters of politics without delay.

The throne itself was fashioned from white granite, imbued with veins of gold that ran through it. Legend held that the throne was exceedingly cold and that any unworthy ruler who sat upon it would freeze to death. The throne room was adorned with white linens, with the symbol of the Baloki people embossed in gold. The council members were seated in one section, while the high lords occupied the other.

"Your Highness, if you can please lend your ears to the words of this lowly servant," said a voice of high pitch, belonging to a corpulent man, Morena Tlou.

Morena Tlou was of the Lefa clan, the wealthiest in the kingdom, yet he spent his family's fortunes in debauchery and gambling. His lord father, Tladi, had coerced the queen to appoint him to the council under threat of withdrawing their patronage of the throne. None respected Tlou, but all feared his father's power and influence.

In the civil war that ensued, leading to Queen Motapo's ascent to the throne, a third of the kingdom supported her sister, the late Queen Motakia. Though the late queen had a greater number of followers, Queen Motapo, formerly known as Princess Letsoba, possessed means backed by Morena Tladi. When Queen Motapo ousted her sister, the reinforcement of the Lefa Clan ensured that she was forever indebted to Morena Tladi.

The Lefa Clan was famed not only for their riches but also for their cruelty, embodying the motto of *gold, pride, and fear*. Morena Tladi had always espoused that fear was their sole protection, for the moment people ceased to fear them, they would seek to usurp their position in the kingdom and appropriate their gold.

"Morena Tlou, can you please give the queen a moment to take seat before you inundate her with your news," said Black Mamba.

"I fear this news brooks no delay," protested Tlou, whose tunic was tight upon his plump form. "This morn, we received a messenger pigeon bearing most unsettling news. What I shall impart to you must not leave the confines of these chambers," he continued.

Black Mamba interjected, "Tlou, I can assure you that the contents of that letter are already public knowledge to everyone present. Sometimes I feel you forget who your audience is."

Laughter and giggles erupted in the room.

"Let him speak," the queen granted him an audience.

"You are most gracious, Your Highness," Morena Tlou cleared his throat before he continued speaking, turning to look upon Black Mamba as he proceeded to read the letter.

"This letter was written by the Gasane, King Shadu's closest councillor. He does fear that a plot to slay the king at his son's funeral is afoot."

"Like I said," Mamba responded, walking towards Morena Tlou, "this council already knows the contents of your letter. Perhaps you could show us some wisdom and tell us how we can resolve this problem. All that fortune, and you are still slow."

Tlou sought to rise from his chair to challenge Black Mamba but struggled to get up from the chair, which was tight on him. Morena Seriti placed his hand upon Morena Tlou's shoulder to calm him and kept him in his seat.

"This manner of behaviour shall not be tolerated in the presence of our queen," Morena Seriti declared.

Morena Seriti was of a small yet significant house of the Metsi Clan, who owned the largest shipping trade in the Baloki. He was the youngest son of the presumed-dead Morena Sehlare. Morena Seriti was but fifteen winters when he joined the council and took over as the head of his clan, following his father's disappearance at sea.

Despite his youth, he was wise beyond his years, and now, at age nineteen, he was one of the most respected members of the council. Morena Seriti stood at six-foot-one, fully built, and handsome.

He had a struggling stubble beard adorning his visage, an attempt to bestow upon himself an elder mien befitting his status in council.

"Tlou and Mamba, this hallowed chamber is no place for your puerile games. If you are so inclined to act as boys, perhaps you should do it beyond the walls of my throne room," the queen declared. Although a glint of mirth shone in her eyes when Morena Tlou struggled to rise from his seat, she still commanded reverence.

"Your Highness, what of the news concerning the prince and the princess? Their very lives are in danger. It seems the culprit who seeks their demise will strike when all three are gathered," said Morena Seriti.

"I propose we dispatch a letter to Gasane and offer our aid," suggested Morena Tlou.

Black Mamba spoke with a sarcastic tone. "Have you any other sage counsel to impart, that we, in our foolishness, have not yet considered?"

Morena Tlou opened his mouth to reply but thought better of it and held his peace.

"My queen, Morena Seriti and I have penned a letter with details of where we believe the deed shall be done, and who might be involved." Black Mamba proffered the epistle to the queen, who scrutinised it with care.

She perused the letter and nodded her assent. "Are you certain of this?" she enquired.

"We are all but sure, Your Highness," replied Morena Seriti.

"I have already apprised some of the council members of the letter's contents, and we are of one mind that it must be conveyed to Prince Moroka directly," stated Black Mamba.

Morena Tlou cleared his throat. "Your Highness, I am unacquainted with the letter's contents."

"I must amend my words. I conversed of the letter's content with the council members whose counsel I held in high regard," Black Mamba made reply.

"Your Highness, I cannot abide Mamba's insults!" cried Morena Tlou in fury, slamming his hand upon the chair and struggling to rise therefrom.

"One more offence from you, Mamba, and I shall remove you from this assembly," said the queen. Like all present, the queen held no respect for Morena Tlou, but diplomatic she must be for the good of the kingdom's relations with Morena Tladi.

Morena Seriti then stood and approached the throne. "Your Highness, if it please you, I can go forthwith to warn Prince Moroka. If the rain gods be kind, the journey shall take me about a day and half. May I have leave to depart after this meeting?"

The queen nodded. "Deliver this message to Prince Moroka directly, no other; give it to the prince alone. Tell King Shadu that our swords are his and we are at his service," added the queen, before Morena Seriti took leave from the throne room.

We Mourn Together

Morena Moroka, his brother Kwena, and Her Ladyship Mapula did make their way towards the grand chamber of the throne. Moroka had commanded that Mapula attire herself in her royal black dress, so as to display her respect for the king. Alas, Mapula was much troubled and irate by the garments her father had coerced her to wear.

"Walk with the manners befitting a lady, and do not forget your courtesies," reminded her father sternly.

Mapula, filled with a great sigh, replied with a sour countenance, "Aye, I shall."

"Take care not to stumble on your gown, Princess," Kwena jested, barely containing his amusement.

As the doors to the throne chamber were opened, the blaring of horns and pounding of drums filled the air, played thrice in unison. Kwena whispered to Moroka, "Is that the scent of lavender that tickles my nostrils?"

"Indeed," answered Moroka.

"Do you recall how dearly our sister cherished the fragrance of lavender?" added Kwena with a tinge of sorrow.

With heavy hearts, the trio advanced towards the throne. The flooring of the chamber was a gleaming aqua blue marble, upheld by towering granite columns. The very seat of the king was wrought from the same blue marble, adorned with a black *seana morena*, representing that the kingdom is in mourning. At the base of each column blazed fires, for the land of Thaba Ntsu was known to be cold throughout the seasons, including summer.

"Hear all, hear all! Before you stand His Royal Majesty, the King of the Mountains, son of the ancient Basoso bloodline, ruler of the kingdom of Soru, King Shadu Thaba, may his reign be long and prosperous!" Thus proclaimed Gasane, as the horns and drums sounded in unison.

"I stand before His Royal Highness in the full capacity of our Rain Queen, Queen Motapo," replied Morena Moroka, bowing down in reverence. "The people of Baloki extend their most sincere condolences. Like everyone else, we are shocked and saddened by the tragic sudden passing of your first-born son and heir, Prince Thubo."

Mapula stood, with her hands together and face towards the floor, as a sign of respect. Whilst Kwena knelt beside Morena Moroka.

"My kingdom is greatly honoured by your presence, and I trust that we will be blessed with rain now that you are here," replied King Shadu.

"Arise!" he commanded, and they all stood up, their heads still bowed in respect.

"Brother, it has been a while since we last saw each other. I see you brought little baby Motakia, the future Rain Queen. I remember when she was born, all the eight kingdoms received rain for seven sunsets nonstop. She's the true Rain Queen," continued the king.

"Well, Your Royal Highness, this is not Motakia. This is my youngest daughter, Her Ladyship Mapula.

She's the youngest of the four royal children," replied Morena Moroka.

"Is she the one whose beauty is rumoured all over the continent? For once, street gossip was correct!" exclaimed the king.

Mapula frowned at the thought of men around the eight kingdoms talking about her like an object. All the king's children, including their mothers, were present except Prince Tlou and Leko, who were noticeably absent from the lineup. However, Morena Moroka had forgotten what the prince looked like, so he did not notice.

"Morena Moroka, you have brought great honour to our house."

"It is a good thing you brought Mapula with you. Perhaps we can find a suitable match for her among my sons. I have many to choose from, though this lot may not be to her liking," the king said, gesturing towards his sons with a sneer.

Mapula's face twisted with displeasure at the king's words. However, she knew her place and kept her composure, curtsying gracefully as befitted her station.

"Calm down, Princess," whispered Kwena, who could sense Mapula's discomfort.

Moroka changed the topic, remarking on the long years that had passed since their last meeting and how much the king had gained weight. The room erupted into giggles.

"Tis been thirteen summers, indeed. Thirteen summers since …" the king trailed off, his expression turning sorrowful.

"The lavender," Moroka finished for him.

"Aye, your sister loved lavender. I make sure the throne room is filled with its scent in her memory," the king said, his eyes meeting Moroka's in shared sadness.

"She was my sister too," Kwena whispered, but loud enough that the king heard him.

"Aye," the king responded, standing and descending from his throne with a grave expression.

When King Shadu was but a boy of six, his father, King Thabang, had sent him to live in Baloki, to strengthen the alliance between their kingdoms and hopefully find a wife. The king and Morena Moroka had grown up together, inseparable like brothers, bound by a love that knew no bounds.

Their bond was strong, the villagers did wag their tongues, saying that their relationship was more than mere friendship. Such gossip, however, was quashed by the lingering eye of King Shadu for women. 'Tis said that he knew half of the women in Baloki intimately before he departed.

In his youth, the king was very comely and wild, with a burning love for battle, a thing that most women did find hard to resist. But now, a slight shadow of his former glory loomed over him.

As the king reached the bottom of the stairs to his throne, Morena Moroka was about to bow, but the king embraced him instead. Although the embrace was brief, 'twas intense, and Moroka could feel the king's pain. Many words could describe King Shadu, but "soft" was not among them. The king could not show his emotions in public, yet in that moment, he felt like a boy of seven in Baloki embracing his friend. But he knew he must not reveal his feelings; he could not break. Nonetheless, that fleeting embrace, which lasted no longer than a second, seemed to stop time itself. The king released Morena Moroka, and their eyes met.

"Our king seems very glad to see this man. What do know you of him?" Perega whispered to Nare.

Perega had recently joined the king's council. A lean man of full beard in his late twenties, who hailed from Sepula Clan, one of the noble houses in Soru.

"Other than he is the brother of the late queen and a close friend of our king, I know very little of the man," Nare replied.

"Learn what you can about him. I am suspicious," Perega commanded.

The two men then withdrew from the back of the throne room.

"I hope the journey through the mountains was not too gruelling. They are known to be harsh to those unaccustomed to their ways," said King Shadu, taking a step back towards his throne whilst still regarding Morena Moroka.

"The journey was pleasant, Your Highness. 'Tis a pity that we have come in such mournful times," replied Moroka.

"It seems the only time you ever visit Soru is when there is death in the royal family," quipped the king, attempting to lighten the mood.

Soft laughter echoed throughout the throne room.

"He speaks truth, my lord," whispered Kwena, his words meant only for Morena Moroka and Her Ladyship.

Moroka turned towards Kwena with an unamused expression before quickly shifting his gaze back to the king.

"Fear not, Your Highness. We have been welcomed with great hospitality. The young prince, towering as you, but more handsome, has been most gracious," responded Moroka, the subtlest of smiles gracing his lips, one which only the king could discern.

The room erupted in giggles, yet not so much as to dishonour the king.

"Shall we observe the usual pleasantries?" the king said. "Tlou, please step forward," he commanded with authority.

Gasane cleared his throat and said, "I fear he is not present, Your Highness."

The king sighed and displayed no sign of surprise. "Where is the young one? Maru, approach me," he demanded.

The young prince stood beside his father, and the king and Prince Maru bore a striking resemblance.

"Son, I shall take a walk with Morena Moroka. I leave you to host the rest of our visitors," declared the king.

Drums and horns were played to signal that the king was about to depart the throne room. Morena Moroka followed him, and his brother and daughter followed suit.

"No, stay behind. I believe the king wants a private audience with me," instructed Morena Moroka.

"Of course, the brother you never had wants a private audience with you," scoffed Kwena sarcastically.

Without causing a commotion, Prince Moroka turned around and took hold of Kwena's hand. "Kwena, there is a time and place for everything, and this is not the time or the place for such jests."

"Well, someone is quite sensitive. Let me find a brothel. The company there might be better," retorted Kwena.

Kwena gave a nod to his brother and excused himself. "Maru, show Her Ladyship around the kingdom. Lira, inform the cooks to prepare something delectable for tonight's supper. My brother has arrived," the king instructed before departing the room with Moroka.

The king and Morena Moroka left through the left door, reserved solely for the king's use when exiting the throne room. "Kara, there is no need for you to follow me. We shall not be venturing far. Besides, this man here shall protect me better than you and the royal guard can," said the king, gesturing for his royal guards not to follow him.

As soon as they left the throne room and the sight of everyone else, the king let out a deep sigh. "Brother, I thank you for making the journey and seeing me in my time of grief."

"Our kingdoms must always lend assistance to one another, Your Highness. You are my brother, and I will always come in your hour of need. We mourn together, we go to war together, and celebrate together," Morena Moroka said, looking into the king's eyes.

"Moroka, you don't need to use formal titles. No one can hear us," an irate King Shadu said.

"Where are you taking me?" Morena Moroka enquired.

"Just follow my lead, and all will be revealed soon," the king replied.

That Throne Is My Destiny

"I, Prince Tlou, am now his heir, yet mine own father does not take a moment to speak with me as he does his friend," the prince said with great fury to his sister, Leko, standing in the middle of an empty hut. Despite the fire's damage, the hut stood firm, thanks to its sturdy wooden walls and stone foundation. Its secluded location on the royal grounds added to its allure, with overgrown bushes and trees creating a natural barrier around it.

The half-burnt roof would be the first thing to catch one's eye as they approached the hut, which used to be the royal guards' chambers.

The charred and blackened walls stood out against the greenery, a testament to the fire that had ravaged the hut several summers prior. As one peered inside the hut through the broken windows, they would see the remnants of the royal guard's living quarters. There were traces of beds, rusted weapons, and broken furniture scattered around the room. The walls were still adorned with old banners and flags that now hung limply from their hooks.

Prince Tlou and Leko would often meet here in secret, as there were but few eyes in this part of the royal grounds.

"That 'friend' is your uncle," Leko responded.

Leko was the firstborn daughter of the second wife of King Shadu, Princess Funi from the Veka tribe in the north. She possessed the fair skin of the Soru people, but her appearance was not considered beautiful by any measure. Her teeth were slightly crooked, and she had a hairy, manly build. She was known as Leko the Angry, for she was always irritated and had no love for anyone except for the now-heir to the throne, Prince Tlou.

As per Soru customs, any children of the king who are not born of a wife from the royal bloodline cannot bear the titles of prince or princess, for they cannot inherit the throne. This includes children born outside of wedlock, as well as any children who are not born of the first wife.

Nevertheless, if the mother is of royal blood, the king may exercise his right to legitimise the child as his heir.

King Shadu could have legitimised Leko and her siblings, but he chose only to designate as heirs the children born of his beloved, the late Queen Karabo.

"I have scarcely conversed with the man," replied the prince. "I have laid eyes upon him no more than thrice in mine entire life."

"He bears a striking resemblance to your mother," observed Leko. "Does seeing him not bring to mind memories of her?"

Prince Tlou let out a sarcastic laugh. "I do not remember her face. I see her in my dreams, but she does not have a face."

Leko moved towards him. "Perhaps you should visit the gardens more often."

The prince's face changed, and he looked away from her.

"Father needs to officially name me his heir. I know not why he has not done it already," he said, leaning against the wall.

Prince Tlou was tall and masculine, with the pale skin of the Soru people. He had thick eyebrows, sharp eyes, and a scar on his left chin. He tried to grow a beard to cover the scar, but his beard was not fully connected on his youthful face.

He was commander of the army, alongside Morena Nare, before his brother died. Soru laws dictate that the second-born son becomes commander of the army and defends his brother, much like the tradition followed in Baloki. From a young age, he had always been a military man. Although he was not particularly popular with the people, he was well respected.

"Maybe he is waiting to do it after the funeral. The fact that he is now including you in council meetings is a good thing, aye?" Leko reassured Prince Tlou.

"Our father is very close with your uncle, and he listens to everything he says. It might be worthwhile to befriend him while he is still here and whisper in his ear," Leko continued, moving closer to the prince.

"I cannot stand that man from Baloki! Our father has never shown any love to us or his wives. The only time our dear father shows any form of happiness is when he is telling stories about him and Moroka. When Father learned of Moroka's arrival, one would think that the man was no longer in mourning for his son, for his face has been transformed entirely."

"Forget your anger towards our father, for your focus should be on being named his rightful heir," Leko said with conviction.

"What do you think I am doing?" He glanced briefly at her before turning his gaze towards the window.

"Remember, the child that grows inside your brother's widow is a threat not to be taken lightly," she reminded him.

"I do not cower at the shadow cast by an unborn child!" the prince exclaimed with great fury.

"If that babe is a boy, he shall lay claim to the throne more rightfully than you," Leko cautioned.

"Much can come to pass between now and the birth of that babe," retorted the prince with defiance in his voice.

"I might have a plan," Leko suggested. "Hear me out, for I offer but a suggestion. Perhaps if you were to take a wife, our father may take you more seriously." She cleared her throat, inching closer to him.

The prince gazed upon her with confusion.

"Though our father has not legitimised me, given that I am still of royal blood, do you think we can be wedded?" she enquired, reaching out her hand to hold his.

"By the mountain gods, Leko! Cast those thoughts from your mind, for you know whom I am expected to wed. What we share shall never be known outside this burnt hut," the Heir Prince rebuked, removing her hand from his.

"I'll do whatever it takes to have you seated on the throne. Anything," she whispered. "I have killed for you, and I …"

Before she could finish, the prince put his hand over her mouth. "Hush now, it is done," he said.

The prince turned Leko about and kissed her.

"My king, my king," she did whisper.

"Shall I be yours forever?" she queried.

"Upon my ascent to the throne, you shall be richly rewarded," the prince responded.

"I long to be your queen."

"Leko," he sighed.

"Make me your queen," she implored.

"You are my sister," he declared.

"Half-sister," she retorted.

"You are my sister." He pushed her away.

"Listen well, and heed me closely. You will never be my queen. You shall receive your reward when I am crowned, but you shall never be my queen."

"I do know that," she replied. "I was but indulging in fanciful playacting."

Prince Tlou's words did wound Leko deeply. She was visibly distraught and turned away from him so as not to reveal her pain.

He was the one person who had always comprehended her. She had felt that she could let down her guard around him, but in this moment, he was a stranger. *Maybe it be the weight of the crown that weighs heavily upon him, as he is now the new heir*, she pondered silently to herself.

In this moment, she did not recognise him. Since the demise of their brother, he had transformed into someone she scarcely knew.

In the past, they had oft talked of fleeing together to the east of scatter islands, perhaps to Macara, a land where they would be unknown.

But now, he was destined to rule as king, and they were no longer the kindred spirits of their youth. They had been inseparable since they were but children, and yet now, she found herself next to a stranger.

"That throne is my destiny," he whispered.

She Was My Soulmate

"The gods know the love I bear for you is greater than that which I bear for any woman whom I have lain with or wed," sighed King Shadu, gazing into the eyes of his friend.

"Yea, even my own children, I do not cherish with such ardour as I do you. What has befallen us, Moroka?" He continued.

"Eight winters have passed since you last wrote me. I have written you oft, yet none of my letters have ever been returned," Morena Moroka replied.

"Moroka, I did write you back. I wrote you before you travelled to Soru," King Shadu responded with a smile.

"Aye, you did write to Baloki Kingdom. But none of the letters were addressed to me."

The king took a deep sigh. "Sometimes I forget the irritation that you stir within me. You know that I am not one for literature or poetry."

"You still could have written me," Morena Moroka responded, eyes cast downward, a hint of melancholy within their depths.

"Things were simpler when we were younger. Oh, how I miss those days in Baloki, where we would hunt and lose ourselves until the early morn. And the women! Do not even get me started on the women," the king reminisced fondly, and they both chuckled.

"Half of the children in Baloki are your illegitimate bastards," Moroka jested.

"Those were different times, Shadu, and we were different men, rather boys," Morena Moroka took a pause, his mind stirring. "We can spend hours reminiscing about the past or bickering about who wrote more frequently. But what I wish to speak to you about is the news that reached us before dawn, from one of our advisors." Moroka continued, his face turned solemn and fraught with anxiety.

"That sounds grave, Moroka. What has happened?" the king whispered, moving closer to his friend to ensure that no ears but his own catch what he was about to learn. King Shadu knew that winds do carry whispers and walls had ears.

Moroka placed his hand on King Shadu's shoulder, gazing into his eyes with great intensity, which conveyed the gravity of the news to the king.

"Shadu, there is a bounty on your he–" said Moroka, before being abruptly interpreted by the king.

"Head," the king finished off Moroka's sentence, jesting at the notion of a bounty on his head, for it had been a common occurrence in his reign.

"I already know about that, Moroka. I thought the news you were about to tell me was life-threatening." The king chuckled and gave a reassuring wink to his friend.

"Your Highness, lend me your ear, for this matter is of grave import," said Morena Moroka, as he placed a gentle hand upon the back of King Shadu's head, fixing him with a piercing gaze.

"I see we have reverted to the usage of our formal titles. Do you remember how you would grab the back of my head like this when we were younger? It would always soothe my troubled spirit," responded the king.

But Moroka's countenance turned cold, and he tightly grabbed the back of the king's head, staring intently into his eyes. "No, Your Highness, this is no laughing matter. They plan to kill you," he said with clarity.

King Shadu was taken aback and removed the prince's hand from his head with force, stepping back in anger. "Moroka, you know well the risks that come with being king. Many have tried to kill me before, and many more shall try in the future."

"From the whispers that reach my ears, it seems even your queen is not beyond peril," King Shadu retorted. Moroka's countenance betrayed his confusion. "What do you mean, Shadu?" he inquired.

"The letter must have arrived after you left Baloki. I dispatched a letter to your queen, apprising her of my advisors' dire warnings to Baloki," King Shadu explained.

Confused by what he was hearing. "But..." Moroka started to interject before King Shadu cut him off.

"Hear me, brother, the price of the throne is steep. I am well aware with this truth, and so is your queen."

To prove his point, the king removed his tunic to reveal a scar beneath his rib cage. Prince Moroka touched the scarred area with concern. "What happened?"

"Aye, two summers past, some treacherous knave attempted to take my life. 'Twas a dark time in our kingdom, for while we may seem peaceful to the outside world, internal conflicts do arise. But fear not, for I overpowered the coward and emerged victorious," said the king with a tone of confidence.

Moroka gently touched the scarred area, studying it.

"I might be old and not as fast as I once was, but I am still able to fight, Moroka. Any fool who dares to challenge me will die a slow, painful death. I had the fool who tried to kill me hauled around the villages naked behind a horse because he assumed I would give him a quick death.

And when he was unconscious, I had my best healers revive him, only to burn him alive in front of everyone," the king boasted.

The king's voice grew sombre as he spoke of his past attempts on his life. "Aye, and four summers past, one of my councillors plotted with my own cook to poison me," he recounted. "But I discovered their treachery, and they paid for it with their lives. The cook was made to run the royal grounds while my guards shot arrows at him. My so-called councillor's family was made to eat the very poison meant for me. He watched his loved ones die before being burned alive for his crimes."

Moroka couldn't help but smirk at the king's liking for brutal justice. "You seem to have a talent for burning people alive," he said. However, his concern for his friend's safety outweighed any amusement. "Why do they want to kill you?" he asked, his eyes betraying his worry.

The king sighed, as if the answer to that question eluded him. "Men want to be me; they want my crown. They think being king is easy. But I will not run or cower like a helpless fool," he declared with steely resolve.

Moroka's grip tightened on the king's head, his eyes pleading. "But why did you not write me? I would have come to your aid."

The king's expression softened, and he rested a hand on his friend's shoulder. "I did not have the time, Moroka. I was busy defending my kingdom."

"I do not care. I would have come."

"Moroka, you speak of a foolish promise. Death is an inevitable fate that awaits us all, no matter how mighty or meek we may be," King Shadu replied, his voice filled with resignation. "But I swear by the mountain and rain gods that I shall fight with all my strength to stay alive, for the sake of our kingdom and the memory of my beloved son."

Moroka shook his head, a look of deep concern etched on his face. "Shadu, do you know who wishes to do you harm and for what cause?"

"Aye, Moroka, I have my suspicions. But I shall not speak of them until I have proof."

"I received a message from one of my advisors, which speaks of an intent to slay you at Prince Thubo's funeral service.

"Does your message say how they plan to kill me?" King Shadu asked, with worry betraying his face.

"I'm afraid not, my dear friend. I have been asked to be cautious as well because my life is also in danger," said Moroka, his countenance displaying deep concern.

"Well then, I will be prepared," King Shadu responded with a wink to Moroka.

"Please take this message serious, Shadu. Tell me, how can I help?" Prince Moroka asked.

"Fret not, brother, I will take care of this. This kingdom is under my protection and guardianship," reassured the king, seeking to ally Moroka's fears.

As they walked through the gardens, a fragrant aroma of lilies and lavender filled the air, enveloping them in a serene calm. The gardens were rich with colours, with rows of lilies and lavender blooming in hues of purple, pink, and white.

However, Moroka's attention was caught by a figure in the midst of the garden, a magnificent seven-foot statue of a comely woman. "Is that who I think it is?" he asked, his voice filled with awe.

The king nodded solemnly. "I commissioned the finest artist in the land to create this statue of my beloved queen, so that I may always remember her beauty. For when she passed, I feared that with each passing day, her image would fade from my memory. And so, I gaze upon this statue, and in her likeness, I find solace."

The statue was chiselled from gleaming white marble, and its intricate details were a testament to the masterful skill of the sculptor.

"This statue is a true masterpiece, Shadu."

"Aye, but even the best artist could not capture her true beauty. She was more radiant than the sun, and her kindness knew no bounds."

The king's eyes glistened with tears as he spoke of his beloved queen. "She was my soulmate, Moroka. I loved her with all of my heart," his voice choked with emotion.

Moroka placed a comforting hand behind his friend's head again. "I miss her too, Shadu. She was my sister."

Together, they stood in front of the seven-foot-tall statue of the late Queen Karabo, carved from white marble and surrounded by fragrant lavender and lilies. The beauty of her likeness captured in stone was a testament to the king's undying love for her.

There Will Be Bloodshed

"Listen to me, young Neo," said Kobo, a banished mage and former advisor to the late Queen Motakia VIII, his words heavy with the weight of experience. "You should be sitting on that throne, for it is your rightful place."

Neo, a comely youth, with short hair and a white streak birthmark that marked his left eye and eyebrow, looked at Kobo with confusion. The very same birthmark that adorned his eye did cause a change in its hue, turning it to grey, which contrasted with his other eye of honey.

"But you know that Baloki has never been ruled by a male heir, Kobo. I do not have a sister, so my mother's line of succession ended with her."

Kobo shook his head, his eyes gleaming with conviction. "No. The customs of our land do not dictate that only women can sit on the throne. It is merely a tradition that has been followed for many generations. Your bloodline is strong, and your claim to the throne is just."

Kobo was an elderly man; his face had been beaten by the sands of time, etched with lines and wrinkles from a long and eventful life. Despite his advanced age, he carried himself with vigour, a sense of purpose, and determination that belied his frail appearance. Though his body had aged, his mind remained as sharp as a sword.

Neo was taken aback by Kobo's words. He had always felt like an outcast in the royal household, despite being raised by his aunt, Queen Motapo, after his parents fled to the Gauta Islands and later died in the great plague that ravaged the north. He had never considered himself a contender for the throne, and the idea was both thrilling and daunting.

"I do not know if I am ready for such a responsibility," he said, his voice barely above a whisper.

Kobo placed a hand on Neo's shoulder, his gaze unwavering.

"You are young, but you have the heart of a true ruler. You have shown wisdom beyond your years, and the people of Baloki will rally behind you. You are not alone, and you will not fail."

Neo gazed into Kobo's eyes, and at that moment, he felt a newfound sense of purpose stirring within his heart. Yet, he dared not confess it, for he knew the heavy price that came with the crown.

"Your Highness," Kobo said in a solemn tone, "you were meant to sit upon the throne. You are the king prophesied to us, born beneath the bleeding moon." Neo had a look of confusion on his face. "When you were born, young Neo, the heavens resounded with thunderous clamour for a span of three sunsets, devoid of gentle rain, yet bursting with thunderous might. Never afore had such an event come to pass throughout history," Kobo continued.

Neo took a moment to consider what Kobo was saying. "But I am pledged to Princess Motakia," he replied. "I would gladly serve as her princely consort," he said, not truly believing the words he uttered.

"Serve?" Kobo scoffed.

"You think you shall be allowed to govern alongside her? Look at what befell Prince Moroka. Our sweet queen has reduced him to naught but her concubine. And mark my words, she will never wed him, and you will never wed Motakia. The council will make sure of that."

Neo hesitated. "I have no desire to rule. Our last male monarch, Prince Noka the Ruler, was the crown custodian until his daughter came of age to ascend the throne."

"Your Highness," Kobo's voice lowered to a whisper, "our nation was founded by King Pula, a warrior king. A man of strength and vision."

The sounds of the Loaba River drowned their voices, but Neo knew that the weight of Kobo's words would remain with him long after they parted ways.

"The hour for a matriarchal rule has passed. Baloki is in dire need of a sturdy leader, and you have the birthright to that seat of power," said Kobo, draped in a cloak of black, nearly unidentifiable amidst the dark night. Neo made haste to conceal himself beneath a tree.

"But ..." Neo could scarcely fathom the words he was hearing.

"Kobo, do you hear the words that slip from your tongue?"

"Oh, Your Highness! Your destiny far surpasses even your wildest dreams. You are the king who shall unify our eight kingdoms. Your birth was prophesied. On the day that you were born, every mage among our tribe felt their magic amplified. You were not birthed to serve behind a queen, but to rule," said Kobo, his words causing Neo great unease.

"Why have you waited so long to bring this to my attention?" asked Neo.

"You are now a man capable of leading and capable of hearing the truth. Had I made this known when you were a babe, who knows what mischief your aunt could have wrought upon you?"

"The queen cherishes me as if I were her own son. She would ne'er do me harm."

"Your loyalty to the queen and her offspring is indeed touching. Yet, when you are ready, I shall reveal to you who the queen truly is, and who you really are."

"I cannot be king. Baloki shall suffer a curse the day a male sit upon the throne."

"Ah, the curse of the male heir." Kobo shrugged. "Listen to me. There are many, many people throughout Baloki who support your rightful claim."

"I make no claim, Kobo. I seek nothing," said Neo, his face troubled.

"Kobo! True, I agreed to meet with you, but it is only for the sake of my mother, because you were her closest ally. You requested my audience in the middle of the night, and I came here because I thought you had news you wanted to tell me about my mother. I am all ears."

"A storm is brewing, and it is important that you choose the right side. There will be bloodshed, and we will need a just and righteous ruler in the aftermath," Kobo continued.

As they spoke, a band of young men emerged along the riverbank, and Neo grew anxious. "Kobo, I must take leave before anyone spots us together."

"Go, but know that I shall summon you again," said Kobo with a nod.

Neo nodded in agreement and swiftly made his way towards the shadows of the night, trying to avoid being seen by the young men.

Who Are You?

"Hurry up, cousin," said Prince Maru in a hasty tone as he sped through the dense forest of Thaba Ntsu.

"Where are you leading me?" enquired Mapula, struggling to keep pace with the prince as they raced atop the hill.

The fog rendered their journey even more arduous.

"Well, you did request an adventure. Are you frightened, little princess?" taunted the prince.

"I am no little princess," replied Mapula, endeavouring to appear valiant, quickening her pace and nearly overtaking the prince.

The prince halted suddenly and clasped Mapula's hand.

"What are you doing?" she asked.

"Cousin, we are about to enter the accursed Khoro Forest," he replied.

"No need to cling to me for protection," she retorted.

"Are you certain, Princess?"

"I fear not, for I am of the bloodline of the ancient rain gods. Nought can scare me," she proclaimed, shoving his hand away.

"Do you want me to tell you the tales of this forest?" queried the prince.

"Surely, I have read it in our library's extensive collection. Did you know that Baloki boasts the second-largest library after the one in Sepoko Island?" remarked Mapula.

"So I am told," he said sarcastically. "However, I will tell you the true accounts, which are not recorded in your fancy library. So, listen carefully," responded the prince, prompting Mapula to roll her eyes.

"Very well, proceed."

"Hear ye, hear ye, in days of old, a time lost to the annals of history, before my ancestors settled in these mountains, 'twas said that the land was cloaked in a dense forest and the Khoro people did dwell here. My father told me that his great-great-grandfather did engage the Khoros in battle and did triumph over them."

"Is that why they moved to the south?" asked Mapula.

"Perhaps so, for in this world, only the strong do survive," replied the prince.

"No, Maru, such words are impolite. The Khoro people are renowned for their peaceable nature; they do not bother anyone. And they were the first humans to settle in Ashari. This entire continent is their land," she continued.

"They are but feeble, mere remnants of their former selves, wandering aimlessly across the face of our continent," the prince scoffed.

"Yet, I have heard that the Khoro people were the first to master the enchantments of the Fefre Crater. However, their reverence for all things sacred hindered them from tapping into its full potential," Mapula responded.

"One day, they can just decide to wipe us all off the face of the continent," she continued.

"If I had such power at my fingertips, I would reign supreme over all the continent," proclaimed the prince, throwing up his hands and shouting, "King of the world!" to Mapula shaking her head and rolling her eyes.

"You speak folly, cousin. How did your forefathers defeat the Khoros and drive them hence?" she enquired, her eyes shining with curiosity.

Mapula was rapt in attention, for the Baloki Tribe had no interaction with the Khoro people. By the time Baloki was an independent tribe, the Khoros had begun their migration to the south, and so she was eager to hear the rest of the tale.

"What has befallen the Khoros sorcery?" Mapula enquired.

"No, but the tale is not yet complete, if you can grant me your patience, little princess."

Mapula, perturbed, did retort with fervour, "I told you, I am no little princess. Address me as such once more, and you shall feel the wrath of my lightning strike."

The prince let out a hearty chuckle, his eyes gleaming mischievously. "Gasane has spoken true, cousin," Prince Maru said, his voice dripping with amusement. "It seems that the curse of the Rain Queen has taken hold of you and deprived you of the gifts that your siblings possess."

Mapula was taken aback, her mind reeling at the revelation that her secret affliction had been made known to people beyond Baloki. She felt a hot flush rise to her cheeks as tears threatened to spill from her eyes.

"I want to go back," she pleaded, her voice quivering with emotion. "I have no interest in your stupid forest or its mysteries."

The prince smirked, his eyes glinting with amusement. "Ah, it seems that I have touched a raw nerve," he remarked, his tone taunting. "But why turn back, my lady, when the wonders of the woods lie before us?"

Mapula's resolve crumbled at his words, and she felt a sense of resignation settle over her. "I want to go back," she repeated, her voice barely above a whisper.

But the prince was not deterred. "Come, come," he coaxed, his hand gesturing towards the depths of the forest. "Let us venture forth and discover the secrets that await us."

The prince's eyes glinted with excitement as he spoke of the forest's cursed past. "No, Princess, the best is yet to come," he declared. "For when my ancestors defeated the Khoros from these lands, the Khoro chieftain placed a curse upon this very forest, decreeing that it would remain uninhabitable for all eternity. And to this day, the spirits of the fallen Khoro warriors still roam these woods."

Mapula's curiosity was piqued once more. "But tell me," she enquired, her eyes wide with wonder and scepticism, "have you ever laid eyes upon these spirits?"

"Aye, Princess, I have," the prince replied with a knowing nod. "And if you would but follow me, I shall show you the very place where they reside."

The prince took off at a sprint, with Mapula hot on his heels. They ran deep into the heart of the forest, until they stumbled upon a dilapidated hut that appeared to have weathered the ages.

The door was adorned with markings that looked suspiciously like fresh blood, and the hut itself was painted a foreboding black. Mapula couldn't help but shiver at the sight of it, but she refused to show any fear in front of the prince.

"Behold, cousin," the prince whispered, gesturing towards the hut. "Within this very abode resides a witch of unspeakable age. It is she who has been tasked with containing the restless spirits of the Khoro warriors, lest they bring ruin upon our land. But she must never leave this cursed forest, else all of Soru shall perish."

Mapula's eyes widened with awe at the prince's words, and she couldn't help but wonder what other secrets lay hidden within the mysterious woods.

"What kind of witch would willingly take up such a task?" Mapula enquired with great interest.

The prince, with a knowing smirk, replied, "One who has made a pact with the dark forces and possesses powers beyond comprehension. She is feared and revered by all who know of her."

Mapula's heart quickened with anticipation as the prince knocked on the door. "Do not touch it, that looks like fresh blood," Mapula cautioned.

"Do not tell me you are scared now, cousin," teased the prince.

"Do you wish to lay your eyes upon the witch?" he asked.

Mapula was hesitant but kept telling herself, *I am courageous, I am courageous.*

"You know, I forgot to mention, she also has the gift of foresight and can tell the future, but for that we should have brought a blood sacrifice. Maybe I shall offer you, Princess," he gestured.

Mapula's uneasiness was now becoming very unsettling to her. It was harder to conceal her fear. Her mother had always warned her that there is power and life in blood and that she should never engage in blood magic, especially with people she did not know.

The small ramshackle hut stood alone in the dark forest. With its blackened exterior and peeling paint revealing the rotting wood beneath, the hut itself was less impressive.

The once strong and sturdy door had degraded to a flimsy piece of wood held together by rusted hinges.

Approaching the hut, the pungent stench of decay and mustiness overpowered. Strange symbols and markings appeared to be painted in fresh blood on the walls. From within, the eerie sounds of wailing foxes and hooting owls filled the air, sending shivers down Mapula's spine.

"If there is a true witch in this hut, I am certain she does not wish to be disturbed, and it is growing dark. I think we should return," Mapula said.

"Today, you shall see the most hideous creature you have ever laid your eyes upon. Have you ever beheld someone who resembles a frog, cousin?" the young prince asked.

Before he could knock again, the door creaked open, revealing a creature that looked like a crossbreed between a frog, a horse, and a woman, sending bats pouring out. This terrified the prince so greatly that he nearly screamed. Nevertheless, he remembered he was with Mapula and attempted to appear brave.

"What do ye seek in these woods alone?" said the peculiar-looking creature, with a voice that sounded as if it had crossed the veil of death.

"Witch, tell us our future," demanded Prince Maru.

"I am no witch, young prince," retorted the creature.

"Wait," Mapula observed with a closer look. "Maru has warned me of your frightful countenance, yet I find you most pleasing to mine eyes. In truth, you are the fairest maiden mine eyes have e'er seen."

The princess beheld an olive-skinned maiden, with piercing cheekbones, a slender form, and a comely figure. Her hair was white, and it coiled elegantly atop her buttocks, while her skin was bedecked with glitter that shone like diamonds.

"Fair maid!" exclaimed the prince.

"Beauty standards must be sorely lacking in Baloki," the prince jested.

The creature then opened the door to her abode, beckoning them to enter.

"Behold, little princess …" before Mapula could utter a word of protest, the woman interjected, "… aye, I know well that you dislike being addressed as 'little princess.'"

"How? How do you know?" asked Mapula, perplexed. The prince had not referred to her as little princess in the presence of this strange woman.

"Little princess, I have knowledge of things about you. Things unknown to you. To answer your question, you see me the way you want to see me. I am unique to everyone who gazes at me; no two people can see the same person. I can be anyone you want me to be. I might be your deepest, darkest yearning or your deepest, darkest horror.

"So, little princess, what do you seek in these forbidden, cursed woods?" enquired the woman in a cautionary tone.

Mapula, who was trying to appear brave, responded, "Maru spoke of your ability to see into the future."

"Are you certain, little princess? Once I reveal your fate, no matter how grim it may be, you can never alter it. Your days shall be spent in torment, waiting for the inevitable," warned the woman, as one of her owls hooted, startling Mapula.

"People oft desire to know their future, but they shun the truth of what it may hold," added the woman, her gaze piercing through Mapula.

"Reveal our futures, witch," demanded the prince, unyielding.

"Ahhh ... the future," the woman sighed. "What is it but a mere concept, young prince?" countered the woman, her words laden with gravity. "Consider carefully before you answer, for there shall be no turning back."

The prince persisted, "Tell us our future, creature!"

It had been several summers since the prince last visited the creature with Gasane, when he was but a child. It had warned them then of a dark cloud looming over the royal bloodline and a shift in destiny.

"As you wish, my prince," acquiesced the creature, bowing her head mockingly. "I am but your servant."

"I see no blood sacrifice, little princess," she continued, eyeing Mapula directly. "For me to discern your future, blood must be shed, for therein lies power of life and death." The woman's words hung in the air, pregnant with meaning, as Mapula understood their significance.

Mapula was filled with terror upon this sight, for she remembered well the teachings of her mother, warning her not to meddle with blood magic. But her pride held her fast, and she could not show weakness before the prince.

Prince Maru had a dagger at his side; she seized it and drew it across her own hand. "If you desire blood, then take it," she said, her wound oozing crimson as she strove to appear bold.

The woman took Mapula's hand in hers and let her blood drip into a skull, mingling it with potions and muttering dark incantations. "Now give me the blade," she commanded, wrenching it from the Mapula's grip and tasting of her blood before cutting her own hand to add it to the brew. "Ah, royal blood! I love its taste," she cackled, fixing her gaze upon Mapula and making the already anxious princess quail with fear.

"Now we shall sing for the dead Khoro spirits to lead us into the unknown. Take my hand!" she cried, and the room began to quake. Prince Maru, who had visited this hut before, but always in the company of his Gasane or his brother, beheld with horror the strange shadows and whispers that filled the now-darkened chamber.

"What sorcery is this?" he demanded of the creature, his voice trembling with fear.

As the prince laid his gaze upon Mapula, he saw that her eyes had begun to glow white, and his heart was filled with a great dread.

"Witch!" he cried out. "What sorcery is this? Release her, I demand you!" He attempted to shake Mapula, but both she and the woman were in a trance and unable to move.

Mapula was almost immobilised, for she could hear and feel her surroundings, but she could not see anything, as if she were transported to a different dimension. "I see rain, thunder," the woman said in a deep, echoey voice. "Destiny calls you to another path, little princess. The road you take now shall not lead you home. Betrayal lurks on the horizon for you. The sun and the moons shall soon dim their light."

"Will our parents unite us in marriage?" the young prince, standing nearby, enquired.

As the woman delved deeper into the princess's future during her vision, she saw glowing white eyes surrounded by pure magical energy and sought to approach and consume some of that energy.

"I must draw closer," she thought as she reached out to grasp the energy.

However, the moment she clasped into the overwhelming energy, there was a mighty thunderclap outside, followed by lightning that struck the hut, piercing through it and striking the woman and Mapula. When the lightning struck both of them, the woman let out a loud scream, while Mapula remained unscathed.

The creature let go of Mapula's hand, wailing in agony. "What have you done? Who are you? Leave my hut at once!"

Observing what had taken place, Prince Maru seized Mapula's hand in terror and ran out of the hut. Mapula was barely conscious, trying her utmost to keep pace with Prince Maru. When they glanced back at the creature, her eyes were burnt, and her eye sockets were hollow. She had been struck blind.

They left the hut to the sound of her anguished screams.

Who Sent You?

The funerals of Soru, akin to most tribes in Ashari, were of great splendour, with royal burials that lasted for three sunsets. The entire kingdom was plunged into grief as they laid to rest their prince and heir, who was well loved by all. On the third day, which was the day of the funeral, the king donned a black *mokorotlo*, a hat of conical shape with a knob at its peak. The knob of the king's hat was crafted from a rare aqua-blue diamond that had been handed down through the Soru rulers. The king also wore a black *seana morena*, a traditional Soru blanket draped over his tunic, embroidered with gold, exclusively designed for kings to wear during royal funerals.

Princess Palesa, consort to the late Prince Thubo, walked on the left of the king. She was with child, bearing the heir to the throne. Despite being four moons pregnant and grieving, her beauty shone like a radiant flower, as beautiful as her name. On the right of the king walked Prince Tlou, dressed in a manner akin to his father, except his *mokorotlo* lacked a diamond. The king commanded his trusted friend, Morena Moroka, to accompany him, along with Prince Maru, Princesses Puo and Lebo, followed by Mapula and Kwena, and the remaining royal children and their mothers.

Amongst the guards surrounding the mournful royals was Kara, a nineteen-year-old who had served the king for the last four summers. Kara was born into one of the lower-class clans but had climbed the ranks to become a royal guard. His father had warned the king about an attempted assassination, earning him the king's gratitude. As a token of thanks, the king offered Kara's father a position in the royal household, to which he requested that his son be appointed as a royal guard. The king granted his request and henceforth, Kara had served the royal household with loyalty and valour.

Kara had shown rare and exceptional talent, and had swiftly advanced through the ranks to become a member of the king's guards. This was his first royal funeral, and he was visibly sweating. Perhaps it was due to the heavy armour he was wearing, he pondered. He had to put on a black *seana morena* on top of his normal armour. The young king's guard, who was tall and masculine, had a smooth, chiselled face. His face bore a semblance of innocence, a token of his tender youth that had not yet endured the trials and travails of war. He looked towards the king, who was but a few steps away from him. His thoughts were racing like a wild steed. *What have I gotten myself into?* he thought to himself. He strove to maintain his composure, yet he was sweating to such an extent that one could almost see him shaking.

This task must be perfect. No, seamless, he thought, recalling the instructions received the night prior. *A simple errand it is; to pour a cup of wine for all, and on the second round, to pour the widow's tears into the king's cup*, he repeated to himself without rest, his lips moving, but not such that anyone could hear what he was saying.

The widow's tears, a fluid that left no mark or hue or scent, could bring about paralysis and death in fewer than ten heartbeats. Though an antidote existed, it was very expensive, and rarely did it arrive in time to save the afflicted soul's life.

At the pyre's head stood the king, surrounded by his retinue, all gathered to pay their last respects to the fallen prince. Princess Palesa stood by her husband's feet, as was the custom. The priestess intoned prayers while the lamentations of the womenfolk filled the air. Then, the signal came for Kara to bring forth the wine.

The king, Prince Tlou, and then Morena Moroka, were to share in the ceremonial wine, a rite of passage to initiate the funeral ceremony.

It was the custom that whosoever served the king a drink must taste it first. In general, this duty fell upon the tasters, but of late, the king had allowed only his royal guards to attend upon him.

I cannot succumb to panic, thought Kara. *I must execute this task flawlessly. Pour the widow's tears on the second round, just after Prince Tlou has been served.*

Kara took a sip of wine from his cup, then poured for Morena Moroka, followed by Prince Tlou, and finally the king. The priestess continued to chant prayers, offering Prince Thubo's spirit to the afterlife and pouring some of the wine upon the prince's chest.

Keep your composure, Kara, he thought to himself. *When the distraction come, pour the widow's tears into the wine before serving the king.*

Sure enough, as soon as Kara moved towards the king, a fight broke out in the crowd, causing enough of a distraction for him to nervously pour five drops of the widow's tears into the wine. One drop could send a man into a days' slumber, while three drops stopped a man's heart within seconds.

"Seize those who create such dishonour during my son's funeral!" the king bellowed.

In that instant, Morena Moroka sensed that something was amiss. It felt like a diversion, but from what, he knew not. He felt that something was about to happen but was uncertain as to what it might be. Therefore, Moroka began silently chanting spells of his own.

"*Metse, mabu, maru, mollo, mahlo*" he repeated the chant four times.

"Stop, Shadu, stop!" cried Moroka, just as the cup was on the verge of touching the king's lips.

The entire funeral came to a standstill, and only the sound of burning torches could be heard crackling in the silence.

The king turned around and perceived the urgency in Moroka's eyes.

Moroka then cast his glance towards Kara.

"Drink it," he ordered.

"But, but my lord, I have already sampled it," Kara replied.

Kara had already filled his cup with wine and imbibed it.

"No. Sip from the king's cup," Moroka insisted.

"But my lord, I am not worthy to drink from the cup of our king," Kara answered, with his eyes filled with terror.

"I am not your lord, I am Prince Moroka, present here on behalf of Queen Motapo, the Rain Queen, who hails from the gods of rain. And I command you to drink the wine from the cup which you have just handed over to your king."

The onlookers murmured amongst themselves.

"What is the meaning of this?" the king enquired.

"This is madness," Gasane added.

"I said drink the wine have you just poured into the king's cup," Moroka persisted.

All eyes were now fixed upon Kara, waiting with bated breath to witness if he would comply and consume the wine.

Kara discerned a gap in the crowd and realised what was about to befall him. He pondered to himself that if he could make a run for it, there was a waterfall in close proximity. If he could plunge into it and survive the descent, perhaps he could swim in the frigid river and flee.

How could I be so stupid? What have I done? he cogitated. *I am about to meet my end.* He reflected upon his father and the sorrow and shame he would have to endure.

With adrenaline coursing through his veins, Kara flung aside the jar of wine that he held and charged through the crowd, making his way to the precipice of the mountain before leaping down into the cascade.

"Oh no! You shall not escape us," declared Moroka, as he cast a spell that froze Kara mid-jump.

The king, visibly angered and yet still trying to comprehend what had occurred, cried out, "Bring him here unto me!"

And so Moroka, chanting his incantation, lowered Kara down to the ground.

Suddenly, the king was encircled by his loyal guards. "Who has sent you?" demanded the king. "Speak truthfully, and I shall grant you a swift death!"

"Forced was I, threatened to do it, Your Highness," replied a terrified Kara, knowing full well the dire fate that awaited him.

"Who sent you, boy?" boomed the king.

A voice from within the crowd cried out, "Let him drink the wine!"

"Who sent you?" demanded the king once more.

Kara, bewildered and disoriented, looked about him until he raised his hand to point at someone who stood behind the king.

In the darkness of the night, an arrow flew and struck him straight in the eye, causing blood to gush forth and leaving him dead upon the spot. In the ensuing chaos and terror, the crowd scattered in all directions.

Princess Palesa remained rooted to the ground at the base of the pyre. Overwhelmed by the events that had unfolded, the princess faltered and dropped the torch she held, setting the pyre ablaze.

"Shadu! Tlou! Mapula" cried out Moroka. "Grasp my hand!" With his spell casting, they vanished into the obscurity of the night, leaving behind the chaotic funeral that had unfolded.

No Turning Back

"Young lad," said Mamba whilst addressing Neo, who was making his way towards the queen's quarters.

Neo was taken aback; forsooth, Black Mamba had ne'er spoken with him afore, except for the casual greetings exchanged between them. They had never had a conversation, and thus Neo was confounded.

"Are you all right?" Neo enquired.

"In times of war, the gravest folly is to find oneself on the opposing side. Tell me, young lord, have you ever engaged in warfare before? It is a grisly affair," remarked Mamba.

Mamba's words were heavy with meaning, and Neo sensed that there was more to the conversation than met the eye. However, his countenance was inscrutable, for he often came across as impassive. "I have heard as much," he replied.

Mamba scrutinised him momentarily.

"Occasionally, we believe we desire to learn the truth, yet as we pursue it, we discern that ignorance is indeed bliss," opined Mamba.

"But can we really ignore the truth just because it might be uncomfortable or inconvenient?" Neo challenged, frowning slightly.

Mamba shook his head. "It's not about ignoring the truth, lad. It's about recognising that sometimes the pursuit of truth can come at a cost. It's about weighing the benefits and risks of uncovering certain truths."

Neo raised an eyebrow, which had his trade birthmark. "And who decides which truths are worth pursuing?"

Mamba shrugged. "That's a difficult question. I suppose it depends on … I think it's important to recognise that there are different versions of truth, and not all of them may be worth pursuing."

Neo considered this for a moment before speaking again.

Neo slowed his pace and regarded Black Mamba, who was of shorter stature in comparison to his tall, brawny frame. "And what is your truth, Mamba?" he enquired.

"The truth is subjective, for it hinges on the veracity you wish to learn. There are several versions of the truth, but some ought to remain buried in the past," replied Mamba.

"The subjectivity of truth does not lend validity to the fabrication of falsehoods. You have served on the queen's council since I can recall, and yet your origins remain a mystery. Why should your truthfulness be trusted?" enquired Neo.

"Never afore have I been asked of my birthplace, and so it seemed none were interested in the veracity thereof," replied Mamba.

As they made their way towards the queen's chambers, Mamba issued a grave warning.

"Listen to me, young one, and heed my words with utmost care. The path you are treading is fraught with danger and leads only to a fate from which there is no turning back. Mark my words well, for the next time we shall converse, it will be in the presence of the queen."

Baffled, Neo said, "Forgive my ignorance, but I fail to grasp the meaning behind your words."

"You are on the brink of a decision that will alter the course of your life forever, my boy," Mamba responded. "Once you have chosen that path, there will be no turning back. The queen must be made aware of the danger you are putting yourself in, and I shall ensure that she is."

With a deep sigh, Neo replied, "Your words confuse me, but I shall trust your counsel and await the queen's judgement."

The two men walked side by side, entering the queen's chamber; the air seemed to grow thick and heavy with tension.

Name Your Heir

"Please tell, what possessed you to nearly expose yourself like that?" asked the first man, his voice tinged with irritation and concern.

"I had no other recourse," replied the second man, speaking through the rustling of hay. "It was either him or us."

"That fool would not have betrayed us; we paid him handsomely," said the first man confidently.

"What is silver when you are facing death?" the second man responded.

"That silver will take care of his family for life; the fool would not have spoken."

But he was pointing directly at you," countered the second man. "I had to take action. I could not risk our exposure. And besides, it is done now. I do not believe they suspect us."

"But—"

"Think on this, my friend. Had I not acted swiftly and did what I did, both our heads would be impaled upon spikes by now," said the second man.

"True enough," conceded the first man. "It has been three sunsets since the funeral, and I hear the mage departs on the morrow. With him gone, the king will be vulnerable."

"What is our next course of action? Have you received any word from the Keepers?" enquired the second man.

"No, I am still awaiting instruction. But have no fear, all shall be made clear in due time. For now, you should return to the feast before someone notices your absence," urged the first man.

The feasting hut was heavily guarded, and all the royal chambers had been similarly fortified since the funeral.

Only the royal family, the king's council, and Moroka, Kwena, and Mapula were permitted in the royal feast huts or anywhere near the king.

"Have you breathed a word of the Khoro Forest to any soul?" Prince Maru whispered to Mapula, as they sat side by side at the rear of the table, far from the reach of their fathers.

"No, I have spoken not of it," replied Mapula.

"Excellent, keep it so. Should Gasane catch wind of it, he shall tattle to my father, and I shall find myself in dire straits."

"Please tell me you are not afraid, young prince?" jested Mapula.

"I am telling you, those woods are off-limits, particularly to outsiders."

"Very well, I will not breathe a word of it," promised Mapula.

"You are such a scared baby," she jested again.

"No, I'm not!" exclaimed the young prince, shoving Mapula to the ground.

"Children, mind your manners. Maru, it is unseemly to strike a lady," scolded the king.

"But she ..." protested the prince.

"I will not hear it," rebuked the king, to the amusement of those present in the hut.

"Your Highness, the guards have completed their search of Kara's chambers," reported Sedi to the king, bowing her head in respect.

"And what news do they bring?" enquired King Shadu with a stern countenance.

"A large pot of silver, which is believed to have been the payment for his treacherous act," replied Sedi.

"And do we know the hand that fed this snake?" asked the king, his voice heavy with suspicion.

"I cannot say for certain, but the whispers that reach mine ears indicate that he was seen conversing with a man who donned a black robe with red lining," she continued.

"That is a most vague description," said Prince Tlou, taking a seat to break his fast.

"Forgive me, Prince, I did not hear you come in," Sedi said with deference.

"Please forgive the intrusion, but I chanced upon Gasane outside and thought that the meal had not yet commenced," the prince replied.

The king shook his head in disappointment and whispered to Moroka, "I fear my son may not make a worthy king."

"Well, it is fortunate that Prince Thubo left behind a widow who is with child. Speaking of which, have you decided upon a succession plan, Your Highness?" queried Moroka.

"Why? Are you plotting to kill me?" jested the king, and Moroka chuckled in response.

"No, I speak in earnest. I have pondered, if the assassination attempt was a success, who would inherit your throne? Who is next in line?"

"Must we speak of such matters now, Moroka?" said the king in a ponderous tone.

"Indeed, Your Highness," replied Moroka, "for the question of succession weighs heavily upon us. Shall the crown pass down to your unborn grandchild or to your son? Please tell, if the gods are kind, the princess will bear a son, but what if it is a daughter?"

"I hear you, but if I am deceased, that means I do not have to worry about who shall succeed me. Either way, they are both of my blood, and my legacy shall endure," said the king dismissively.

"Listen to yourself, Your Highness. You will start a civil war because you are too indolent to name an heir," retorted Moroka with a hint of frustration.

To change the subject, the king turned to Sedi and enquired, "Any other information on finding out who tried to slay me?"

"Your Highness, at present, I have no further information, but my whispers are diligently working on the matter," replied Sedi with deference.

Morena Perega then spoke up. "If I may interject, Your Highness. The whispers that I have heard suggest that when Morena Moroka asked the traitor who sent him, he pointed to someone who was standing behind you before the arrow pierced his eye. Now, I am not making any certain accusation, but those who stood behind you that evening were Gasane, Masega, Sedi, Prince Tlou, Nare, and myself. Perhaps the perpetrator is in this very room."

Gasane, who had just entered the room, overheard Perega's words and sternly replied, "Take care with your words, boy. Those are grave accusations you are making."

"I too was behind the king, Gasane. I am merely recounting the whispers that are borne on the wind," Perega replied, unperturbed.

"You said you had more information?" Sedi asked. She did not like being in the dark; she made it her job to know everything that occurred around Soru, no matter how big or small.

"Well, before I was interrupted. On the same night that the hooded man was seen interacting with Khara, he was also seen entering the royal grounds. Khara's wife, who is now on the run, was overheard boasting about her husband's plans to purchase a large plot of property. Being in charge of the royal budget myself, sire, I know how much royal guards are paid, and I can tell you that no low born can afford to acquire a plot of land after only four summers in your service. My ears are on the trail of her, and when we find her, I'll have her brought back for questioning."

"Good job, Perega," Morena Moroka added.

"Now he is on Father's council," whispered Leko rhetorically to Prince Tlou.

The prince shook his head and rolled his eyes, to show that he agreed with what his sister was saying.

Sedi was not happy that Perega knew all of this before she did. However, she tried to conceal her disdain. "Very good work indeed, Perega," she said.

"What about his father?" the king asked.

"He was seen travelling to Swarai. I have instructed our guards to pursue him and bring him back alive," Sedi said proudly.

"My whispers inform me that a man matching his description was travelling with a lot of coin, also travelling to Swarai. I believe it is him," Perega interjected.

"Does the father have a wife or another child?" enquired Gasane.

"The wife passed away a few summers ago, and no records indicate any other child," answered Sedi.

"'Tis good work, but we must still uncover who amongst us colluded with Khara," declared Morena Moroka.

"Are you implying that wolves surround me?" asked the king.

"It will not be the first time that one of your advisors has attempted to take your life," Moroka replied, causing the room to fall silent.

"Well, does anyone have anything to say? Shall I remind you of the fate that befell the last person who tried to poison me? Answer me!" roared King Shadu in anger.

"Your Highness, I can assure you that we toil day and night to uncover the culprit behind this vile act," Perega responded, diffusing the tension in the chamber.

Sedi cleared her throat. "Sire, I know not if there will ever be a most opportune moment to bring this up. The council has been in discourse since the passing of the prince, and recent events at his funeral have spurred us to act with haste."

King Shadu, now more composed, nudged Moroka to indicate that he comprehended the topic at hand. "Speak on," he commanded.

"Your Highness, the matter does pertain to your succession," Sedi finally revealed, bowing low before the king.

"My succession remains unchanged, for I am still alive," responded the king, his voice tinged with concern.

Prince Tlou appeared ill at ease, and Princess Palesa, who had been silent thus far, with her head bowed low, suddenly sat up straight.

Since the funeral, Lera had provided comfort to Princess Palesa, even now, she was by her side for support.

"Your Highness, forgive my impertinence. But our customs dictate that the coronation of the heir be held a fortnight following the funeral of the last heir," Perega said hesitantly.

"Sire, the princess is with child. Should she give birth to a son, if the gods be good, he shall be your heir. However, if she bears a daughter, Prince Tlou shall become the heir," proclaimed Gasane, who was seated beside Sedi.

"Indeed, I perceive no hindrance to my succession. In a few moons' time, the identity of my heir shall be known. Why must we debate this now?" queried the king.

"I pray that you shall live a long life, and we all shall strive to keep you safe at all times. But the truth is, if Morena Moroka had not been present at the funeral, you would have perished," Sedi said carefully.

"Then my council and the guards would have failed in their duties," the king retorted.

"My king, you must name your heir," urged Sedi.

"I will hear no more of this conversation! I shall name my heir when my grandchild is born. Until then, the line of succession shall not alter," the king thundered, his voice resounding throughout the hall.

All in attendance were confused by the king's reply.

"Does that mean you are the heir?" Leko whispered to her brother.

"I do not know," Prince Tlou responded.

"But my king, who is …" Perega began.

"I have said I shall hear no more of this conversation! I am still mourning the death of my son, and you would have me discuss my succession?" the king bellowed, his eyes ablaze with fury.

Morena Moroka gently and subtly placed his hand on the king's thigh under the table to calm him down.

Please Do Not Die

A skilled rider mounted on horseback would take a day and a half, or perhaps just a day (without rest), to make the journey to Baloki from the base of the Molotli Mountains. But they would have to exchange horses a few times along the way to make such a time. Meanwhile, the entourage of Moroka would take just shy of four sunsets to complete their trek on the open Shari Road, given their size. Morena Moroka desired to depart at dawn, but the king insisted he wait until after the daybreak meal.

"Your Highness, I know it has been long since our last meeting, and these circumstances are not ideal. However, I pledge to make efforts to visit often," Moroka said humbly as he knelt before King Shadu in the throne room.

"I extend my sincere condolences to the great Soru Kingdom on behalf of Queen Motapo and her people," he continued, scanning the room carefully as he chose his words.

"Your son would have made a great king. Though saddened, I find solace in knowing that your true heir will rule with honour and integrity."

Prince Tlou sat on the right-hand side of his father, whilst Princess Palesa sat on the left. The king attempted to lighten the mood with a jest, saying, "It appears I am spoilt for choice in selecting an heir." However, the quip did not amuse Prince Tlou.

"If it pleases Your Highness, we humbly request permission to depart after the daybreak meal. Though our journey is long, we pray to the gods for safe travels," Moroka said with respect.

"My son, Prince Maru, will be accompanying you on your journey to the north. I hope he has a memorable adventure, just as I did at his age. Please take good care of him, Moroka. He is still an heir to my kingdom." The king looked towards Prince Maru, who stood beside Mapula, with a subtle grin.

"Maru, when you depart from this place today, you are to consider Morena Moroka as your father. Show him the same respect you show me. Remember always that you are Soru's Prince, and as such, you are an extension of our kingdom wherever you go."

The chamber echoed with mirthful cries and joyous ululations.

"Father! I will conduct myself with propriety and acquire as much knowledge as I am able. I shall write you often," declared the youthful prince.

"And I will ensure he behaves himself," Mapula chimed in, prompting laughter among those assembled.

"Please convey my warmest regards to the good people of Baloki, and most especially to the queen. Farewell, Moroka. May the gods watch over you and keep you safe," pronounced the king, bidding them farewell.

Once more, the chamber resounded with jubilation.

But then the king requested Moroka to stay behind for a private audience. As the king made his way towards a nearby door, Moroka followed close behind. The royal guards wanted to follow them, but the king dismissed them, making an offhand comment that Moroka's protection is better than all of them.

"Close the door and listen carefully," the king instructed Moroka as they entered one of the chambers immediately behind the throne chamber.

"Your Highness. Tell me, what troubles you?" Moroka enquired.

"In truth, I suspect this shall be the last occasion on which we meet in this life," the king disclosed in a grave tone.

The only times Moroka beheld the countenance of the king this worried was on two occasions: during his sister's funeral and the time when they were young lads, when Moroka fell ill and the healers feared for his life.

"Shadu, is this one of your jests? You are causing me to fear," Moroka entreated.

"Promise me one thing, brother," besought the king.

"No, first you must tell me what troubles you." Moroka clasped the king's head and looked deeply into his eyes.

"Moroka, I am filled with terror. I fear for my life. Which is why I have sent Maru with you. Keep him safe, I ask of you."

"You have my word. I shall love and guard him as my own," Moroka pledged. "But you still haven't told me why you think this is the last time we will see each other."

"When I am gone, I wish for him to reign as king."

This pronouncement caught Moroka off guard, and he released his hold on the king's head.

"What are you saying? Maru is third in line. You should not utter such words, lest you ignite a civil war," Moroka cautioned.

"Let us be honest; Tlou is not fit to rule. He is my son, and I love him dearly, yet he lacks the qualities of a great king. He knows it, and the people know it. If he takes the throne, Soru will suffer."

"But what of Thubo's widow? Her child shall be your heir," Moroka reminded him.

"True, but until the child is of age, who shall rule Soru?"

"His mother and your council," Moroka replied.

"No, Moroka. Do you know who has always coveted my throne?"

The king and Moroka spoke in unison. "Gauta."

"Do you think he is behind your assassination attempt?" enquired Moroka.

"No, he is not that cunning, but I do believe that someone on my council is pulling the strings to seat a mere babe upon my throne," replied the king.

"How do you know that it is one amongst your council?" queried Moroka.

"Call it a king's intuition. Though I may appear to play the fool at times, mine eyes are ever upon my councillors. They have been known to sneak away under cover of night, conspiring on matters of the kingdom in my absence. Be assured, there is a traitor in my council, yet I bide my time, laying a snare and awaiting the moment when the rat shall be caught in its own deceit."

"Whom amongst your council do you trust?"

"I trust none of them. They will betray me to the highest bidder!" exclaimed the king in frustration.

"Surely, there must be someone," pressed Moroka.

The king took a step towards Moroka and seized the back of his head, an unusual gesture for King Shadu, as Moroka was usually the one to do so.

"You are the only one I trust, Moroka," declared the king.

"Allow me to remain here in Soru until I am assured of your safety. I can send Maru with the rest of my entourage back to Baloki," suggested Moroka.

"You cannot let them travel on the open road without you. There are many opportunists along the Shari Road. If news breaks that you are not accompanying them, the worst may befall them," replied the king.

"Do you underestimate the Baloki guards? I think …" began Moroka before being interrupted by the king.

"No, you must go. You have already done more than enough here. I shall never be safe, and I cannot bear to put you in harm's way," insisted the king.

"Put me in harm's way, Shadu. When we were but children, I was always in danger because of you," retorted Moroka with a laugh.

The two shared a moment of nostalgia before the king grew solemn again.

King Shadu produced a blade from his tunic, which Moroka examined closely.

"I did give you this blade," said Moroka.

"Aye, but I had the handle changed," King Shadu replied.

"I cannot believe you have kept it. I gave it to you at your coronation," remarked Moroka.

"Indeed, and now I desire for you to have it. Give it to Maru once he is of age," said the king.

The king heaved a great sigh and proceeded to remove his ring.

"This ring has been in my family for generations, passed down from one king to the next. It can never fall into the hands of the unworthy ruler. Give it unto Maru, and tell him it was meant for him," the king instructed.

"Shadu, why are you doing this?" enquired Moroka.

The king looked at Moroka intently before responding. "The final item I cannot give you physically, but it is my heart. You have been more of a brother to me than words can express. Your loyalty and devotion have been unwavering.

The pact you and I made when I arrived in Baloki as a mere lad of six still holds true. I would not have ascended to the throne were it not for you. I owe you my very life. Most men go their entire lives without experiencing true love. Although I do not believe in them, the gods have been kind to grant me two soulmates, you and your sister. If I am to fall, I am content to have known this love, and I am overjoyed that my soul shall be reunited with my love, who does wait for me."

Moroka's eyes were as teary as a spring's dew, but he tried to withhold his tears. Although he did not want to admit the truth to himself, Moroka knew that his stay in Soru would but prolong the inevitable, for there were many who sought to end the king's life.

"Why do you speak in such a manner, Shadu?" he asked.

"I am bound for war, brother," King Shadu replied, producing a letter bearing his seal and presenting it to Moroka.

"And what manner of letter be this?" Moroka enquired.

"'Tis a letter declaring mine heir," answered Shadu. "You are the lone soul I trust to safeguard this. Keep it close to your chest, and should I perish, reveal its contents to the council."

"Please do not die," Moroka entreated.

"You have sought my benediction to depart, and I grant it with all my heart. May the gods of rain and mountains watch over you," Shadu declared, embracing his brother, their spirits heavy with unspoken fears, for the future lay uncertain and fraught with peril.

For the Greater Good

It had been two sunsets since Prince Moroka left Soru. In the streets of the marketplace and the royal grounds, whispers and rumours echoed, as everyone speculated about who would be the rightful heir to the kingdom.

Prince Tlou, the eldest living son of the king, had been chosen by the council to be crowned as the temporary Heir Prince, until Princess Palesa's child was born. The kingdom was split in two, with one side supporting the young prince and the other advocating for Princess Palesa to be proclaimed as Regent Princess until her heir came of age.

The prince was a striking figure, with the typical features of the Soru people. At the tender age of seventeen summers, he had proven his worth as a seasoned warrior, having fought in two battles. However, his grim countenance and rare smile left many people in the kingdom wondering about him. He rarely made public appearances and was viewed as a mysterious figure.

Despite his lack of public engagement, Prince Tlou had the backing of the army and the majority of the council. They valued his strength and military prowess, believing that he was the best choice to lead the kingdom. Some asked why he, rather than the widow of the late Heir Prince, was chosen as the temporary heir, but the council felt that a man would be a stronger heir in these troubled times.

As the day of the coronation approached, Prince Tlou found himself deep in thought, contemplating the weight of responsibility that would soon be placed upon his shoulders. Although he had never aspired to be king as a young lad, he knew that he now had a duty to his people and that he must prove himself worthy of their trust and respect.

For the kingdom of Soru needed a leader who was strong, capable, and just, and he was determined to be that leader.

The prince had spent much time in the company of his father and the council since the passing of his brother. This night was no different, for he went to keep company with his father in preparation for his coronation.

Prince Tlou stood in front of his father, with a look of frustration etched on his face. The two were in the king's private chambers, where the king had come back to after meeting with his council. Tlou had been hoping to have a conversation about his future.

"Tlou, who has sanctioned this coronation?" King Shadu asked. "Might we delay it for a brief while? What is the haste?" the king continued.

"Father, it is our custom to crown an heir or a king a fortnight following the funeral of a monarch," replied the prince.

"Aye, do not tell me about our customs, boy! I am well aware of them. Also, your brother's heir shall be born in a few moons," said King Shadu.

"Father, I am your living heir. And who can say that child shall not be a girl?"

"Perhaps we should wait until then?" suggested the king.

"Would you rather break with tradition and await the birth of this child than crown me as your heir?" queried the prince.

"What is the urgency? Do you plan to have me slain?" the king asked in a mocking tone.

The prince sighed deeply, gazing at the moon outside through the window. "And risk the wrath of the gods? You think so little of me, Father?" he said, turning his gaze upon his father.

"I merely enquire as to the haste," replied the king.

"Father, since the day of my birth, you have made it plain that you do not hold me in high esteem," lamented the prince.

"That is not so," his father retorted, putting down the jar of ale he had been drinking.

"I have come to accept that I shall ever live in the shadow of my brother. Even in his passing, he does cast a long shadow upon me.

I was the second-born son, and that was a place that I had come to accept, discharging my duties with honour.

Today I stand before you as your eldest legitimate son, requesting that you name me your heir. Yet, you would sooner gamble your throne on a foreigner," the prince said sorrowfully, approaching his father, who sat in a chair by his bedside.

"Watch it, boy. I am still your king."

"You are my father afore you are my king," replied the prince angrily. "All my life, all I have ever desired is to make you proud and to know that my father loves me."

"Tlou, I am weary. I have no time for this," King Shadu sighed.

"No, you must make time," demanded the prince, looking at his father. "Why do you not love me?" He wept.

The king took a moment to collect his thoughts. "I care for all of my children equally," he said carefully.

"The happiest I have ever seen you was when your friend was here," the prince pointed out.

"He is your uncle," corrected the king.

"You never shown me any love or appreciation. And now, you sit here and attempt to deny me my rightful inheritance."

The face of the king was rife with ire, yet he remained composed to mitigate the situation. "Let us reconvene on the morrow, for I am exceedingly weary."

"No, I shall have my coronation," Tlou retorted, departing from the king's chamber.

At the entranceway, Lehlo, who had been promoted to safeguard the king, was stationed. The council had carefully selected him. Bonolo, another veteran warrior, in service in the army for ten summers, stood alongside Lehlo.

"Permit none entry, do you understand?" commanded Prince Tlou before shutting the door. The prince was well acquainted with both men and trusted them with his very life, having personally recommended them to the council.

"We shall safeguard His Highness with our very lives," answered Lehlo, a towering and intimidating figure clothed in the garb of the royal guard.

"Excellent. This does bring to mind, Lehlo. I shall have need of the army soon," Prince Tlou said, scratching his head like his mind was racing.

"Of course, my prince, I obey unquestioningly. Yet, if the men enquire, 'Shall we go to war?' what shall we say?" asked Lehlo, piqued by curiosity.

"No, we shan't go to war. But inform the men that I remain their chief commander," Tlou replied.

"As you command, my prince." Lehlo bowed as Prince Tlou departed.

Meanwhile, the king, having retired to his bed, found slumber elusive as his thoughts raced. "Who is the rightful heir?" he pondered.

The king lay restless upon his bed, his mind in great turmoil. He sought to make a decision that would not lead to war, yet he was torn between the unborn child of Thubo and Tlou. Perhaps he should make it known that he desires Maru to be his heir, but he feared the outcry such a proclamation would cause. The lad was too young and naive to understand the ways of politics, and he would surely be devoured by the council. As the night wore on, the king's weariness grew, and he felt himself slipping into slumber.

His chamber door opened, and he roused himself, thinking it was one of his guards. But a dark figure loomed in the doorway, and the king felt a weight settle upon him. He sat up in alarm, demanding to know why this familiar figure was in his chambers at such an hour.

The shadowy figure said naught, but swiftly approached the bed. From beneath the black cloak, the figure produced a glimmering object that shone to the light of the full moon outside. Before he could utter another word, the king felt a sharp, icy pain in his chest, and he gasped in shock as the metal blade penetrated his night garment and pierced his heart. He seized the figure's cloak in a desperate attempt to hold on to life, his eyes wide with sorrow and anger, but above all, disappointment. His voice failed him, and he could only utter words. "It is you, they sent you!" he whispered, gasping for air, as a dagger did pierce through his heart.

The shadow then shoved the king onto his bed, tearing his garment in the process, due to the king's strong grip on it, and whispered, "For the greater good."

The shadow stood over the king's body, staring down at him with an unreadable expression.

The figure watched as the life slowly drained from the king's body, his eyes losing their glimmer and his chest becoming still. All of a sudden, the stillness of the night was broken by echoes of voices outside the king's chamber, calling out, "Unbar the door! The king is in danger!"

As the door creaked open, the shadow vanished into the darkness of the blustery night. Lehlo then opened the door to find the king lying in a pool of blood, lifeless.

"Ring the bells! Seal off all entries to the royal grounds!" he shouted to Bonolo.

Bonolo rushed out to do as Lehlo commanded, while guilt-stricken Lehlo knelt beside the fallen king. "My king, I am so sorry," he whispered, his voice breaking with emotion. "Who could have done this?"

The other guards burst into the room, weapons drawn, ready to avenge their fallen king. Lehlo stood up, his face grim. "Find the killer," he ordered. "I want him brought to justice."

As the guards searched the royal grounds, Lehlo knelt once more beside the king's body.

He noticed something clenched tightly in the king's hand, and he gently pried it open to reveal a small, crumpled note. He unfolded it and read the words written in a spidery scrawl: "For the greater good. We are the keepers of men."

And Now, You Will Suffer

Princess Mapula was abruptly awoken from her slumber by a ghastly dream. "Father! Wake up, wake up now," she cried out.

With bleary eyes, Prince Moraka struggled to find his footing within the royal carriage. "What troubles you, my sweet daughter?"

"They are coming, Father! They come to slay us! I saw it in my dream!"

Princess Mapula had never shown any magical potential or had prophetic dreams in the past. However, in this moment, Prince Moroka's instinct told him to listen to his daughter's cry.

After all, the women of the Rain Queen lineage were known to have prophetic visions; perhaps Mapula's was manifesting for the first time in this very moment.

Before he could fully rise to make sense of his daughter's words, the piercing cries of men echoed through the night.

"Take cover!" one voice shouted.

"Protect the royal carriage!" cried another.

The prince couldn't discern what was amiss, but his intuition warned him that all was not well. Suddenly, the serene moonlit sky was bathed in an eerie red hue. Having seen enough battles in his lifetime, Prince Moraka understood the gravity of the situation.

The clanging of swords could be heard outside the carriage, striking against steel.

"Kwena! Wake up, we are under ambush! Protect the princess! I am going outside to put an end to this!"

"What is happening?" slurred Kwena, still muddled from drinking and drowsiness.

The prince dealt Kwena a fierce slap, jolting him awake. "Fool! I have no time for your foolishness! Rise up at once! In the name of our queen, I command you to protect your princess! We are under attack!"

"I also want to fight! I am not a mere child, and I can defend myself," said the princess, taking a step towards the door.

"Mapula, I have no time for this!" roared the prince. "Remain inside the carriage!"

The princess was taken aback by her father's demeanour, for she had never seen him so fierce. As she was about to sit down, a loud bang resounded on the carriage door. The princess recognised the voice of the young horse keeper, Mohale, whom she had acquainted with during their travels.

Just as the prince opened the door, an arrow pierced Mohale's head, and the young man fell lifeless into the prince's arms. Princess Mapula let out an ear-piercing scream, and a frightened Kwena rushed to comfort her.

As the prince stepped out of the carriage, he beheld their dire situation, for they were greatly outnumbered, and it seemed certain that death awaited them. Yet the prince had fought against worse odds before, like the time during the war with the Swarais and Shangas. Though his army was outnumbered three to one, they emerged victorious.

Taking a deep breath, the prince reminded himself of his prowess. "I am the great mage of Baloki."

With unwavering determination, Prince Moroka charged towards the front of the battle. The clash of steel against steel and the cries of men filled the stillness of the night. On his right, the prince beheld a youth battling for his very life against a towering giant. He recognised the young man, thought to himself, *That is Tlou's boy.*

He then cast a spell, which unleashed a powerful blast from his staff, sending the giant hurtling through the air. "Come hither, behind me," the prince cried out. Tlounyana, with innocent countenance, witnessed his first battle, his eyes widening as his innocence was lost in that very moment.

"Have you perhaps seen Prince Maru?" Prince Moroka enquired.

"No, Your Highness, I have not seen him, but I believe he remains in his carriage," stammered Tlounyana, struggling to articulate his words.

"Boy, be valiant now," Moroka commanded. "I will shield you. Go hence to the young prince's carriage and convey him to safety in mine carriage, where he may join the princess."

As Tlounaya set forth to run toward the carriage, fiery arrows rained down upon it. Upon seeing the arrows, Tlounyana hesitated and sought refuge.

"Run, boy!" cried the prince, invoking a spell that created a force field, deflecting the arrows.

"We require greater cover," Moroka pondered. "Fog. Yes, fog shall provide cover." Prince Moroka then conjured a spell that enveloped the area with a thick fog.

As Tlounyana drew near to the carriage, he heard a voice shrieking, "We shall all perish!"

"I beg of you, spare my life," Prince Maru entreated as Tlounyana opened the carriage door.

"Fear not, Prince of Soru, you shall not die this night," assured Tlounyana. "My lord, Prince Moroka, has dispatched me to convey you safely to his carriage. Follow me."

The young prince was attired in his evening finery.

"My prince, let me help you dress," said his squire, who was travelling with him.

"No! there is no time for that. We need to go now!" Tlounyana shouted.

I must be bold and stout hearted, he pondered, as he accompanied Prince Maru towards the royal carriage.

"Follow my lead," Tlounyana directed as they manoeuvred through the fog, making their way towards the royal carriage. As more arrows were released towards them, Maru and Tlounyana deftly evaded them. Yet, lo and behold, as Maru looked back, his heart sank at the sight of a piercing arrow that struck his squire's breastplate. This grievous sight filled the young prince's eyes with terror.

Tlounyana unfastened the carriage door to reveal a petrified Princess Mapula and Kwena within.

"Your Highness, I have brought his lordship at your father's command," Tlounyana said, "and he assured me that Prince Maru will remain secure in your custody. I must return and help Prince Moroka and the rest of the men."

"Did my brother specifically request my presence?" enquired Kwena.

"My lord, His Highness only commanded me to bring the young prince of Soru here," replied Tlounyana.

"As you see, Princess, I am ensconced in this carriage not for lack of valour, but to safeguard you," Kwena jested.

"I believe the royal carriage is safeguarded by spells that shield it from magical assaults," retorted Tlounyana.

As he hastened back to the prince, Tlounyana espied that the fog had indeed helped to conceal him. From his vantage point, Prince Moroka seemed to be in control. *Perhaps they might survive this ordeal*, he hoped.

The prince stood side by side with Sello, a formidable warrior from the Metsi Clan. Baloki's entourage of nearly forty individuals, including the Soru soldiers who were escorting Maru, had dwindled to a mere few.

A shadow emerged from the fog. Although the prince tried to conjure lightning bolts from his staff, nothing availed.

The shadowy figure effortlessly deflected them. A chill ran down Prince Moroka's spine at the sound of a deep, resounding voice.

"Moroka, you still seem as weak as the day we departed from Sepoko Island," the voice intoned, carrying a weight of ancient wisdom and experience.

Sepoko Island was a place shrouded in mystery; a land accessible only by invitation. There, aspiring mages trained for years to master the art of magic and serve their respective kings and queens.

Prince Moroka recognised the voice at once. "Noga, is it you? What did they do to you?" the prince asked, his face contorted with terror.

"They have bestowed upon me the gift of immortality," Noga responded in a terrifying deadpan voice.

Despite being of similar age to Prince Moroka, Noga looked to be at least two decades older. He was nearly bald, with only six dreadlocks trailing down his back. His face was gaunt, his eyes bloodshot, and he had a long white beard braided into a thin plait. He was tall and skeletal, with black nails and serpentine tattoos that slithered across his hands.

"Old friend, do you call this immortality? You know full well the cost of forbidden magic. It shall only consume your humanity," Prince Moroka said, still attempting to discern the situation.

"Moroka, this shall be your sole and final warning: cast aside your staff and come with me. I pledge to spare your men," Noga demanded.

"Noga, if you release us, I swear upon the rain gods that all shall be forgiven as a mere misunderstanding," the prince pleaded.

Moroka had never delved into the depths of forbidden magic before, but he knew the price one paid for accessing the proscribed dimension.

"I deemed it wise to show you mercy, for the sake of our past camaraderie, yet you do not value your life nor that of your men," Noga said, a wicked smile playing at the corners of his mouth.

"Noga, what impels you to do this? Who sent you on this course?" the prince enquired urgently.

"I have not a moment for this," said Noga, as he uttered a chant of chaos magic that hoisted Sefefe, a Baloki guard, who was still fighting.

The prince endeavoured to weave a counter-spell to bring Sefefe down, but to no avail. Sefefe wailed in torment, his body being crushed from within, and blood pouring out from every aperture, as well as his skin.

"Noga, release him. Your fight is with me. Allow the others to go."

"As I warned you, Prince. Lower your staff and come with me."

The prince sought to counter Noga's spell, but his attempt proved futile, for Noga's power was too great. Moroka knew that he was outmatched; he could not combat this chaos magic alone. Though Princess Mapula lacked manifest magical capabilities, perhaps he could harness her latent magic to bolster his own. However, the risk of this venture was the princess's life, a risk he could not bear.

Noga cast Sefefe's corpse aside like a sack of grain and then fixed his gaze on the carriage transporting the princess and Prince Maru.

As Noga raised his staff to cast another spell at the carriage, the prince uttered a fog spell, one of the densest fogs he had ever conjured, with near-zero visibility. Within a heartbeat, he loosed more than ten lightning bolts at Noga.

Laughter resonated from the thick fog.

"You fool! You wormy creature! You think you can defeat me with that?" said the dark mage, levitating towards the moon, seemingly unharmed by the lightning bolts.

The men kept casting spells at each other, each one more powerful than the last.

Wind gusts, lightning bolts, and fire filled the moonlit night.

Without chanting a spell, Noga pointed his staff, and the entire fog dispersed.

Noga once again focused on the royal carriage. He cast another chaos spell, and a dark cloud enveloped him, raising the royal carriage into the air and slamming it down, with all aboard.

"Surrender now, or I shall crush this entire carriage with all in it."

Prince Moroka knew this was no idle threat. Beside him were Sello and Tlounyana, who quivered with fear, unable to speak.

"Boy, I need you to do something every important. I need you to be brave one last time.

I may not survive what I am about to do," he said to Tlounyana. "Run back to Baloki and make haste to our queen. Inform her of what has befallen here. Let her know that Noga was behind this ambush. Tell her that war is coming, and urge her to prepare the Baloki army. Await my signal, then depart without delay."

Tlounyana prepared himself.

"One last thing – if I do not make it here alive, I want you to take this dagger and ring." The items, which King Shadu had given him, he shoved into Tlounyana's tunic. "And give this note …" which he had scrabbled quickly, to echoes of Noga shouting, "surrender now, prince, or I crush this carriage".

"…with this ring and dagger directly to the queen, no one else. The queen." To which Tlounyana nodded, in his innocence, he understood the magnitude of what was about to happen.

The prince could hear the distressing cries of his daughter emanating from the royal carriage.

"This is your last warning, Moroka, or I crush this entire carriage!" Noga exclaimed. Prince Moroka had to think swiftly and act with even greater speed. He recollected a spell, one that bordered on the realm of forbidden magic, yet not quite. Nevertheless, he had never before uttered this spell, for it could potentially claim his life.

"*Maru, pula, metse, maru, pula, metse,*" the prince intoned as he readied himself to cast one of the most potent spells he had ever attempted.

Levitating in the air, he bellowed, "Boy, go now, and do not look back. Sello, cover Tlounyana," he instructed.

Tlounyana swiftly untethered one of the horses and set off towards Baloki, leaving behind the anguished cries from the royal carriage.

With his staff, Prince Moroka launched a blinding blast towards Noga. The intensity of the blast was such that it could be observed from Baloki. The sky shone so brightly that it seemed as though it were daylight.

This ought to do it, thought the prince as he collapsed, blood trickling from his nostrils. This spell had consumed all his strength, and his body had given out.

Attempting to deflect the blast, Noga let out a piercing scream of anguish. A dark cloud enshrouded Noga, and eerie whispers could be heard surrounding him.

Once the night had resumed its darkness and stillness, Noga was discovered to be partially charred on the right side, where he had held his staff. As Noga fell to the ground, a dark cloud surrounded him and entered his mouth and nose.

Although weak and partly burnt, he managed to land on his feet beside the lifeless body of Prince Moroka. The cloud began to dissipate, and Noga emerged, a sinister smile on his face. "You really thought you could defeat me, Moroka?" he sneered. "You are nothing compared to my power. And now, you will suffer for your arrogance." The dark mage then took a spear, which lay next to Prince Moroka, and pierced the prince on his side.

Bring Me His Head

In the aftermath of the king's assassination, the entire kingdom was thrown into disarray. The kingdom was split in two, with one half proclaiming Prince Tlou as the lawful successor to the throne, while the other half supported Princess Palesa.

"Gathered here this eve, my lords and lady, I speak in light of the events of the past night," Prince Tlou addressed the council, draped in mourning attire. "My father, your king, was slain in his sleep. Justice must be served, and I vow to turn this continent upside down until the guilty party is brought to justice."

"Our best spies and armies have been dispatched to find the perpetrator of this heinous crime," declared Morena Nare boldly.

"Well spoken, Morena," said the prince. "I know this kingdom can always count on your unwavering loyalty."

"Sedi, you were my father's most trusted confidant, and he entrusted you with his very life. Perega, as the head of the royal treasury, you have been entrusted with a great responsibility. Gasane, you have been the royal mage since my father's youth, and he held you in great esteem. And Nare, you have been our stalwart defender for many years. I have learned much from you and have come to greatly admire your leadership," the prince continued, pacing around the council chamber.

"Thus, I stand before you, esteemed council, and humbly request that you crown me as your king and rightful ruler, without delay," Prince Tlou said with authority and conviction.

All in attendance were yet attempting to discern the boundaries and loyalties of their fellow councillors.

This meeting had been convened to address the grievous matter of the king's murder, yet Prince Tlou had redirected the discourse towards his own coronation.

"My father and my brother are no more, slain by foul treachery," he proclaimed. "Our nation cannot wait until a fortnight of mourning is over before a new king is officially crowned. Our enemies lurk among us, cloaked in wool, and we must take action to thwart them before they strike again," Prince Tlou asserted vigorously.

"Yet, my prince," interjected the venerable Gasane, coughing to clear his throat, "please forgive this old man's presumption. We have not yet granted your father the proper rites to usher him into the next world and join his ancestors. How can we, in good conscience, crown you as king before we have fulfilled this solemn obligation?"

Gasane was a man advanced in years, his head mostly bereft of hair, but his mind yet sharp as a honed blade. He was renowned throughout the realm for his magery and wisdom.

"Listen to me," said the prince with conviction.

"You all did lend your support to my father, and now I ask you to extend your allegiance to me, his rightful heir and the next king of Soru. Why must my coronation be delayed? The throne is mine by birthright, and if you had true love for my father and your kingdom, then tonight you shall crown me."

The councillors were taken aback and began to murmur among themselves in consternation. "I fail to see why we ought to defer your coronation, my prince," declared Nare, whose allegiance to the prince was plainly evident.

Sedi, seated at the head of the table, surveyed the situation carefully before weighing in. She apprehended that the events of this evening would have profound repercussions, irrevocably dividing the council and cementing loyalties.

"There have been far too many deaths in this kingdom," the prince pronounced solemnly.

"Indeed," Gasane interjected, "two royal deaths within the same moon are no mere coincidence."

"We all saw what happened at your brother's funeral. Someone tried to kill your father. 'Tis a perilous matter, and we may not chance it. Therefore, we must crown you without delay," declared Nare.

"Aye," agreed Gasane, who had altered his tune and now seemed to be standing with the prince. "Might I suggest that we hold a swift funeral for His Highness, as soon as the morrow, and you, my lord, shall be anointed the day after."

The prince pondered a moment, then turned to Sedi, who remained stoic. "Sedi, Perega, neither of you has spoken a word since this council began."

"Well, my prince," said Perega, directing the prince's attention to him. "I must raise the matter that all present seem to forget: your brother has left behind a widow, great with child. Please forgive me, but the babe she carries is the true heir to the throne. You do summon us in the dead of night to commit treason against the crown by placing a coronet upon your head? No, for the night belongs to witches, and I shall not be party to such foul deeds." So saying, he flung open the council chamber door and was met by the guards of the army stationed outside.

"You cannot keep me here against my will. Sedi, tell them that what they are doing is wrong."

Sedi cast her gaze upon Perega, and many a message did her countenance convey, yet her lips remained sealed.

"Bring him back," commanded the prince with a firm voice, his eyes set upon Perega.

Tlou then turned to Sedi and enquired if she had aught to add to the matter. The chamber fell silent, all eyes upon her.

"My fealty lies with the throne, my lords. Whosoever sits upon it is the king I serve," Sedi responded, her words measured and cautious.

"Am I to understand that you pledge your unflinching support to me?" the prince demanded.

Sedi knew well the dire consequences of refusing such a request. "I await your coronation, my prince. Once it is confirmed, you shall have my allegiance," she replied with a respectful bow.

"Aye, this is the loyalty I seek," the prince said, an uncomfortable smirk on his lips. "Behold, Perega, this is what true allegiance looks like."

"As you can see, I already have the army. I wished for a peaceful transition, but if needs must, there shall be bloodshed in this very hall tonight," he added. Bonolo was one of the guards unsheathing his sword.

Upon witnessing the imminent danger, Sedi stepped forth, her resolve unwavering. "You have my loyalty, Your Highness," she declared.

Nare, with a smile upon his lips, spoke next. "The army is at your command, my sword is at your disposal, and my loyalty is unwavering, my prince."

"I am but your servant, Your Highness. Command me as you see fit," echoed Gasane.

All eyes then turned to Perega, waiting for his response, yet he remained steadfast, holding his head high.

"Do with me as you wilt, boy," he said.

Nare slapped him very hard across the face. "Careful, remember who you speak with."

Parerga never liked the prince; he had always allied himself with the deceased Prince Thubo and his widow. When he looked around the council chambers, he knew he had to make a decision and make it fast.

Princess Palesa had a valid claim; he knew that everybody in that room knew that. She could gather enough people to overthrow the kingdom and would see him as a traitor. But that was not the point. He had made an oath to King Shadu that he will always protect the throne, and now more than ever, the throne needed protection. Perega took few steps away from the guards.

"I have always acted in the best interest of the throne. I was loyal to your father, and I will be loyal to him now, even at his death," Perega said as he leaned against a wall with a window close by, overlooking a hanging cliff.

His mind was racing. Taking big breaths, he looked outside the window again. *It is a bad fall*, he thought.

He noticed that the women who were washing the royal linens earlier had left a pile just outside, down the cliff. Without hesitation, he jumped out of the window, to the voice of Prince Tlou shouting, "Guards, bring me his head!"

For Your Eyes Only

"Two sunsets have passed since we last did hear from the prince. Has any of you heard anything, or has any of your spies brought news? They were due to arrive yesterday ..." the queen asked but was abruptly halted by a mighty knock upon the door, which did not tarry for an answer before it burst open. This meeting was not an ordinary one, for the queen had summoned her council twice within a single moon. Alas, her concern for her daughter and Prince Moroka weighed heavy on her heart, and thus she summoned an urgent meeting forthwith.

"What is the meaning of this?" Black Mamba demanded.

"Morena, a messenger has arrived from Soru, bearing news of the prince," Selo, one of the guards, said with urgency.

Completely dazed, bruised, and besmirched with blood, Tlounyana did rush in, and fell prostrate at the feet of the queen. Though he had transgressed many protocols, he had insisted that the news he bore be delivered solely unto the queen.

"Arise and speak what you know, my son. Someone, bring him water, for he does appear parched," the queen said, with Mamba taking his hand and offering him a vacant chair.

Tlounyana drank the water as if his very life depended on it, for he had travelled throughout the night to arrive at Baloki.

"They ... they did slay him," he said, his countenance contorted in terror. "I am so sorry, Your Highness. The prince is dead. They have slain him. I beg your forgiveness."

All in the room were frozen, and the queen's face grew cold, but as the queen, she could not display her emotions to any. She must remain a symbol of strength for her people.

She heaved a deep sigh and looked to Motakia, and together, they endeavoured to process the grievous news they had just received. Motakia arose from her seat and stood beside her mother.

"What news of the princess? Is she alive?" enquired the queen with an air of composure.

"Your Majesty, they have clapped her in irons and cast her into a cage, along with Prince Maru and Kwena. They are now prisoners," replied Tlounyana.

The queen breathed a heavy sigh of relief. "Please tell me, have you learned where they are taking them and the identity of their captors?"

"Upon the prince's command, I took leave and withdrew to a nearby hill. His Highness bade me to tell you that Noga is behind this ambush, using dark sorceries of forbidden magic," explained Tlounyana.

All those present in the chamber were still reeling from the jarring news.

"Your Majesty, if I may interject, if Noga is behind this scheme, it stands to reason that he now serves as King Shaza's lapdog," said Black Mamba.

"Aye, and if Shaza is indeed the puppeteer, then he means to take our princess to the south," added Morena Hlogo.

"No, I believe otherwise. Should Shaza be the culprit, he would not chance traveling such a great distance upon open Shari Road, for the Baloki and Soru tribes would ensnare him. He has no allies in the north, except Swarai," countered Black Mamba.

"Then perhaps he has taken them to Swarai?" ventured Princess Motakia.

"That would be my surmise, Your Highness," replied the messenger.

"Then we march to Swarai. We have to do everything in our power to get them back," Princess Motakia commanded.

"Did you see which path they took?" enquired Mamba.

"No, Morena, I know not. I cannot fathom their destination. Perhaps they journeyed east, I know not," stammered Tlounyana, his tongue faltering as he struggled to articulate himself.

The queen's face altered suddenly from surprise to fury. "How did you survive? Where is the remainder of the entourage? You did pledge an oath to guard this throne, to safeguard the royal family. Where were you when your prince was slain?"

"Your Highness, by the rain gods, I swear I would have fought unto my final breath. I was battling when the prince bade me go ahead and tell you that they were being ambushed. I left with haste, and when I reached a hill that provided a clear view of the route, I turned back and saw him falling to the ground."

"How did he meet his end?" enquired the queen.

"I witnessed the wicked mage thrust a spear into his belly and then chain and cage his corpse. That is all I saw, I swear it. I have ridden ceaselessly all night without pause, Your Highness."

"What good is a council if you are unable to provide us with intelligence concerning the affairs of Ashari? How many spies do you possess in your collective, and yet none of you has heard anything? By the rain gods, I shall not forget this.

But for the nonce, I demand that my daughter be returned to me hale and whole. As for the prince, I want his remains brought back to Baloki so that he can be buried with his people," the queen said calmly, yet in a tone that conveyed anger and fury.

"Your Majesty, rest assured that we shall bring back the princess unscathed, even if we must raze every village from here to Zuka. Should that boy Shaza seek war, then war we shall give him," declared Morena Tlou, whilst his son stood by his side.

"Morena Tlou, we have allies between here and Zuka. Instead of laying waste to every village to Zuka, maybe we ought to write letters to our allies, summoning them to join our cause," remarked Black Mamba, taking a step forward to approach the queen.

"You speak true, Mamba. We mustn't err in our actions, and all our plans from here forth must be thought carefully with due strategy. No soul outside this chamber shall act without first consulting me. These tribulations are but the birth pangs of what is yet to come, and I can foretell that it shall be no easy feat. History shall remember this war," the queen declared firmly.

"Your Highness, I shall dispatch messenger pigeons to our allies with all haste and commence the assembly of our army," pledged Morena Hlogo, idly fiddling with two marbles in his hand.

"And we are to simply summon our allies and raise an army without a plan, I suppose?" queried Black Mamba with biting sarcasm.

"Stop your prattle," the queen chided, visibly irritated. "I shall –"

Her words were abruptly cut off by the sudden intrusion of Princess Seroka and Morena Seriti into the council chambers.

"Mother, forgive our impudence. Morena Seriti, do tell them," implored Princess Seroka.

"We are aware, Seroka," Princess Motakia replied.

"Who informed you?" enquired a stunned Princess Seroka.

"Mamba thinks that they are being taken to Swarai," offered Princess Motakia.

"Taken to Swarai? Whom are you speaking of? What is the meaning of this?"

"Father and Mapula; they are taking them to Swarai," said Princess Motakia.

"No, that is not the reason I am here. Morena Seriti, please tell them what you just told me," replied Princess Seroka.

"Princess, I think 'tis best they hear it from you," interjected Morena Seriti.

"We know, Seroka. Father is dead," responded Princess Motakia with valour, struggling to hold back her tears as she broke the news to her sister.

Struck by the shock of the news, Princess Seroka stood there trying to comprehend the message.

"What? What do you mean Father is dead? This cannot be! That is not what Morena Seriti has told me. Father is to arrive anon," cried the princess.

"Seroka, my daughter, your father has been slain, and your sister has been taken captive," added the queen.

For a moment, everyone in the room fell silent, allowing the princess to process the news.

"Where is my sister? What has befallen Mapula?" Seroka enquired, looking perplexed.

"Is that not the purpose of your visit?" asked the queen, looking bewildered.

"No, Mother. I am here because King Shadu is dead. He was slain in his bedchamber!" exclaimed the princess.

"What!" exclaimed everyone in the room in unison.

Even Neo, who had been quietly contemplating everything, stood up.

"Are you certain, Princess?" Black Mamba enquired.

The entire chamber was taken aback. The queen, now visibly distressed and confounded, said, "Please, all of you, leave us. I would converse with my daughters in private."

All were departing the chamber. "Mamba and Neo, you stay. Someone find Prince Thebo and tell him to come at once. The rest of you shall remain within the royal grounds, for I shall summon you anon."

As the company made to exit the chamber, Tlounyana tarried. "Your Highness, I almost forgot, the prince instructed me to deliver these items into your hand, meant for your eyes only," he said, tendering a letter and a ring unto the queen.

Morena Seriti glimpsed what Tlounyana had proffered yet could not devise a swift excuse to stay behind. "You are dismissed. I shall summon you anon," commanded the queen.

We Have a New King

"What word have you concerning the traitor?" Prince Tlou enquired.

"Whispers have reached mine ears, Your Highness, that Perega was sighted crossing the Madi River, near Ha-Muleti village, making his way to Batana. It is likely that he seeks to collude with your brother's widow," replied Sedi, as she approached the prince and delivered a letter from one of her spies.

As Prince Tlou read the letter, his countenance changed to one of fury. "Somebody, anybody, bring me the head of that harlot and her child! I shall reward you beyond measure."

"What about the traitorous Perega?" Gasane enquired. "What are we to do with him?"

"I desire Perega to be captured alive. I shall make an example of him," replied the prince.

"And what of the princess?" Gasane then asked.

The prince roared, "Did I not say that I wish her dead? Have you not heard me correctly? Old man, perhaps you should consider taking a step back from the council and let a younger mage take over."

"I assure you, Your Highness, that my mind is still as sharp as a sword," retorted Gasane.

"Then prove it with your actions," Prince Tlou commanded.

The prince paused and looked around. His cupbearer, his younger half-brother, Khutso refilled his jar with ale.

"Your Highness, with regards to your brother's widow and the traitor, I shall arrange it and send word," said Nare with a bow.

"Thank you, Nare. I know I can always count on you" the prince responded with a grin, pointing and looking towards Nare.

But Nare cleared his throat to remind the prince of a matter he had yet to address. "Oh, aye, before I forget why I summoned you here. When is my coronation?" Tlou enquired.

"After the funeral, Your Highness. The high priestess has already arrived to conduct both the funeral, which is today, and your coronation on the morrow," Gasane replied.

Growing up, Tlou never harboured any aspirations of being crowned as king. He had always accepted his fate as a prince, content to serve as a member of his brother's council. However, when the Keepers approached him with an offer of a kingdom, it was an opportunity too good to be spurned.

For years, Nare had been whispering in his ear that he would make a better ruler than his brother, citing his control over the army as proof.

"I desire a long and peaceful reign," Prince Tlou declared.

"The very words that every king that has sat upon that chair has wished for," proclaimed Sedi, scrutinising her words with utmost care.

The prince, though he concealed it well, was not convinced, but he knew he needed Sedi, and thus he suppressed his enmity towards her.

"Nare, you are the commander of our army. What do you think we should do?" enquired Tlou.

"Your Highness, I suggest we assail their feeble, disordered kingdom and crush them utterly," Nare proposed.

"Nare, I have thought many things of you, but never a fool. When have we ever conquered a nation by force? Our might lies in these mountains, in our impregnable defence. You must be mad to think we ought to sacrifice our men to sate your pride," countered Leko, now a member of the prince's council.

"How dare you speak to me like that, girl! I have fought wars long before the king sowed his seed in your harlot mother!" retorted Nare, his anger boiling over.

"Silence your tongue in the presence of your future king," admonished Gasane.

"I must concur with your sister, Your Highness. Soru is not known for its attacks. If we march our troops to Batana, we will surely be marching to our deaths. We should stay put, sheltered by these mountains. Let them come to us," added Sedi.

"War is not a woman's concern. I am not my father, nor his fathers before him. I am here to usher in a new era. History shall remember me as the king who did not cower behind these hills," Prince Tlou responded, with a prideful tone.

"As you wish, Your Highness," Sedi replied, bowing her head, and acquiescing to the prince's plan.

"Your Highness, the people await you outside. It is time to usher your father to the afterlife," Gasane said, rising to his feet. The others in the room followed suit.

The prince led them out of the council chamber, his councillors trailing behind him, the two royal guards, Lehlo and Bonolo leading the way.

As they made their way through the streets, the wails of mourning women filled the air, and men sang songs in honour of their fallen king.

One particular song caught the prince's attention.

Killed in his bed, by his most trusted.
The king we all loved, the king who was.
Now we have our nation divided .
Who is the true heir?
The prince or the babe,
Who shall rule, who shall rule?

"Guards, stop," Prince Tlou commanded. "What is your name?" he enquired of the man singing in the crowd.

"Peno, Your Highness, my name is Peno."

"Take heed, guards! Ensure that Peno shall sing no more, and bring me his tongue!" Tlou commanded.

"Please, Your Highness, show mercy! I ask of you!" Peno beseeched, prostrating himself at the prince's feet, as the crowd looked on.

"No, mercy shall only be shown by removing your tongue. Lehlo! Fetch me his tongue!" bellowed the prince, not swayed by Peno's supplication.

Three other guards held the hapless Peno, as Lehlo hesitantly drew his blade and severed the man's tongue from his mouth. The agony was so intense that Peno let out an anguished cry and swooned, blood spurting from his gaping mouth.

The prince showed no pity and strode away, leaving the wounded Peno writhing in pain.

The burial of the king was to be held in the village square. A towering pyre, ten feet high, was raised, and atop it was laid the body of the king, clad in the regal aqua blue hues of Soru.

"My father has been taken from us, murdered in his sleep," said Prince Tlou, his voice resonating across the crowd. "I swear to you, by the mountain gods, his death shall be avenged. He has left behind great shoes to be filled, and I fear I may not be worthy to fill them. Nevertheless, his final wish was for his oldest heir to be crowned without delay. It is a pity that the coronation shall no longer be for an heir, but for the crown itself. Know this – once I am crowned as your king, those who have conspired in the murder of my father, your king, shall face justice. I promise you this. I also promise you peace and prosperity. With our new ally, King Shaza, a new dawn is at hand."

At his words, the crowd erupted into cheers, momentarily forgetting that they had lost their king.

Meanwhile, the entire council looked confused by the events unfolding before them.

The high priestess, Masega, took a step forward, flanked by two young stable hands who brought forth two sheep for sacrifice. With a sharp knife, Masega slit the throats of the sheep one by one, their dying cries piercing the solemn silence of the onlookers.

The heavily guarded Prince Tlou stepped forward, holding a torch, which he used to light the pyre on which his father lay.

"A royal funeral in broad daylight," whispered Gasane to Sedi, who looked upon him before turning her gaze back to the pyre. "This is the end of the peace we have known."

"We shall have a new king on the morrow, all hail," responded Sedi.

The cries of the gathered mourners drowned out the beating of the drums, which echoed across the royal grounds as the pyre consumed their king.

The solemn beats of mourning drums had given way to the triumphant rhythms of coronation, causing all who were present to take notice and the atmosphere to become hushed.

Sedi, inquisitive as she was, whispered to Gasane, seeking to discern the reason for this sudden change. Being unaccustomed to surprises, she yearned to be included in the know.

Gasane, rising from his seat, approached Prince Tlou, who stood boldly in plain view of the multitudes. "Your Highness, the tune that the drums now beat is the coronation tune. 'Tis a most outrageous act and a lack of respect to your father."

The prince's face spoke volumes, conveying a message that needed no words. Gasane, perceiving the prince's displeasure, humbly bowed before him. "As you wish, Your Highness," he shook his head, walking back to his seat next to Sedi.

Observing from her seat, Sedi desired not to draw too much attention to herself, even as she too was baffled by the sudden turn of events.

The prince signalled for the drums to cease their sound and beckoned for Nare to step forward.

"People of Soru," Nare declared to the murmurs of the crowd, as they sought to unravel the reason for this unexpected gathering.

"Our nation has been wounded, robbed of a ruler whom we all cherished. We shall not rest until justice is served," Nare continued, his words solemn and weighty.

"Soru now needs a ruler, a ruler strong and able. As per the tradition of Soru, established during the founding of our nation, the king is to be succeeded by his oldest heir, Prince Tlou."

Though some murmurs could be heard in the crowd, with some believing that Prince Thubo's unborn child should be the heir, Nare's announcement could not be gainsaid. The prince was visibly angry at the murmurs and objections, for he was the true and rightful heir to the throne.

"Hold your tongue!" Nare bellowed, silencing the murmurs. "As I said earlier, the council has agreed not to tarry a fortnight before the crowning of our new ruler."

Gasane leaned in to whisper to Sedi, "Did you agree to this?"

Sedi, looking bewildered by the sudden turn of events, scanned the surroundings, only to behold an army surrounding them.

"We have agreed to an immediate coronation. I now entrust the high priestess to conduct the ceremony," Nare continued, much to the confusion of the council.

The prince advanced towards Masega, whilst the drums played a tune of coronation, eliciting cheers from the crowd. "It does seem as though they did not mourn for their king," Sedi whispered, clapping softly along to the cheers of the crowd.

"Good people of Soru, I stand afore you, representing the mountain gods and our forefathers," Masega proclaimed, holding a *mokorotlo* to place upon Prince Tlou's head, prompting cheers and ululations from the royal grounds. All save for those who did not acknowledge Tlou as the rightful heir to the throne.

Masega proceeded to place the *mokorotlo* on Tlou's head. "You knelt before the people of Soru as a prince, and now you shall rise as a king."

Sounds of women ululating filled the atmosphere.

Masega poured oil onto Tlou's head, as per custom.

"It appears we have a new king," Sedi said to Gasane.

"Yes, we do. All hail," Gasane responded.

Queen Palesa

Princess Palesa had returned unto her father, King Gauta, ruler of Batana, a kingdom in the northwestern part of the continent, accompanied by a few loyal people who supported her unborn child's claim. King Gauta was a corpulent man, standing six feet tall with a prominent belly, owing to his excessive drinking. The people of Batana were renowned for their practice of forbidden magic, as was evidenced by the king's burned face on the right side, caused by a spell gone awry many summers past.

The king's face was seldom seen to smile or laugh. He had eight daughters from three different women.

The law of Batana stipulated that the king could only marry one woman at any given time. Nonetheless, rumours abounded in the villages that King Gauta had ordered the murder of his first two wives for their inability to bear him a male heir. Having failed to produce an heir of his own, his designated successor was his younger brother, Prince Futhuma. Palesa was his eldest daughter, whom he cherished above all else. She alone could soften the rugged and uninviting features of his face. He was also gratified that she had wed Prince Thubo, for even though his direct heir might not inherit the throne of Batana, they would still inherit the Soru Kingdom. Initially opposing the union, King Gauta could not deny his daughter's wishes, as Thubo had fallen madly in love with Princess Palesa, and her beauty was beyond compare. After months of beseeching her father to allow her to wed the love of her life, the king was unable to refuse his daughter, for he loved her more than anything.

"If that boy thinks he can lay claim to my daughter's kingdom, he shall have me to answer to!" King Gauta exclaimed, with the princess seated beside him in the throne room.

At the centre of the chamber stood a grand and intricate throne wrought of exquisite wood and the most noble of metals, platinum. Two pillars of great size stood at either side of the throne, bearing upon them detailed etchings that spoke of the kingdom's rich history and culture.

"Sire, I received a messenger pigeon this morn," said Kolobe, presenting unto the king a letter.

With careful hands, the king unfurled the parchment and perused its contents, his face contorting into a fierce scowl. "The boy wears the royal *mokorotlo* and claims himself king now?" he read aloud.

"Father, Soru belongs to my son, Thubo's heir. The late king himself wished to wait until my child was born before he confirmed his heir. When last we spoke, he made known his desire for my son to continue his legacy," declared Princess Palesa, now garbed in *moshweshwe* (traditional women's clothing) dress made of the finest *leteisi* (fabric print) representing Batana's colours.

Commotion from beyond the door could be heard within the throne room, where the king's council was deliberating on their next course of action.

"Sire, if it is war they crave, then war we shall give to them," added Kolobe, a rotund man with a round face and ears that protruded from his head. Kolobe had gained his seat in the council by virtue of his family's immense wealth in Batana. His great-grandfather, Kolojwana, a former farmer, had stumbled upon a precious and lustrous mineral upon his land. Thus, Kolojwana abandoned farming to establish platinum mines, the largest in all of Ashari. Platinum was more valuable than gold.

"He has not even observed the fortnight required by our tradition before proclaiming himself king," added Nonyana.

"He knew full well that I held a stronger claim. He knows that my son is the heir. I should not have journeyed hither; I ought to have remained in Soru," lamented Princess Palesa.

"Princess, your decision to come here was wise. That usurper would have slain you and your child if you had remained in Soru," replied the king.

"I concur," said Kolobe, and the rest of the council did nod in agreement.

"What clamour is this outside the door? Can someone tend to it," the king bellowed, his ire rising.

As Nonyane arose to investigate, the door did burst open.

"Your Highness, we have a visitor from Soru who demands an audience with Princess Palesa," said the royal guard as he opened the door.

Princess Palesa readily recognised the man who had entered and leaped as if he had fled for his life.

"Bring water, urgently!" cried the princess, pointing to the jar of water next to the jar of ale upon the table where her father sat.

"Do you know this man, Princess?" enquired the king.

"Aye, he was one of my most trusted companions whilst I was in Soru. He aided me in my escape. Perega, you are injured," she observed, rising to aid him and offer him water.

"Ve- very well, anyone who is your friend i- is surely a friend of Batana," Legomo who struggled with a little stutter said, rising from his seat and offering it to Perega.

Perega could scarcely stand, so grievous were his wounds from his leap through the window.

"They are after me. They want to kill your baby," Perega gasped before collapsing upon the cold, hard floor of the grand throne room.

The princess, being of noble bearing and steadfast heart, commanded her loyal servant Lefefe to tend to the fallen man. "Lefefe, you are charged with the care of this man. See to it that he is tended to with the utmost haste and care," she said in a firm but gentle tone.

"Guards, take this man to my workshop and summon my apprentice, Fika. Bid her to administer *muringa* [a healing plant] and wash his wounds. I shall come to attend to him personally when my duties here are done. And mark ye well, let not Fika open the door for anyone until I come. Place two guards to keep watch over the entrance," said Lefefe, turning his attention to the guards and issued forth his orders.

Lefefe was the elder amongst the Batana mages, a man of many winters, with furrows etched upon his face, bearing witness to the seasons he had beheld.

He wore a resplendent robe, cascading down to the very earth, draped gracefully over his hunched back. As the guards hastened to carry out their assigned tasks, Legomo spoke words of warning to the king.

"Sire, d-do you not hear the d-dire news this man has brought? Th-they are after the queen's babe!"

Legomo, the esteemed hand of the king, was a man of lesser stature, yet nigh approaching forty summers. His face, fair and pallid, bore a full and flourishing beard, while his gaze, swift and keen, mirrored the sharpness of a falcon's sight. He was the brother-in-law of the king through Palesa's mother, thereby entwining their noble lineages.

"Aye, we have heard his words," the king responded. "But perhaps we should wait until the child is safely born before we take action."

"No, Sire, we cannot afford to tarry. We must march our army to Soru without haste," declared Nonyane, the army commander.

Nonyane, a man of years slightly greater than the king's, bore a stern face, ne'er graced by a smile, akin to the king himself in this regard.

Towering in height, he stood like a noble oak, his skin adorned with an olive hue, and his physique imbued with a rich, brawny frame that bespoke his strength and vigour.

"Nonyane speaks the truth. Delay shall only serve to strengthen our foes and weaken any allies we still have in Soru. We must strike while the people are yet on our side," said the princess.

"I implore you, Sire, heed the wisdom of the princess. My mother, may she rest in peace, hailed from Soru. She oft spoke of the Soru pride and the people's unwavering loyalty to their own. The babe must be born on Soru lands, and to do so, we must seize the throne forthwith!" said Lefefe with great fervour.

The king, moved by the words of his daughter, stood up from his throne. "I swear by all the gods, my daughter, that you shall sit upon the throne of Soru, even if it kills me."

At this, the princess gave a subtle nod and a smile of approval to her father.

"Sire, and all who are assembled here, let it be known that Palesa is the rightful queen of Soru until her son and true heir is born," Lefefe interjected.

The court erupted in cheers and jubilation at the declaration of Palesa's rights.

The winds of change had begun to blow, and all knew that the days of the usurper king were numbered. "Queen Palesa, Queen Palesa!" the men shouted.

If I Must Perish

"Your Highness," Kubo whispered amidst the sound of the river's gentle flow on that chilly, serene night. The half-moon hung low in the nighttime sky, casting a silver light that created an eerie yet exquisite ambiance. "The king of Soru is dead, and Prince Moroka is assumed dead. Our kingdom has ne'er been weaker than this moment, and we direly need a strong leader."

"Kubo, I bear no inclination to sit on the Baloki throne and bring forth its curse," Neo answered, resting against a tree with a straw in his mouth. "Do you think the people will still support me during a time of drought and famine?"

"Your Highness, this kingdom is rightfully yours. When your mother … may she find solace with the rain gods … departed, the throne was left for you. True, we may quarrel over technicalities, but you could have passed on the throne to your female heir, and the succession should proceed through you," Kubo continued.

"You are of the purest royal blood, a direct descendant of King Pula. A war is looming, and we must brace ourselves."

Neo breathed in deeply, unsure of how to respond.

"Everyone keeps prating about an imminent war, yet these eight quarrelsome kingdoms have been clashing against each other for as long as I can recollect," Neo responded.

"This war is unlike any other. Prophecies have foretold of a child of rain and thunder, born under an eclipse, who shall unify the eight kingdoms," Kubo asserted.

"But is not Shaza parading himself as the king of the eight kingdoms?" Neo queried.

"But he lacks the blood of rain and thunder," Kubo answered.

"Kubo, what you are suggesting is high treason. The only reason I have not reported you is because you were a cherished friend of my mother," Neo replied.

"An accusation of treason would not be laid upon me if my words were not true. You are the king," Kubo insisted with conviction.

"Baloki has not been ruled by a male heir since the reign of King Pula," Neo countered.

Kubo, however, was not deterred and presented a counterargument. "Prince Noka, the Ruler, did reign peacefully for sixteen summers until his daughter ascended the throne."

"You forget that Prince Noka never sat upon the throne, ruling only in name. Furthermore, for fourteen of those peaceful summers, our land suffered from drought. I shall not bring such a curse upon my people," Neo replied, appearing displeased. "Moreover, I have pledged to marry the Heir Princess in the upcoming harvest season."

"Your Highness, time is running out. I knew that you would not heed my advice, so I have brought someone who may persuade you," Kubo replied with urgency.

"A man? You think he can sway me?" Neo asked, perplexed and scanning the dimly lit forest.

Suddenly, a man in a black robe materialised out of nowhere. Neo recognised him and was taken aback.

"Morena Seriti! You are involved in this?" Neo exclaimed in disbelief.

"Your Highness, my father regaled me with tales of the kindness your mother bestowed upon our family when I was younger," Morena Seriti replied.

"Morena Seriti, this is high treason that could lead you to be drowned!" Neo warned.

Morena Seriti knelt afore Neo, took his hand, and gave it a kiss. "Your Highness, there be much that you do not know. You have been kept in the dark for far too long. Our kingdom needs you. A new dawn is nigh, and if I must perish to ensure the rightful ruler ascends the throne, then so be it."

Neo looked upon Morena Seriti and Kubo with perplexity and unease. He knew that there were factions within the kingdom, but ne'er did he expect anyone to risk their lives to establish him as the king, let alone someone from the queen's council.

"But what of the queen and the princesses?" enquired Neo.

"All we require is your agreement that when the time come, you will be ready to take the throne," answered Morena Seriti.

"And when shall that time come, and what shall occur?" queried Neo.

"Trouble not yourself with the particulars. When the time arrives, you shall know," answered Kubo.

"When the time arrives, you shall know," echoed Morena Seriti.

"Morena Seriti and Kubo, I do appreciate the loyalty you seek to show me, but I cannot condone any actions that may cause violence or bloodshed. I will not allow needless strife to besmirch my mother's legacy," declared Neo resolutely.

Morena Seriti and Kubo exchanged a fleeting glance before nodding their agreement.

"We do sympathise with your concerns, Your Highness. We desire only to restore our kingdom to its former glory, without any violence," Morena Seriti said while Kobo nodded.

Neo heaved a deep sigh and gazed out over the kingdom, hearing the chirping of crickets and the croaking of frogs.

"What are you thinking about, Your Highness?" queried Kobo.

"I ponder upon the fate of Morena Seriti and how the queen shall soon deliver him to a watery grave for his heinous treachery."

"If I must perish for my beliefs, then so be it," said Morena Seriti, steadfast in his conviction.

In that moment, they heard a twig snap amidst the dense forest yonder. The three men exchanged anxious glances, for they knew it bode ill if they were caught congregating so late in the day.

"Did you hear that?" queried Kobo.

"Aye, I fear we are being watched," replied Neo.

Kobo turned to look at Neo and Seriti and whispered, "We must depart hence. 'Tis unsafe to linger. Fear not, we shall continue anon and impart our news."

"Your Highness, you must leave forthwith. As you have seen and heard this day, I am not alone in my support for your cause. An army stands ready to rally behind you," said Kobo.

"Remember, sire, treat me as you would normally do in the royal grounds. We must not arouse suspicion," Morena Seriti instructed.

"But I scarcely speak with you," replied Neo.

"Indeed, keep it that way," responded Seriti.

With that, the three vanished into the forest with all due haste.

The Prisoner Is Awake

"Father, Father, Father, wake up," Mapula whispered, with tears streaming down her face.

Princess Mapula and Kwena were locked in a cage, bound in chains. Behind them, in a separate cage, was Prince Moraka, also imprisoned and enchained. The chains that held the prince were enchanted with spells, making it difficult for him to escape through any magic. Blood covered his body, with a wound above his brow.

As the rain pour down mercilessly on the muddy Kgosi Road, a procession of wagons slowly made its way through the thick forest. The front of the line was guarded by two heavily armed guards who kept watchful eyes on the prisoners in the back.

Kwena took a small stick from his cage and prodded the prince, hoping to wake him. "Brother, brother, wake up," he pleaded. But the prince remained unconscious until this moment.

"Princess, do not despair," Kwena consoled her. "Your father is not dead, for one does not chain a dead man." He tried to reassure her, though he could not be certain of the prince's injuries.

Just as Kwena was about to prod the prince once more, the prince's eyes flickered open for the first time since the ambush. He tried to move but was wracked with pain from his wounds, especially the spear wound in his stomach. He suppressed his cries and met the princess's gaze, knowing that she had not seen him so weakened before. His lips were dry and cracked from the lack of food and water over the past two sunrises.

"Ahh," Prince Moroka wailed as he flickered his eyes. "Mapula, is that you?" he reached out to just barely touch his daughter's hand.

"Father!" the princess exclaimed in relief, handing him her skin of water to quench his thirst.

Prince Moroka cleared his throat, "are you hurt, Princess?" he enquired, as he tried to drink the water using whatever little strength he had.

"We are both well, brother. Thank you for your concern," said Kwena in a relived yet sarcastic tone, still bleeding from a leg wound sustained from an ambush.

The prince noticed the blood on the princess's chest and, though still weak and in pain, gained enough consciousness to orient himself.

"Mapula, you are bleeding? Are you hurt?" he asked again.

"Father, I …" Princess Mapula struggled to find her words, overwhelmed with sadness and the joy of seeing her father awake.

"Fret not, brother, the princess is safe and sound. The blood on her chest is from my foot. She was very brave and tried to stop the bleeding from my wound," Kwena responded.

"What happened?" Moroka enquired.

The princess burst into tears. "We have failed you, Father. We have failed to protect everyone. All those valiant men died for nothing."

The prince looked at his daughter with sorrowful eyes, struggling to speak. "No, my sweet child. You have not failed me. You did everything you could to protect me and our people. You have shown great bravery and courage in the face of danger."

"Kwena, what happened?" Prince Moroka asked, still trying to regain consciousness.

"Well, you have been sleeping for the past two sunrises. I think they are taking us to be slaughtered by King Shaza, and your friend is an evil warlock, who wants you dead," said Kwena.

"Are you telling me the blast did not work? How did he manage to survive?" enquired Moroka.

"Well, that hinges on your definition of 'work.' You did manage to burn half of his body. But now he seems more pissed with us, and our heads shall soon adorn the spike of Zuka, unless your warlock friend cuts off our limbs to use in his dark magic," Kwena retorted.

"Where is he now?" demanded the prince.

"He seems to have an aversion to daylight, perhaps due to the burn you inflicted upon him, or perhaps because pure evil does not abide in the light," replied Kwena, prompting Mapula to give a hint of amusement.

"And where is the Maru? I see him not with you," Moroka enquired as he tried to sit upright.

"You have a keen eye, brother. It appears our nephew has escaped. Maybe he died of starvation, was devoured by beasts, or was waylaid by thieves. The lad is no warrior," Kwena scoffed.

"I could say the same of you," the prince retorted, struggling to catch his breath and grieved by the news of Maru's absence.

"I was charged with guarding the royal carriage and protecting the princess. The princess is safe. Are you not, Princess?" Kwena stated proudly.

The princess nodded in agreement.

"There you have it; I reckon I have fulfilled my duty. I cannot say the same of you. Your charge was to safely return us home," Kwena added.

"Enough, Kwena. Where is my staff?"

Prince Moroka attempted to cast a spell, but he was too weak, and it failed to take effect.

"Ah yes, by the way, your warlock friend said that your cage is impervious to magic. Therefore, you are as powerless as I, trapped inside. How does it feel to not have magic at your disposal?" Kwena taunted.

Prince Moroka spoke with a voice filled with ire. "Kwena, must every word from your mouth be a jest?" His eyes surveyed his surroundings, noticing the intricate inscriptions of forbidden magic that enveloped him.

He knew he was outmatched and outwitted, and he needed a plan to escape this cage of his. "We require a plan of escape."

Kwena let out a boisterous laugh. "Ha! Princess, your father awakens after a two-day slumber, and now we must conjure up a plan. What do you think we have been doing all this time, braiding each other's locks?"

"Behold, my brother, Moroka, the hero to every story. The world shall not crumble without your stratagems," Kwena continued, sitting upright in his cage.

"Kwena, you know what I mean. Surely you have contemplated an escape," the prince said.

"We may not have a definite plan, but that does not mean we have not been pondering one," Kwena replied.

The prince sighed. "You disappoint me, but I cannot say I am surprised."

As the day waned and the sun began to set, the company stopped at a small outpost by the Olive River, one of the major tributaries from the majestic Loaba River.

"Why did we stop?" Moroka enquired.

"The hour is late, and the soldiers pause to sup and care for their animals before nightfall. We are likely spending the night here," the princess responded.

"You said they were taking us to the south. I am assuming we are going to Zuka?"

I did overhear some soldiers conversing yesterday," said Kwena, attempting to find comfort in his position. "I believe that is the direction we are headed."

"No, I have my doubts. This path is familiar to me, though I have not trodden upon it in many moons. I am nearly certain we are not bound for the southern lands. If we have been traveling for two sunsets, as you say, we should have arrived at the Fefre Crater. But look! The vegetation here is lush and verdant, and we have been journeying toward the Olive River, to the east," said the prince.

"Tell me, who in the east is in allegiance with King Shaza?" enquired Kwena.

"Are we making way for Swarai?" queried the princess.

"Aye, I believe that is our destination. Shaza would not take the risk of sending us southward, for he would be caught between Soru and Baloki. Moreover, if Noga is indeed working for Shaza, he knows full well that he cannot risk my traversing the crater, for my magic would be amplified in that place," Prince Moroka responded.

The Fefre Crater was a colossal impact site from an ancient meteorite that was thought to be the original source of magic in Ashari. It was believed that the Khoro Tribe, who had inhabited Ashari before the arrival of modern man from the north, had harvested most of the magic from the crater. Though the crater now lay dormant, it still heightened the magic of all those who crossed over it.

"I do recall reading about the Fefre Crater in the books of magic housed in our library. The high priest Selo informed me that the impact of the crater nearly decimated all living creatures on the continent. He related that the Khoro populace was reduced to a mere handful," said the princess. "And those who did survive were able to harvest the magic brought down by the gods."

"Very well done, Princess, you are smart. Yet not all sorcery was deemed goodly. Balance is required in this continent, as the meteor's great magic also brought forth vile and dark magic into Ashari, which the Khoros did contain, until the arrival of the first man. When we slew the Khoros and drove them southward, the dark magic was left to run rampant. It is the same forbidden chaos magic that Noga has channelled," the prince explained.

"Why do you think the school at Sepoko Island was established? It was not originally a school, but a sanctuary where great mages who kept watch over all magic lived. They did chant spells unceasingly to ensure that chaos magic remained contained. But they …" continued Moroka before he was interrupted by two soldiers who brought them sustenance and drinks.

"Oh great, here is our friend coming to give us something to eat," said Kwena.

"The prisoner is awake," said Terego, one of the guards who was responsible for the captives.

Terego was a veteran soldier, with piercing eyes, bushy brows, a broad and prominent forehead, and a face that spoke of determination and seriousness. He had also lost an eye and bore a scar above it from a blade.

"You two," he said to the coachmen who were drawing the cages that held the prisoners. "What did I bid you to do? Your task was to alert me when the mage awakens. You shall be punished for this transgression. I shall ensure it."

"Please, forgive us, Morena. We, we, we did not realise that he was roused," replied one of the coachmen.

"How could ye not discern this, idiots?"

"In all fairness, these two buffoons were engrossed in a heated debate over whose wife cooks *mogodu* (tripe) the best," quipped Kwena in jest, trying to make acquittance with Terego. Alas, Terego was not amused.

"Tonight, the comedian does not eat," Terego instructed to the guard who was with him bringing food to the prisoners.

"You," pointing to one of the riders, "go tell the Great One that the mage is awake."

Avenge His Father's Death

"I was raised in the mountains of Soru, Father. I have long dwelt in Soru since I was but ten winters old. I know Soru like the back of my hand. We cannot win victory in this battle alone. We ought to summon aid from the Baloki, Veka, and Shangas. I doubt the Gauta Tribe may wish to leave the comforts of their islands," Princess Palesa declared, her voice brimming with authority, still garbed in her mourning garments.

"My lord, I have already dispatched messenger pigeons to the Baloki queen, yet no reply has reached us. I doubt they will come to our aid, especially now that their princess is a prisoner of war. They would rather observe our downfall than offer aid.

As for the Vekas and Shanga, they remain fiercely loyal to the Rain Queen. They will not come unless she does," replied Nonyane.

"We boast the most formidable mages in Ashari. We shall use our forces to reclaim your throne, my daughter. For too long have these kingdoms spurned us. It is time we earn our rightful place and seize that which is ours. We shall unleash upon Soru the mightiest terror they have ever beheld," King Gauta said, donning his full battle regalia.

"Your Highness, the Princess …" Perega began before being interrupted by Kolobe.

"She is no mere princess. She is your queen, and the child she bears is your king. You should show her due reverence," Kolobe chastised.

Perega, who was still healing from his wounds, cleared his throat, somewhat abashed.

"Yes, Your Highness. I concur with our queen," Perega replied, looking to Kolobe as he corrected himself.

"My queen! I do not trust this one. Maybe he be Tlou's spy sent here to gather information, and strike at a propitious time" Kolobe said, pointing to Perega.

"I agree, do not trust me, nor any man. In these warlike times, men will resort to anything to save their own skin," Perega did reply.

"I shall keep your words in mind, Perega," said Palesa, her countenance alight with displeasure towards Perega.

Perega, who was using a walking stick for support, limped towards Palesa with measured steps. "I too am well acquainted with those mountains. Nonetheless, my escape was a harrowing ordeal, and I barely survived. Your Highness, no one has ever breached the borders of Soru in our lifetime," Perega cautioned.

"My king, the Molotli Mountains are impregnable. Should you decide to march to Soru, you'll be sending your men to the slaughterhouse," Perega cautioned.

"You dare question the authority of our king? Watch it, boy, this is not Soru. We have respect for our king and queens," said Kolobe, with evident disdain towards Perega.

"I meant no disrespect," said Perega, limping back to his seat.

"There's a way to force them to meet us in battle. We'll lay the greatest siege these kingdoms have ever seen. We'll cut them off and hit them where it hurts the most," the king suggested.

But a voice, feeble and trembling, spoke up. "Your Highness, King of Kings, if I may be so bold, the boy usurper acts under the orders of King Shaza. I have heard that he has allied himself with the south. If we lay siege, we shall be vulnerable to attack from the southern kingdoms," Lefefe spoke in a cautionary tone.

The king's expression turned to one of pride. "You see, Lefefe, your old age has now dulled your mind. Legomo, tell the council what you have told me today."

Legomo, though stuttering slightly, explained the news he had received. "I-I have received ne- news that the Rain Queen has called on all her allies t-to raise an army to march t-to the east t-to demand the release of her daughter and Prince Moroka."

The royal mage, as old as the kingdom itself, added,

"Old age catches up with us all, Your Highness. If this be true, King Shaza shall not spare a single man from his army to defend Soru's civil matters. He is more interested in Baloki than he is with us. He needs Baloki in order to capture the entire north."

"E- everyone knows that Baloki army alone is enough t- to send shivers down the spine o- of any man," added Legomo, bravely attempting to speak despite his slight stutter.

"Aye, I agree with His Highness. We must assail Soru with all our might and show them the mettle of Batana. King Shaza will want his army by his side, and I am certain he has called upon his allies to prepare for war in the north," Kolobe chimed in.

"Very well. We shall set forth for Soru in five sunsets. Summon every able-bodied man and lad in Batana, including our temple priests. The usurper seeks war, and we shall grant him blood," declared the king, to the joyous applause of his council.

"Forgive me, Your Majesty, but we still have loyalists in Soru who support Queen Palesa's rightful claim to the throne. They shall rally behind us if we but call upon them. Allow me to send them a letter," added Perega.

"Be it as you say, but first bring it to me for my approval. Meanwhile, let us plan for battle."

"Father, I too shall go with you. If my people are to follow their unborn king, they must know that he fought valiantly for his rightful place in the kingdom. They must know that my son, the son of the soil and king of the mountains, shall never yield. My blood runs Batana, but his runs Soru, and he shall avenge his father's death," declared the Palesa with great fervour.

"The daughter of Batana shall ascend to become the queen of Soru," King Gauta proclaimed proudly, his voice resonating throughout the chamber. The entire chamber resounded with joyful cries and cheers.

We Made an Oath

"Thebo, do you understand the gravity of your father's passing?" enquired Queen Motapo.

"Yes, Mother, it means that I am the royal mage now. But I have not yet completed my training," replied Prince Thebo, a boy of thirteen who looked innocently young.

Prince Thebo, being a late bloomer, was a little shorter than his peers, and his voice had not yet changed. The dimples on his cheeks made him seem younger than he was. He bore the royal emblem of a white patch of hair on the right side of his head, as all royal children except Mapula did.

"You are going to learn fast, baby brother, for your people need you," advised Princess Seroka.

"I am not a baby," retorted Thebo.

Princess Seroka ruffled his afro and bestowed a smile upon him.

"Mother, Shaza wants war. I say we give him war. We have strong allies. I suggest we call on all of them and wage a war the eight kingdoms have never seen," the princess continued, seated across from her mother.

"My darling child, you are ever full of passion, but at present, we must be prudent. I desire to retrieve your father's remains and bring your sister home alive. I suspect that your sister is being held captive for some sort of bargaining. Should war come, I believe Shaza shall bring it to Baloki," stated the queen.

"But, Mother, I concur with Seroka. We cannot idly sit here while our sister languishes in some cage or prison cell," added the Crown Princess, seated next to her mother. It had been several sunsets since the news of the prince's death spread across Baloki and the surrounding kingdoms.

The queen had sent out their best spies to find any information regarding the prince and the princess, but none of the spies had returned with credible information so far.

"Your Highness, my prince and princesses," said Black Mamba as he entered the royal chambers to join the royal family for the daybreak meal. "It smells great in here. Maybe I should have had my meal here instead of the council chambers."

"Should I order the sister wives to prepare you something to eat?" Princess Motakia offered.

"Thank you, princess, however, my belly has reached its limit," Mamba gave a nod of gratitude and subtle smile to Princess Motakia.

"My queen, forgive my intrusion. I bring news that concerns you," Mamba continued, taking a sit next to the queen.

"Speak, Mamba," Queen Motapo commanded.

Mamba cast his gaze about the room and beseeched the queen, "If it please you, I would prefer a private audience."

"Attend me," ordered the queen. "All those who are not of royal blood, you are excused."

The chamber was emptied of all but the royal children, the queen, Black Mamba, and Neo.

Mamba cleared his throat and began, "I have received two messages this morn. My whisperers inform me that Princess Mapula and Kwena were spied heading toward Swarai."

"I knew it! If Swalazi is behind this treachery, he shall pay for it," fumed Princess Seroka.

Mamba continued, "There is more, Your Highness. A third prisoner was being conveyed with them. Although their identity is uncertain, I believe it to be the prince."

"I cannot say whether or not the prisoner was dead or alive, but you wouldn't transport a corpse in a cage," he continued.

At this, the room erupted in cheers and relief. Prince Thebo, unable to contain his excitement, asked, "Is our father yet alive?"

"I do not know, young prince."

"He is alive. I know it. I know it in my heart. He is alive," the queen responded.

"It is settled then. We are riding to Swarai," Seroka said.

"Mamba, you said you received two messages. What is your second message?" Queen Motapo asked, her eyes alight with curiosity.

"Your Highness! A message has been received from Batana, bearing news of Princess Palesa's flight unto her father's. They plan to amass an army and wage war against Prince Tlou, who has declared himself King of Soru.

"'Tis a strange turn of events, for Prince Tlou to wear the crown, whilst his brother's widow carries the kingdom's heir. He is a foolish lad to think he can maintain his reign."

"What news of Princess Palesa's intent?" enquired Princess Motakia, seated beside her mother.

Mamba, with a clearing of his throat, continued, "Princess Palesa now also calls herself the queen regent of Soru. Her message came directly from her father, King Gauta, bearing his seal. He implores us to march with our army and take back his daughter's rightful place."

The fiery Princess Seroka, not one to mince her words, spoke vehemently. "By all the gods, we shall not heed that treacherous man's call! He has no loyalty in his bones, and I will not risk our people's lives for him!"

Princess Motakia, taking umbrage at her sister's coarse language, reproached her. "Sister, let us comport ourselves with the grace befitting our position."

"Ladies, let us put aside our differences and remember our duty to our allies." The queen, the voice of reason, reminded them all of their oath to be Batana's shield, despite their personal feelings towards them.

"No, Mother," Princess Seroka interjected, "we cannot spare our army to fight in King Gauta's war. We need to prepare ourselves for the war Shaza brings upon us."

Black Mamba, who agreed with the princess, was about to speak, but he observed the queen's face and remained silent. He saw that she was displeased with Princess Seroka's interruption.

"I am still speaking, child," chided the queen.

"Listen to me, children. We need not send our army to aid King Gauta's war. Long ago, the eight kingdoms forged a pact in the Fefre, wherein we agreed not to meddle in each other's civil strife. Therefore, if Palesa leads this war, it is deemed a civil matter, and we cannot interfere."

Neo, who had remained silent until then, rose from his seat and approached Black Mamba. He spoke in a calm, reassuring tone. "You speak true. I read somewhere in the library that the eight kingdoms have pledged not to interfere in each other's internal affairs. But we all know that this war is not Palesa's doing. King Gauta covets power, and I would be much surprised if he does not seize the throne and declare Soru as his own."

Black Mamba regarded Neo with suspicion. "Read, you said? You must have a lot of interest in politics of the eight kingdoms for someone who will not rule them."

"What are you insinuating, Black Mamba?" Neo asked, taking a step towards Black Mamba. The room grew slightly tense. Neo often did not talk during royal discussion; he would often keep to himself and had very little interaction with Mamba.

"I am not insinuating aught, my lord," Mamba gave a nod to show respect to Neo.

Princess Motakia stood up and paced around the chamber. "I think Neo is on to something. This is not Palesa's war but King Gauta's war. Why do men love going to war so much?"

Black Mamba shrugged. "I would not know, Princess, for I serve under a queen." The queen gave a hint of a smile.

"Think of this for a moment. The moment Palesa brought her father into this, this matter ceased to be civil," Princess Seroka chimed in.

"But we made an oath. Baloki is not an oathbreaker," the Heir Princess responded.

The queen took a moment to ponder. "I think ... Mamba, do not respond to the letter. We need a few sunsets to consider this carefully. This is something we should consult with the rest of the council. Politics are a very messy affair."

"Mother, time is not on our side. Give me your blessing to ride to Veka and Shanga kingdoms to ask them to join us to march down to Swarai to rescue Mapula and Father," Princess Seroka requested.

"On one condition: take Morena Seriti with you," the queen demanded. The queen hesitated to send Seroka away from Baloki, given that two of her family members were captives. But she knew she could not control Seroka.

"I will."

"Perhaps I should go with the princess, Queen Mother," Neo suggested.

"That does seem a most excellent notion, Neo. 'Tis decided then. Seroka, you and Neo shall make haste to Veka to convey my message," said the queen. "Mamba, you and Morena Seriti go to Shanga."

Mamba gave a nod of acknowledgment to the queen.

"But Mother, I wanted to go to Shanga," declared the crown princess.

"Me too," Thebo chimed in.

"No, I need you here, Motakia," the queen said to a disappointed Motakia. "And Thebo, you have to catch up on your training."

"But …" The young prince was about to say something.

"This is an order, not open for discussion," the queen commanded. "Mamba, summon the remainder of the council that we may contrive a plan."

"As you command, Your Highness," Black Mamba responded, departing the chamber, yet casting a wary glance at Neo, causing him to feel ill at ease.

Stay Alive

"Kwena! Do you remember when we were young, we would venture to these mountains?" Prince Moroka reminisced, lost in thought and nostalgia of his past.

"Aye, indeed. How could I forget? I did dislike those escapades. You and Shadu were faster, better climbers, leaving me always behind," Kwena responded.

"If you did despise it so, why partake in such journeys?" Moroka queried.

Kwena sighed mightily, pondering his musings. "If you seek the truth, 'twas because I wished you to favour me as you did Shadu," he revealed, drawing a deep breath.

"He has always been the brother you wanted." Kwena cast his gaze downward, concealing the sorrow within his eyes from Moroka.

"But …" Moroka began.

"Do not pity me," Kwena interjected. "Once I discovered mine own lack of speed and bravery, I turned to the solace of reading. 'Twas then I realised mine intellect surpassed both of you combined."

Mapula emitted a soft chuckle. "Indeed, Princess, I could outwit your father and Shadu at any game we played."

"Well …" Moroka began before he was interrupted by the sound of horns announcing that the prisoners were entering the kingdom of Swarai.

"Oh, behold! We have arrived at the slaughterhouse," Kwena quipped, sending shivers down Mapula's spine.

The prince could only shake his head in discontent.

"Father, are they going to kill us?" enquired the princess.

"No, child. We are captives of war now, and our lives will be used for bargaining," Moroka responded.

"But what purpose do they have for me?" Kwena interjected. "I am naught but a commoner, with no royal lineage to speak of."

"You wouldst have been put to the sword already if death was their intent," reassured the prince. "Also, you are still my brother."

For several nights, the three prisoners traversed the roads until they neared the gates of the Swarai kingdom. Although they found solace in the knowledge that they would soon sleep in quarters more comfortable than their carriages, the journey had not been kind to them.

As they approached the two pillars marking the entrance to Swarai, the sun began to set, bathing the lush landscape in a golden hue. Although the mountains were easily accessible by foot, carriage, or horse, the Swarai Kingdom had a poor trading record with the neighbouring northern tribes, which was likely due to their secession from the Ngori Tribe. Upon arriving in Swarai, the stark contrast between the affluent lifestyle of the royals and the abject poverty of their subjects became apparent.

There was a clear divide between the poorly maintained huts that bordered the royal grounds, separated by a massive gate.

A rank odour hung heavy upon the air, whilst children, dressed in tattered clothes, stood in waiting along the wayside, eager to behold the procession of captives being escorted unto the throne hut.

Mapula looked into their eyes, and she remembered the eyes of the children that bid them farewell when they left Baloki, except these eyes were cold.

As the gates swung open, a sudden tumult ensued, with the children rushing towards the gates and the guards casting leftover food in their direction.

Mapula looked away from the scene, yet tears betrayed her. "It is unjust," she murmured.

"Life has never been just, Princess," Kwena replied, his hand gentle upon Mapula's shoulder.

Another horn resounded. "Father, why have we come to a halt?" enquired the princess, noting the abrupt stop to their journey.

As she looked around, she noticed they had arrived at the Swarai royal grounds; the main throne hut could be discerned to their right. Kwena, with a touch of malice, did jest, "I don't suppose your warlock companion shall be arriving to escort us to our demise?"

Moroka just looked at Kwena and shook his head. As usual, Mapula, who had now composed herself, just smiled.

Whilst they were still conversing, eight guards, led by Terego, approached to remove them from their cages.

"Where are you taking us, and where is Noga?" enquired Prince Moroka, yet the guards remained mute.

"Bring forth your hands," demanded Terego, to which Prince Moroka hesitated.

"I demand to speak with Noga." But when he enquired about Noga once more, another guard inflicted him with a spear in the same spot where Noga had pierced him afore. The agony was unbearable, and the prince cried out uncontrollably.

"Where is Noga?" Prince Moroka asked again.

Another guard seized his spear and smote him with it. The prince struggled to refrain from screaming, but the blow to his wound was so excruciating that he let out an uncontrollable scream.

Princess Mapula attempted to intercede, shouting, "Stop it! You are harming him!" But the guard advanced towards her cage with the same spear as if to strike her.

"Lay a hand on her, and I shall kill you first when I escape these chains!" Prince Moroka shouted, swearing by all the rain gods. Despite being in immense pain, he subdued it.

"You do not issue commands here, mage," said the guard binding his hands.

The prince looked upon his chains and beheld with his own eyes the enchantments that bound him, knowing full well that Noga would not dare to chance their release.

The captives were then led to the throne hut, situated within the royal grounds. The chamber was a grand edifice, the tallest of all the royal huts, known as "*emalawu*" or beehive huts.

As the prince, Kwena, and Princess Mapula were dragged in chains before King Swalazi, they could sense his imposing presence. King Swalazi VI was a harsh man who had taken over fifty wives and sired countless offspring. His temper was infamous, and he had changed his royal councillors annually, for they dared to oppose him. One such councillor had been fed to his pet lion as punishment for suggesting that the kingdom could not afford another extravagant royal wedding. The king had replied, "Find me the funds or find me another treasurer."

Such was his reputation that those around him bowed to his every whim without question. The nation of Swarai had just celebrated the wedding of King Swalazi to his latest bride, a maiden of mere fourteen summers, not much older than Princess Mapula.

Queen Motapo had received an invitation to the wedding but had chosen not to attend, a decision that did not sit well with the king. In fact, the Rain Queen had not attended any of the king's weddings. Representatives from the Baloki Tribe had only been sent to the first wedding and not since.

Once inside the throne room, Prince Moroka swiftly noted the presence of Noga standing beside the king.

"Swalazi.

Uyimbube uyingwenyama! (You are the lion; you are the king!)

Bayethe! (All hail!)

Wena waphakhathi! (Your Royal Highness!)

"You find yourself in the presence of His Majesty King Swalazi VI, ruler of the great Swarai Kingdom," proclaimed Ntombe, an advisor to the king.

Prince Moroka, Kwena, and Princess Mapula humbly bowed before the ruler of Swarai, showing reverence to their captor. The king, sitting atop his throne with a stern expression, peered at them with disdain. Though held captive, the royal protocol dictated that they never lose their courtesy.

"What brings you to my court, Prince Moroka, and the Rain Princess? I am shocked to receive such an audience," King Swalazi enquired sarcastically, as he endeavoured to rise from his throne, with his child bride by his side attempting to assist him.

"I lament that our reunion is in such unfortunate circumstances. It has been too long since our last encounter. As you can see, time has not been too kind to me," the king stated, pointing to his portly belly.

"I have recently wed, a joyous occasion that you have missed. However, I did send an invitation to your queen, but it seems the messenger pigeons must have gone astray," he continued with a sarcastic tone.

"Behold, my bride, a gift from King Shaza, to unite our great nations once more," the king proclaimed, pushing his child bride forward.

Prince Moroka gazed up at a young child, who reminded him of his own daughter. Though her skin and structure were that of a child, her eyes burned with fire, revealing one who had already endured much in her tender life.

"Your Highness, the entire Baloki Tribe send their well wishes on your marriage. May your bride bear you many children and expand your kingdom," the prince replied, carefully scanning the room.

"His child bride," whispered Kwena.

The prince turned and gave Kwena a severe death stare.

"The great prince," the king said in a biting tone. "All you northerners think you are better than me. None of you ever invite me to anything.

None of you has graced my weddings with your presence. Mine offspring, countless in number, yet none has made a marriage match with any of your children. Please tell me, is their blood not royal enough for you?" said the agitated king.

The youthful queen sought to calm the king, placing her hand on his shoulder. But the king was unamused, and she withdrew her hand, taking her seat.

"I perceive that you have encountered your old friend," said the king, pointing towards Noga.

"I commend your little trick, for it must have taxed you greatly," Noga said as he unveiled his hood, revealing his disfigured face, half of which was burnt beyond recognition, exposing his teeth.

There was a gasp in the room, as the gruesome visage of Noga was unveiled before them.

"That should have killed you. What forbidden magic are you channelling, Noga? Are you still even human?" the prince enquired in wonder.

"Join me, join our cause. You can end this conflict right now, Prince of Baloki.

I can furnish you with a letter, which you can use to summon your queen to bow before King Shaza and declare him the one true leader of Ashari," Noga responded, his voice eerily haunting, ravaged by the battle with the prince.

"You are a very talented mage. Imagine the potential you could unleash if you were to tap into the powers of true magic," he continued.

"Noga, this is an act of treachery," the prince retorted.

"How long do you intend to keep us captive?"

"As long as you are needed alive. You have until the morrow to decide whether you will pen that letter to your queen or not," Noga replied.

"Prince of Baloki, perhaps you will take some time to consider a marriage proposal between your daughter and my son," the king said, motioning for the guards to take the prisoners to their cells.

"I shall never consent to wed any of his sons," whispered Mapula.

"Fret not, Princess, I shall ensure that such a match never come to pass," replied Prince Moroka.

With a spear, Terego shoved Prince Moroka, who was heavily chained and could scarcely move, ordering the prisoners to be placed in the royal cells reserved for highborn captives. The cells were in a hut that was frigid and dim, lacking any windows to the outside.

"Make yourselves comfortable, for you might be here for some time," Terego said, handing the keys to Legatlo, the prison guard.

The prisoners' cells were adjacent, but Prince Moroka's cell had magical inscriptions to prevent him from using his magic.

"Father, will you pen the letter as requested by Noga?" the princess asked.

"Baloki shall never yield, and your mother will not bow to a foreigner," Prince Moroka responded boldly.

"Then I guess our heads will soon adorn the spikes of Zuka gates," Kwena jested.

"I hunger, Father," Princess Mapula said, weariness from the journey finally catching up with her.

"Mapula, remember your training. I cannot say for certain how long we will be in these cells. I will need you to be strong," Prince Moroka said. He knew the implications of being a prisoner of war and didn't want to offer false hope to his daughter.

"Princess, when I free us from this nightmare, I promise you all the *magwinyas* (fat cakes) in the world. I know how much you love them," Kwena reassured Mapula with a smile.

"Free us, you say, and how do you…" Prince Moroka began, before being interrupted by the sound of a key turning in the lock of the door.

"Ahh, Legatlo, you have brought us food," Kwena said, trying to discern who the figure entering their cell was.

"I am afraid not, old friend," said a familiar voice echoing forth from the obscurity of the dreary, dark, and icy prison cell. "Could it be?" enquired Prince Moroka, his voice tinged with surprise.

"How? How did you find your way here, Kazi?"

"You can thank your brother and his spies."

"Remember when I said I did not have a plan?" Kwena said with a smirk. "Well, I lied."

"But how?" Moroka asked.

"Umm ... well ... certain guards who were carrying us did us a favour," Kwena taunted.

Moroka was still trying to process what was happening.

"See, Princess, I might not be as handsome or as fast as your father, but I am smarter," Kwena said, looking at Mapula, who was very impressed by her uncle.

"Old friend, we have scarce time. The guard has left his post to relieve himself," replied Kazi urgently.

Kazi was a hairless, portly fellow who presently served on the council of King Swalazi.

"But behold whom I have discovered, trying to move unnoticed," he continued, shining his torch towards a figure in the gloomy cell.

Prince Moroka, Mapula, and Kwena were astonished. "How is it that you still draw breath?" enquired Kwena of the figure shrouded by a hood as it approached the faint light of the torch in their cell.

"The lad is sharp witted, albeit lacking in sagacity. 'Tis fortunate for him that mine own spies were the ones to espy his presence. The gods know what could have happened if the wrong eyes gazed on him."

"I have been tailing you closely since the ambush, avoiding the guards. They know not my face, so it was easy for me to move about under the cover of night. I survived by pilfering sustenance during their encampments," explained the figure.

"How did you survive when the carriage fell? I had deemed you dead," Kwena enquired.

"I know not how, but I tumbled out of the carriage and was unconscious for a little while. When I came to, all was quiet. I clambered up a tree to discern my bearings, but I spotted lights that I reckoned to be the army which had apprehended you. I trailed them from afar and have been doing so ever since," Prince Maru replied.

"Kazi, how did you find him?" Prince Moroka queried.

"Well, it was not too difficult, especially for those who just recently attended his brother's funeral.

Sorus do stand out in the Swarai crowd. I have eyes everywhere and make it my responsibility to know what goes on in this kingdom."

"I thought I was being careful," said Prince Maru.

"You have acted valiantly, my son. Firstly, we must dispatch a letter to your father, informing him that you are yet alive. Is there anyone you trust in Soru? Secondly, we must devise a means to communicate with Baloki and let them know that we live and where we are," declared Prince Moroka.

With tears nigh brimming from his eyes, Maru responded, "Uncle, my father –" He took a pause. "My father is dead. I overheard the guards say that he was murdered in his own bedchamber. And my brother now calls himself king."

Fury and sorrow in equal measure surged within Moroka. "Are you certain of what you have heard?" Prince Moroka asked, his voice almost breaking.

"The lad speaks truth, my lord," Kazi echoed.

"What happened?" Moroka's voice broke with sorrow.

"My lord, all will be explained soon. We must make haste before Legatlo's return," Kazi said.

"This is the last time I will be visiting you. The risk is too high. From now on, Maru will visit you alone," Kazi continued.

"Thank you, old friend. Leave now, before the guard returns."

"Stay alive," were Kazi's words as he and Maru left the prison cells.

Yield unto the Darkness

Princess Seroka and Neo did journey to Veka Kingdom to seek an audience with King Mikado, to plead for his aid in rescuing her father and Princess Mapula from Swarai.

The Veka and Baloki tribes had known strife in times past yet had since kept peace for the last few generations. Veka people were renowned for mastery over all manner of sorcery, only second to Batana mages. Their kingdom provided the only land access to Sepoko Island, where all mages are trained.

While not the most skilled in warfare, their enemies trembled at the sound of their secret weapon: the *ngoma ngoma*, a drum made from human skin that brought on bouts of unyielding diarrhoea and nausea when played in battle.

It was whispered that the *ngoma ngoma* was fashioned by the hands of the gods themselves, bestowed upon the first Veka king, Masha, who used it to defeat all his enemies as he and his tribe journeyed to Ashari. Though the tribe had adopted many of the customs of the other tribes in Ashari, their own faith remained resolute, untouched by the winds of change. Their god, who they called Nali, was believed to be the one who handed the *ngoma ngoma* to King Masha.

The tribe made their homes atop easily defendable hills, providing them with a strategic advantage against attackers. Their kingdom covered the northernmost lands of Ashari, with semi-arid terrain.

As they approached the gates of the kingdom, Princess Seroka and Neo were met by Crown Prince Rendu, the king's advisor Musha, and Queen Naki, the king's first wife. The Veka folk had a complexion of dark hue and were strongly built.

"My lady, your very presence graces our land. Your gods shall surely smile upon us and bring us much-needed rain now that you are here," said Prince Rendu. "I am grieved to hear of your father and sister's plight. I pray they are yet alive. But let it be known, if King Shaza dares to declare himself ruler of Ashari, he shall first have to face us." Clad in the dusky skin of the Veka people, he stood tall, just over six feet, adorned with a full beard, though his youth be just of eighteen summers.

"My lord prince, please forgive my words, but my father and sister are yet alive," Princess Seroka reassured, with a hint of irritation in her words.

At this moment, Neo intervened, perceiving Seroka's agitation. "Your Highness, my lady speaks nought but the truth. News from our spies confirms that Prince Moroka yet draws breath."

"The prince did not intend any slight, your ladyship," said Queen Naki, her hand resting on Seroka's shoulder, assuring her. "Be at ease, our tribe is your ally, and we have fought countless battles shoulder to shoulder. Fear not, for we shall do all in our power to retrieve your father and sister, alive."

Queen Naki, a lady of diminutive stature and dusky complexion, was possessed of great comeliness and meekness. She was clothed in *minwenda*, the attire of her people, which did grace her shapely form with utmost elegance.

"The queen speaks true," the prince added.

"Forgive our manners; this is not the conversation one has at the gate. Although emotions run high, we must proceed to meet the king, who shall guide us on how best to aid your people," advised Queen Naki.

With Neo's aid, Princess Seroka regained her composure and entered the throne room, where she awaited King Mikado's counsel. As she entered, a sense of unease stirred within her, for this was her first trip as the foremost messenger and representative of Baloki. Nonetheless, Neo's presence served to soothe her, and she stood with poise and dignity.

"*Mavu, iwe ne makole, iwe unori ifa nda fa,*" (*My soil, you of heavens, you who say I should die, and I do so*), the king's right man, known as Thileli, chanted as Princess Seroka and Neo entered the throne room.

The throne room was bedecked with red, blue, and silver, the colours of the Veka people, with paintings of the *ngoma ngoma* drawn on behind the throne. The king sat atop his throne, clad in regal attire crafted from animal skin and adorned with splendid gems. He was a tall, balding man, exuding an air of command, with a beard that was greying at the edges.

"Princess Seroka and Neo, 'tis an honour to receive you in my kingdom. I have been apprised of the trials that afflict Baloki, and I offer you my deepest sympathies," proclaimed King Mikado in his resounding voice.

"'Tis a blessing for my kingdom to bask in your radiance. A pity that we are brought together under such dire circumstances. I trust that my son and wife have accorded you a warm reception," he added.

For many years, the king had sought to arrange a marriage between his son and Princess Seroka. However, Baloki tradition forbade the marriage of the spare princess before the first princess has produced an heir, particularly to a foreign land. Further complicating matters was the fact that Seroka was the commander of the Baloki army.

"Your Highness, we are humbled to be in your presence. My father has oft spoken of your virtues, and it is an immense honour for me to stand before you in these troubled times," replied her ladyship Seroka.

"I am very honoured, my lady," King Mikado responded.

"Your Highness, we have need of men. We have good reasons to believe that King Shaza will be marching his troops north, and we cannot withstand his onslaught without you. Should our defences falter, rest assured that he shall set his sights on Veka." Neo spoke with conviction, with a subtle tone of arrogance.

"If Baloki falls, so will Veka," Neo continued, his tone rising.

The king appeared displeased with Neo's tone.

"Mind your tone, boy, you dare question the strength of our defence?" interjected Thileli, who did not hide his irritation with Neo.

"Your Highness, my brother meant no disrespect. What he wishes to convey is that our two kingdoms are interdependent, for we have been allies for countless generations.

The people of Baloki shall ever remain beholden to your kingdom," her ladyship said with a serene demeanour.

"I assure you, the Veka Kingdom shall stand with you in this war. We have battled together ere now, and we shall not forsake you at this time," said the king, his words giving comfort.

"Princess, I shall offer you three thousand of my finest men …" began the king, but Neo cut in abruptly.

"But we need more…" he interjected.

"Your Highness, my brother means to express our gratitude," Princess Seroka intervened, seeking to mollify the king's feelings.

"Thank you, Your Highness. We are grateful for your support," Neo added, bowing respectfully.

The princess, who was evidently agitated, whispered something in Neo's ear, prompting him to excuse himself from the king's presence.

As Neo strode out of the throne room, he noticed a figure following him. Neo had never seen this man before, so he increased his pace to confirm that the man was indeed following him. The man increased his pace also. Upon exiting, the man caught up to him.

A tall, gaunt man with dark skin and bleary eyes approached Neo. "Your Highness, may I speak with you?" he enquired.

Neo appeared baffled, for none but Kobo and Morena Seriti addressed him as Your Highness. "Morena, are you addressing me?" he asked, puzzled.

"Yes, Your Highness, I speak to you. Please follow me; I am a friend of Kobo's," the man answered.

Neo's countenance shifted from bewilderment to inquisitiveness.

"Follow me this way. Here in these parts, I am known as Mulafa," said the man as he gestured for Neo to accompany him. Mulafa proffered a black hooded robe for Neo to conceal himself, and they embarked upon a sojourn through the winding alleyways of the royal grounds, where the common folk made their abode.

As the night did draw nigh, they traversed the streets unnoticed until they arrived at a brothel. "I understand that this is not fitting for someone of your position, however, I ask you, decline not my invitation. I assure you that this is the most secure place to converse in private," Mulafa implored of Neo, who was looking very uncomfortable to be there.

As they entered the brothel, Mulafa greeted a corpulent woman, whose face was heavily rouged and adorned with finery. "Sister, 'tis a pleasure to see you," he uttered whilst proffering her a sum of silver coins. "Make certain none disturb us whilst we are within your establishment."

Thereupon, Manaka, Mulafa's half-sister by their father's side, ordered her ladies to leave the premises. "The hour is still young, and the good folk have yet to partake in the merriment of ale. You have a few hours ere the masses shall arrive," said Manaka.

"I offer you gratitude, dear sister," Mulafa replied.

"The hut is wholly yours to claim. Select any chamber that does please your fancy. Perhaps the chamber of torment would suit you well, for 'tis said that hushed whispers does not traverse within its walls," suggested Manaka.

"Let us proceed forthwith." With a sweeping gesture, he beckoned unto Neo, who concealed himself beneath the black cloak.

As Neo was about to cross the doorway, two of the harlots approached him. "Handsome fellow, summon us when you have finished," whispered Duvha lasciviously.

Neo, who was trying to hide his face, had a look of abhorrence and hastily pushed the lascivious women aside and followed Mulafa across the room, which smelled of very expensive perfumes.

"Your Highness, please forgive me for having led you here. Yet, I deem it of great importance that you should know what I have to impart." Mulafa spoke with a contrite tone.

"Please tell me what is it that you would have me know?" enquired Neo, visibly agitated.

"Your Highness, a storm brews on the horizon and the darkness draws nigh. The hour is dire, and we must unite under a mighty ruler to weather this tempest. Please, consider that you are the rightful heir to the throne. When your mother left us, may her soul rest well with the rain gods and the other rain queens, you became her heir."

"Sir, if you are as wise as you are trying to appear, you will be aware of the Baloki curse. No man can ever sit upon the throne," Neo responded.

"'Tis true that no man may sit upon the throne, but if your aunt was never coronated, you as the only surviving heir of your mother, forgive me if I am wrong, but you would be allowed to rule until you bore a daughter.

Do you not yearn to carve you name in history, to lead your people through the storm to a brighter dawn? The hour is late, and we cannot dally any longer. The right bloodline must lead us in the coming war," Mulafa's voice resounded with conviction.

"You are not the first person to say this. What war is this, and why do I need to be on the right side? There is only one side," Neo insisted, "and that side is of my people and my queen."

"Ahh, the queen. She is not my queen. She will not be queen for long."

"Chose your next words very carefully, or I will have you arrested and killed for conspiring to murder the queen."

"Apologies if I have spoken out of terms, *my king*."

"There's that word again. I am not your king, and please tell whoever sent you that I am not interested."

"What do you want from me?" Neo commanded.

"Your Highness, you need not do anything; when the time come, you shall know. For now, I only desire you to know that you have support throughout Ashari."

"What meaning does this hold?" queried Neo.

"Before long, the throne of Baloki shall be empty," Mulafa said, causing Neo to be taken aback, sending shivers across his spine.

Neo pushed Mulafa, his mind awash with shock. "This be treason! I shall not partake in this! Whate'er plans you have, I entreat you to notify Kobo, Seriti, and all others involved that I have no interest."

With haste, Neo departed from the room, almost colliding with Manaka, who was standing at the main entrance.

"Hold your horses, good sir," said Manaka, with a mug of ale clasped in her grasp.

"Morena, you do appear agitated. Allow me to offer you a solution," suggested Duvha, who was standing just outside the brothel.

"By the heavens, restrain yourself, wench, or I shall order your tongue removed," Neo snapped, storming out of the chamber.

Having visited Veka on several occasions, Neo was familiar with the royal grounds. Moreover, locating the throne hut was a simple feat, as it was the main attraction positioned atop the highest peak of Mount Thavha Zim.

As he tried to make his way back, he recollected a prophecy relayed to him by a seer during his previous visit to Veka alongside Prince Moroka. The seer instructed him to seek Mulemba, informing him of his vital role in the impending war. Though Neo had not granted the prophecy much attention at the time, it was now resurfacing within his thoughts.

All around him, they spoke of this war in which he was to have a significant role, yet no clarity had been given as to its nature. With haste, Neo set forth towards the very place where he had encountered her, his mind stirring trying to piece everything together.

As he made his way through the streets, Neo encountered a young lad, standing idly by the roadside. Approaching the boy, he enquired as to the whereabouts of Mulemba's hut.

Without hesitation, the boy seized Neo's hand and took off running down a narrow alleyway, with the robe Mulafa gave him flowing behind him. It was a desolate place, with barely any movement in sight. As they came upon a small, doorless hut, the boy pointed at the entrance without saying a word and stretched out his hand for payment.

Though Neo had no coin on his person, he bestowed upon the boy a small neckerchief of meagre value to him, yet of great worth to the common folk.

With a grateful nod, the boy vanished as quickly as he had appeared, leaving Neo to ponder his next move. He felt hesitant to venture into the mysterious hut before him, but then he heard a deep voice call out from within.

"Who goes there?" Neo cried out; his curiosity piqued.

"Mulemba," he whispered.

"Follow my voice, Neo," the voice responded, beckoning him forward.

With a great deal of hesitation, Neo stepped inside. At once, he was assailed by a powerful light that left him momentarily blind and mute.

"Your Highness, resist not the pull of destiny," the voice boomed. "The power that draws you here cannot be denied."

A bellowing voice, like a creature from the depths of one's worst nightmare, did resound. "Yield unto the chaos that draws you," it commanded.

"No!" did Neo retort, yet his words did not escape his lips. Suddenly, he collapsed, and upon waking, found himself amidst a vast desert.

"Where am I? What do you want from me? Who are you?" enquired Neo, his voice restored.

"Release me!" he did scream, realising his predicament.

"Destiny calls, Neo," the voice echoed.

"Let me go," Neo called over and over again.

Then, a familiar voice did beckon him, calling out his name. "Neo, Neo, Neo, Neo, wake up."

With a deep inhalation, like one emerging from the depths of the sea, did Neo stir. And when he had regained consciousness, he realised he lay naked upon the earthen floor of an ordinary hut, with two familiar figures in front of him.

As he gathered his wits, he did behold the face of Seroka.

Quickly, she took a blanket and draped it over him.

"Neo, we have found you. Praise be to the rain gods! Are you injured?" she enquired, with great relief in her eyes.

A befuddled Neo shook his head, striving to comprehend the situation. His lips were cracked as one who had not drunk water for a few days.

"What is the meaning of this? Where am I?" he asked. "I thirst."

"Thank the heavens you are alive. Get him some water," Seroka said to Rendu, who gave Neo a mouthful from his waterskin. "Three sunsets have you been missing, Neo," replied Seroka.

"What do you mean?" Neo said, trying to quench his thirst. "I did see you but three hours past."

"Neo, what has occurred? Three sunsets have passed. Were you drugged?" queried Seroka.

With grave concern, Prince Rendu spoke unto Neo, "It is true; your sister has searched for you without cease, and she vowed to turn this entire kingdom upside down until you are found. Tell me who has done this to you, and we shall seek them out and bring them to justice."

Neo, sorely distressed, replied, "There was a lady, and her name was Mulemba. You must know her, Rendu, for this is her hut. She brought me inside, and the darkness was profound. I heard a voice, but I saw no one."

"No, Neo," replied Prince Rendu, "you are mistaken. This is but a common hut, and you are alone. And there is no one here that goes by that name, I can assure you. Can you recall where you had been before you came here?"

"I was with Mu–" Neo began, but then he bethought himself that speaking of Mulafa might bring him to suspicion. "Forgive me, my lord, for my mind is yet clouded, and my words do falter."

"Take your time, Neo," advised Seroka.

Neo sighed heavily, striving to remember how he had come to this place without revealing his secret. "After I left you in the throne room, I wandered through the royal grounds and ended up here. That was three hours past, and now I find myself naked upon the floor of this strange hut."

Keep My Enemies Close

"From my whispers in Batana do I bring news, my king," Sedi said in a hushed tone, drawing a note from her bosom and extending it to the newly crowned king. "They report that Princess Palesa calls herself queen regent to the Soru throne and deems her unborn child to be the rightful king of our kingdom."

The king received the letter and read it with a scoff, his face darkening with ire. "There can only be one true king in Soru," he replied in a biting tone, his lips twisted with disdain. "Let it be known to all that I shall tolerate no rival to my sovereignty."

"My king, rest assured that all of Soru recognises you and only you as the rightful ruler," Sedi responded in a measured tone. "Your council will labour tirelessly to ensure that the eight kingdoms understand this truth. Yet, even as we do so, we must prepare ourselves for the war that King Gauta threatens to bring to our mountains."

"We have sufficient men to prevail in battle," Gasane interjected. "You have our full support, my king."

"If they seek to challenge my throne, then so be it. I shall flay that wretched woman and impale her head upon our gates for all to see. Let it be known that those who would dare contest my reign will suffer a similar fate. I am not my father. I will not show mercy, for they must know who I am," King Tlou continued, his voice brimming with fury.

"Tell me, what is our strategy?" the king demanded.

Nare, who had been waiting patiently for his turn to speak, presented a map and beseeched the servants to clear the table. "Might I humbly request, my lord, that all who are not of your council do depart the chamber? For I possess a plan that shall guarantee your triumph in the impeding war."

King Tlou gave the signal to clear the room, and the council began to devise their strategy.

"My king, for our plan to succeed, we require King Shaza to send us reinforcements. By now, the Batanas, the Balokis, and their northern allies have doubtless joined together to march upon Soru," said Nare as he unfurled a map on the table.

"I have dispatched an urgent letter to King Shaza, impressing upon him the criticality of sending aid. Should our kingdom fall, he shall never claim the northern kingdoms. I made it clear that his united Ashari can only come to pass if he sends us assistance," added Gasane.

The king nodded in acknowledgement to Gasane.

"Your Highness—" Nare pointed to the map. "—if you look upon this, you shall see that we may lay traps at the base of Molotli, where the terrain is flat. This shall give our archers, who shall be stationed upon the mountains, a distinct advantage. We can launch our attack from there," Nare continued.

"With all due respect to Nare, whom I am certain is a great commander of our army, our utmost efforts should be devoted to devising our defence.

The Soru Mountains are harsh and impenetrable. Only a fool would be ignorant of this to attack us. I do not believe that Palesa and her father, are fools," Sedi cautioned.

"Warfare is a task for men. Women should remain at home, caring for their children," Nare retorted.

"I advise you to choose your words with prudence henceforth, Nare. This woman shall win this war," Sedi replied, her voice calm, but her tone sharp.

"Cease your bickering," the king commanded, fixing his gaze upon Nare.

Nare composed himself and declared proudly, "My king, for centuries, we have cowered behind our mountains. However, we now have King Shaza as an ally. He is arguably the feistiest warrior who has ever lived. With him on our side, perhaps it is time we meet the Batanas on the open battlefield."

"We cannot prevail; we must remain within our fortified walls," Sedi cautioned again sternly.

"Your Highness, you must make an example of the Batanas," Nare continued.

"This is how we shall solidify your kingship and ensure that your name is feared from all corners of Ashari. You cannot permit anyone to challenge your throne."

"I must concur with Nare," Gasane added in his old, trembling voice. "If you do not extinguish this fire now, your reign shall never know peace. Any who dare may think they can challenge you. Make an example of the Batanas."

The aged man stood up and approached the king. "I also received another letter," Gasane said, unrolling a parchment from his robe and handed it to the king.

"Why does everyone insist on keeping their information stored in such a manner? Is there no better place to keep such correspondence?" the king enquired with annoyance, to Nare's amusement.

"It reads that Baloki has sought allegiance from Veka and Shanga. Their combined forces shall march upon Swarai. If this be true, then we need not concern ourselves with them. They shall be too preoccupied with their own battles."

"I suggest we attack Batana whilst the other kingdoms are still otherwise engaged," Gasane added.

Sedi shook her head in stark disagreement. "Hear me, oh, long live the king. Should we not spare the unnecessary shedding of blood for our young men? If there is a siege, we have enough supplies for six moons. Remember, your grandfather stood firm against King Shaza's father during the two-winters siege when Zuka marched north in the last war," Sedi reminded the council.

Leko who remained silent nodded her head in agreement. King Tlou, with an air of disdain, turned to Nare and disregarded Sedi's counsel altogether.

"Nare, how many men do we have?"

"Sire, we have twenty thousand men. We have enough gold to buy an additional five thousand men from the Scatter Islands. In the letter I wrote to King Shaza, I asked him for at least five thousand men. We will march thirty thousand strong. Our army will be two for every man they have," Nare said proudly.

"I like those odds!" exclaimed the king, a grin spreading across his face.

"My king, I must agree with Sedi on this. These odds Nare speak of assume that Gauta and Palesa do not call upon any allies, and that King Shaza will indeed send us five thousand men," Leko, who was struggling to keep her silence cautioned.

"Also, we are not taking into account the many mages they have," Sedi interjected.

"Sire, the week past, I had a dream where birds were flying towards Thaba Ntsu, and our mountains grew ever larger. I consulted with the seer, and she confirmed that it portends victory in our favour," said Gasane, giving the king a respectful nod.

"Are we now planning the war by placing our trust in the dream of birds to secure our victory?" Sedi pointed out.

"Your Highness, I advised your father, may his soul rest in peace, in many battles, and he hearkened to my counsel. It saved us much unnecessary shedding of blood," Sedi continued.

"I am not mine own father!" roared the king, smiting his hand upon the table in great anger. "Sedi, the reason why I kept you in this council is because my father always told me to keep my enemies close."

"My king," replied Sedi, bowing low and retreating a pace, yet still within the council's purview.

"Your Highness, the scheme we do propose is to confront the foe in Mokotong whilst maintaining our hold upon Thaba Ntsu," added Nare.

"History will remember my name," King Tlou grinned.

May the Gods Be with Us

"The Queen has issued a command to march to Swarai in three sunsets," Morena Seriti said with great urgency.

"No, Morena Seriti, you must persuade the queen to send but half of our army to aid King Gauta. If we divide our forces, King Shaza may yet receive our letter in time to send aid to Swarai," replied Kobo.

Morena Seriti, however, was not swayed by this counsel. "Are you suggesting that we must help Swarai? That feeble tribe has not the strength to defend itself from any who seek to assail it!" he exclaimed.

"Aye, you are right," Kobo agreed. "If King Shaza be wise, he shall send Prince Moroka to Zuka with all speed. His forces will not reach Swarai in time, but if the queen rescues the prince and her daughter, the war shall be lost before it has truly begun."

Morena Seriti pondered this proposal for a time. "This is a thorny matter, Kobo. If we do send half our army to aid the Batanas, King Tlou may yet suffer defeat. Such an outcome would go against the Keepers' plans to seat him upon the throne."

"Fret not about Tlou, for arrangements have been made," Kobo replied cryptically.

"What arrangements?" Morena Seriti enquired.

"I said worry not about it. You must focus on convincing the queen to divide our army."

"That shall be a hard task," Morena Seriti sighed. "The queen has made it plain that she desires the safe return of Moroka and the princess, even if it means the death of all in Swarai. Such were her words."

"You must depart now. Have you not a meeting with the queen?" Kobo reminded Seriti.

"For the Watchers ne'er sleep," said Kobo ere he vanished into the dark night. "The Watcher protect," replied Morena Seriti, as he made his way to the throne room.

Princess Seroka had just returned from Veka, accompanied by Neo. Despite Neo's poor reception from King Mikado, the princess had succeeded in securing aid from Veka.

"My lords and ladies, we find ourselves in trying times, unforeseen and unwelcome," said the crown princess, giving her first address to the council.

The queen had descended into the depths of the Loaba River, to seek counsel from her ancestors for guidance in the looming war. Such was practice for the rain queens when they needed guidance and strength. She had entrusted the governance of the kingdom to the heiress princess whilst she was away. This was the first time the Heir Princess had been left in charge of the kingdom, without her father guiding her. However, the presence of Black Mamba made her feel at ease and more confident.

"My father, your prince, and my sister, your princess, have both been taken as prisoners of war. We have good knowledge that they and my uncle are all safe and well," she continued, with the poise and authority of a true queen.

"I am pleased to announce that our mission to Shanga was a triumph, thanks to the great work of Morena Seriti and Mamba. King Mogwena has pledged two thousand five hundred of his men to our cause. Furthermore, I have just received confirmation from my sister that King Mikado has pledged another three thousand men to aid us in this war."

"Princess, do you deem such a force to be sufficient? What if King Shaza sends his forces against us as well?" asked Black Mamba, with a hint of uncertainty in his voice.

"Our army already stands strong at fifteen thousand," countered Princess Seroka, her gaze unwavering upon Black Mamba. "Do you doubt the might of our warriors?"

"I do not doubt our people's strength, my princess, but King Shaza is unlike any man. Those who have witnessed his combat prowess claim that he fights as though blessed by the gods, with no mercy shown to his enemies," explained Black Mamba.

"I have also heard that his warriors possess the strength of ten men, and are willing to give their lives for him," added Morena Hlogo with a sombre nod.

The council fell silent, the weight of uncertainty heavy upon their shoulders.

"He has the blood of the ancient Khoros coursing through his veins, and his followers claim he can transform into a lion come nightfall," added Morena Tlou.

"Have you seen him take on the form of a lion, Tlou? What then shall we do to our enemies? Shall we cower in fear at the mere whispers of hearsay? Have you not witnessed the might of our house? The strength of your queen?" retorted Princess Seroka, her tone both proud and resounding.

Mamba gave a hit of amusement as the princess spoke to Morena Tlou.

"No, Princess, I seek not to offend. I but offer a word of caution, that we may not underestimate this man," replied Morena Tlou.

The room grew cold to the exchange between Princess Seroka and Morena Tlou.

"A kingdom divided cannot stand. We must unite as one front, and this quarrelling must cease," said the Heir Princess with a soft yet commanding voice.

"Well spoken, Princess. 'Tis why I believe we ought to display our unity with our cousin nation and dispatch a contingent of men to Batana," suggested Seriti.

"Are you out of your senses?" shouted Seroka.

"And where did you come from?" Mamba asked.

"I had some errands that needed my attention," said Morena Seriti, who had just walked in, stealing a glance at Neo, who was sitting at the corner, quiet as usual.

"Princess, please forgive my insolence, but I must speak my mind on this matter. As a humble servant of the kingdom, I must say that our army needs to be dispatched to Soru without any delay and fight alongside the Batana army. We swore an oath to King Gauta.

We cannot afford to have two enemies, King Gauta and Prince Tlou. If we do not choose a side, whoever comes out victorious will join hands with Shaza and march north to attack us. No, we must take sides in this war and fight alongside the Batana people; we made no vow to the usurper," Morena Seriti continued, to the nod of the other counsellors, except Mamba.

"If Batana falls, it will be a disaster for our kingdom. King Gauta has no heir, and his brother will succeed him. This might result in the same situation as Soru, and we cannot allow that to happen," Seriti continued.

"It sounds like someone was rehearsing his words," Mamba said with suspicion.

"Let him speak," the Heir Princess commanded.

"Princess, you are wise to raise your concerns about the safety of your father and sister. Yet, we have but a small window to act. Shaza would sooner dispatch his army to Swarai, leaving Soru and Batana to settle their civil strife on their own. If we tarry, we put at risk Shaza transporting the prince and princess to the south, where he is strongest. Thus, we must act forthwith, sending one-half of our army to fight in Soru and the other half to Swarai.

"'Tis the proper course of action for the security of our kingdom," Morena Seriti advocated.

"I am struggling to comprehend your suggestion, Seriti," Princess Seroka said, her expression puzzled.

"Consider this, Princess: If we do not send aid to Batana, and Tlou emerges victorious, he will seize the Batana Kingdom and place whomever he wishes on the throne. This means we will have no allies in the south."

"Okay…" Princess Seroka nodded, her mind piecing together the puzzle and apprehending what Seriti was saying.

"If we support Batana, and Palesa emerges victorious, we will gain both her and her father as strong allies, thus solidifying our stronghold in the south," Seriti continued.

"If we have Palesa as an ally, we can block any attempts to transport Prince Moroka and Princess Mapula to the south," Morena Hlogo added.

"Aye, now you understand," Seriti responded confidently, seeing that the council agreed with his plan. "Please tell me, Morena Seriti, how are you so certain that Shaza will not march upon Soru, to aid his new ally, King Tlou?" asked Princess Motakia in a measured tone.

"Aye, Seriti, how do you know?" Mamba chimed in, seeking clarification.

"A hunch strikes me! Whispers in the air say that Shaza, with a heart set on war and conquest, seeks to capture all the northern kingdoms. And to reach the north, Baloki must fall. The lives of your father and sister shall be used as bargaining for the queen to surrender her kingdom."

"Whispers, you say? Were you present in the room where such plans were made?" Mamba said in a sarcastic tone.

"Listen to me. Shaza seeks not peace or harmony, but rather blood and power. Thus, we must act swiftly and decisively before he unleashes his wrath upon our lands," declared Morena Seriti, with conviction in his voice.

"I agree with Morena Seriti," said Morena Hlogo. Seriti gave a nod of gratitude to him.

"Let us send half our men to fight alongside Batana. When we emerge victorious, we shall have a stronghold in Soru to hold Shaza at bay. The rest of our army, with the Vekas and Shangas, shall march to Swarai," Morena Seriti echoed his argument once more.

Mamba, still suspicious of Seriti's plans, interjected, "If we are victorious, Seriti. *If.* We first must win the war, then we shall have a stronghold in Soru."

"Your words ring true, Seriti. We shall heed to your counsel, it does seem wise to send some of our solders to fight alongside Gauta," Princess Seroka, in agreement with Seriti's proposal, decreed.

The other councillors gave a nod in assent, except for Mamba, whose suspicion of Seriti was obvious.

"May the rain gods smile upon us in battle," declared Princess Seroka.

"Aye, may the rain gods be with us indeed," echoed Mamba, solemnly nodding. All eyes in the room turned to the Heir Princess, who pondered thoughtfully over Morena Seriti's proposal.

"You make valid points, Seriti. But I wonder if we can risk delaying the march to Swarai?"

"Indeed, it is a difficult matter, Your Highness. Nevertheless, I firmly believe that this plan shall succeed."

"I gave you enough time to speak, Seriti, now 'tis my turn to speak," said the Heir Princess, to Mamba's amusement.

"Forgive me, Your Highness."

Seroka and Motakia whispered between themselves. "Neo, Thebo, come here," Princess Motakia beckoned, and the four of them engaged in a private discussion.

"Morena Seriti, you presented compelling arguments. The four of us concur that we should sleep on this decision. We must first consult with the queen upon her return from the river. Mamba shall communicate with the council of our decision on the morrow during the break-of-dawn meal."

He Came for Blood

The sound of drums resounded in the distance, an impossible thing to ignore. Leading the army of nigh unto fourteen thousand men were mages and seers, who chanted their enchantments on the road to ensure a triumph. Men struck their shields with spears and swords, singing Batana war songs. Even the rain could not stop the Batana army from marching down to Soru; the seers interpreted the rain as a good omen, a blessing from the gods.

The Batana warriors stood tall, their armour shining in the light of day, swords, and axes ready.

They had trained for many days in preparation for this moment, and they were determined to take back the crown from the self-appointed usurper king.

As the army advanced towards the field of battle, the landscape transformed into a daunting sight. The once-peaceful villages in the countryside had been ruined by deep furrows carved by the heavy chariots' wheels and the trampling of horses' hooves. The ground had turned to mud, and the air was thick with the sweat and fear of the unknown and the bravery of men ready to die.

Following the mages on regal horses and chariots were King Gauta and Palesa. Palesa was already seven moons along in her pregnancy. Despite this, she was resolved to march alongside her army to Soru and would brook no dissuasion.

Her reason for such daring was clear: she wished not for her son to inherit the throne without a fight. This declaration of her intent did not fall on deaf ears, for many men in her father's army beheld her bravery with admiration and respect.

Palesa had chosen black-and-purple armour, the colours of her father's house.

Next to her was Perega, who had risen to be Palesa's right-hand man. He had given her much advice in preparation for the war.

"Your Highness! Your bravery does impress," Perega proclaimed with great reverence.

"Maiden she may be, but the blood of war does course through her veins," replied King Gauta, bedecked in his resplendent platinum-and-gold armour, with a regal cloak of black and purple.

"This land is my home, my son's home, and if the gods are just, we shall reclaim his birthright," Palesa declared, though she struggled in her armour, wary of showing any weakness before the men surrounding her.

"My queen, this is your son's kingdom, all these men will die to have you seated on that throne," added Perega, to which Palesa nodded in approval.

Drummers followed Palesa and her father, singing and chanting war songs. Behind them rode Nonyane, commander of the Batana army, atop his black stallion and wielding his trusty war hammer. The rest of the army followed suit, brandishing their weapons and beating their shields, a clear message to their enemies that war was nigh.

For three long sunsets, they had marched towards the kingdom of Soru, passing deserted villages along the way. Finally, with Thaba Ntsu in full view, they made camp.

The war banner of Soru surrounded the field, a bold statement by King Tlou that the Batana army was on his land. His most trusted warriors mounted powerful warhorses and stood at the front lines, ready to charge into battle at his command. Archers, hidden behind hills, took aim with their strung bows, while infantry stood armed with pikes, spears, and halberds, waiting for the impending clash.

When the Batana army came into full view of the Soru army, they went into formation. The sound of drums died out, leaving the sound of men hitting their shields. Nonyane gave his signal to silence the men. In tense silence, the two armies faced each other, waiting for the signal to begin the battle. Upon the battleground, the setting sun did cast its light, casting long shadows o'er the warriors. The sole sounds that could be heard were the wind's gentle rustling through the blades of grass and the occasional bird cry.

"That harlot thinks she can set foot upon my land, with her vile father, and steal my throne," declared King Tlou, with a clear view of the army from Thaba Ntsu.

"Your Highness, the army stands ready. As the commander-in-chief, we await your command," said Nare, ever loyal to his king.

"On the morrow, a *lekgotla* is scheduled. Perhaps we can entreat her to spare the lives of these men so that they can return to their kin and lay with their wives," added Gasane.

A lekgotla was a customary meeting between two kings before battle, where they would seek common ground to convince the other to accept defeat under certain conditions, in order to prevent bloodshed.

As Palesa, accompanied by her father and their retinue, neared the grounds where King Tlou awaited, tension hung heavy in the air. Seeing that all eyes were on her, Palesa raised her hand in a fist, a roar erupted from her men, their shields resounding with the rhythmic beat of their chant, "Queen Palesa, Queen Palesa."

Observing the tense atmosphere, King Tlou and his retinue advanced to meet Palesa, his archers poised with arrows, yet he gestured for restraint. The distance between the two groups diminished as they closed in on each other, the intensity of their gazes palpable as Palesa and Tlou locked eyes in a silent exchange fraught with anticipation.

"If it isn't the face of a traitor," remarked Leko, her voice tinged with contempt as she cast a pointed glance towards Perega, whose expression remained unreadable.

"Tlou, we can end this war here and now. You know well that the *mokorotlo* upon your head rightfully belongs to my son," Palesa asserted firmly, her tone unwavering in its resolve.

"This is my daughter's kingdom, and we shall not depart until she is crowned queen," declared King Gauta, his voice echoing with steadfast support for his daughter.

"Our demands are as follows: declare Palesa's unborn son as the true heir to the Soru Kingdom. Proclaim Palesa as queen regent, to govern until her son comes of age.

Should you agree to these terms, you will be granted a seat on the council and given the best piece of land in Soru," Nonyane stated, addressing the impassive faces of King Tlou's entourage.

"You have until noon on the morrow to accept our demands," King Gauta added, his tone leaving no room for negotiation.

In response, King Tlou emitted a boisterous laugh, his confidence apparent as he dismissed their ultimatum.

"Let these men return to their wives and children, Tlou," urged Palesa, her voice tinged with defiance.

"Mark my words, the next time I set my eyes upon you, it shall be over your corpse," retorted Tlou, turning his horse and leading his retinue back towards the mountains.

"My King, this is not Palesa's war. Her father has always coveted Soru's throne. I do not think King Gauta has brought all these men and mages here to fight for an unborn babe," argued Sedi, her eyes ablaze with conviction, riding next to the king, wearing her full war amour.

"He came for blood and a crown," she continued.

"Very well then, if he desires war, on the morrow we shall dance," declared King Tlou, his voice filled with pride and fury.

Message of Importance

"Have you heard of the great war between the Sorus and the Batanas?" exclaimed a youth in the bustling market of Swarai.

"My father has told me that King Gauta has assembled the mightiest army in all Ashari, which is led by very powerful mages," a second boy answered.

"No, I have heard otherwise," retorted the first. "My father said that the land of Soru has ne'er been conquered and so, King Tlou shall emerge victorious. Also, King Tlou has pledged his fealty to King Shaza, who has ever been a loyal friend to his allies."

The second boy was struck with a sudden realisation. "If Soru be our ally, does that mean we shall also be called to war?"

The first boy chortled in amusement. "You, fight? You can scarcely wield a wooden sword and are known to faint at the sight of blood!"

With that, the two boys darted off in pursuit of each other, leaving the prince to his own thoughts. Prince Maru, disguised so as to escape detection, clutched a pilfered loaf of bread and a sack of provisions. He was on his way to the prison where Prince Moroka, Princess Mapula, and Kwena were being held captive.

These past few moons had been fraught with danger and hardship, and the reminiscence of his carefree days in Soru, when he would frolic about the throne room causing chaos and merriment, only served to deepen his melancholy. But there was no time for such reveries now. As he trudged through the putrid, damp tunnels of Swarai, he could not shake off the foreboding sense that he was being watched by spies lurking in the shadows. Nevertheless, he pressed on towards the prison, making sure no one was trailing him.

Prince Maru had discovered a way to sneak into the cells where Prince Moroka was detained. Though it was a difficult task, he succeeded by traversing through hidden tunnels, using the map provided by Kazi. He cautiously peeked outside to observe who was on duty and realised that it was Legatlo. Over the weeks past, the prince had kept an eye on Legatlo and observed that he had poor eyesight and took longer breaks during his post, perhaps to visit a nearby brothel. Nonetheless, he paid no heed to such information and waited patiently for Legatlo to leave for his usual break.

Meanwhile, in the chilling darkness of the prison cell, Prince Moroka stirred restlessly, his slumber disturbed by troubled dreams once more. Sensing his brother's distress, Kwena reached for nearby stones, tossing them gently to rouse him from his troubled sleep.

"Brother, brother," Kwena called out softly, in the silence of the cell.

"Why do you awaken me, Kwena?" Prince Moroka murmured groggily; his consciousness barely tethered to the waking world.

"Wake up, Moroka. You are talking in your sleep again," Kwena whispered, taking care not to wake Princess Mapula.

"Let me return to my rest, Kwena," Prince Moroka pleaded wearily, his weariness palpable.

"No. Thanks to you, I am struggling to fall asleep. You keep calling out his name," Kwena paused, and sighed. "He is gone, Moroka," Kwena spoke, seeking to offer comfort to his grieving brother.

Struggling against the chill of the prison walls, Prince Moroka slowly sat upright, his heart heavy with the weight of loss and longing.

"I grieve for him," Moroka lamented, his voice heavy with sorrow.

"I know," Kwena responded, his voice above whisper.

"My heart is shattered; he was very dear to me. I should have remained in Soru. Perhaps he would still draw breath, perhaps we would not find ourselves in this wretched prison cell." Moroka's eyes brimming with unshed tears, as he struggled to contain his emotions. "He was a mighty man, now he is fallen," Moroka continued, his voice faltering with grief.

Not wanting to show his emotions, Prince Moroka cast his face towards the wall.

Kwena, sensing his brother's profound despair, remained silent, his heart heavy with sympathy. Never before had he witnessed Moroka so broken, and he knew that his normal jests were ill-suited for this sombre moment. "It's okay, you did the best you could," were the only words Kwena managed to utter, offering what solace he was able to.

"When last I saw him, he spoke of foreboding, fearing it might be our final meeting," Moroka recounted, his voice trembling with emotion. "He told me how much I meant to him, and I, in my folly, failed to return his sentiment," he confessed, his attempt to withhold his tears proving futile as his voice wavered with grief.

"I am…" Kwena began before being interrupted by a key turning in the door.

Using the key Kazi had given him, Prince Maru opened the prison door carefully. "Prince Moroka," he whispered, catching sight of Prince Moroka, whose face looked withered.

Imprisonment had taken its toll on him, and he appeared feeble, having lost a substantial amount of weight. His hair and beard had grown out, revealing the thinning hair that he usually kept short. However, he was holding himself together, maintaining a facade of strength for his daughter and brother.

"Shouldn't you be fighting alongside your brother against your sister-in-law?" Kwena remarked in a sarcastic tone, trying to distract the young prince so Moroka can compose himself.

"My brother is dead. That usurper is no brother of mine. He slew my father," Prince Maru replied.

"By the rain gods, even your mockery is dull. I need some amusement. Can you arrange to smuggle a woman during your next visit?" Kwena enquired.

"Kwena, I implore you to watch your tongue in the presence of your princess and cease your foolishness. Prince Maru risked his life by coming here," Prince Moroka scolded.

Prince Maru handed a letter to Prince Moroka. "Uncle, the man who gave me this letter requested that I pass on his regards," he said.

"Of whom do you speak? Did you not have an audience with Kazi?" Prince Moroka enquired.

"He did conceal his face; I did not ascertain his name nor glimpse his face. All he said was that Kazi was aware I met with him, and that I should trust him."

Prince Moroka studied the letter he received from Maru and instantly recognised the sigil within.

"Your Highness, I do beg your forgiveness for not coming to see you. It is too dangerous. I am praying for your good health and rescue. I have forwarded your letter to Queen Motapo and relayed all that I know, which might aid her in your rescue. May the Rain Queen reign forever," the letter read.

"Who is your secret admirer?" Kwena asked.

"The letter is from an old acquaintance, who might be the key for us to return home."

"Ohh, how mysterious," said Kwena, looking at Princess Mapula, who was now awake.

Prince Moroka reached out and passed the letter on to Kwena, who was in the opposite cell.

"The sigil," Kwena remarked, fixing his gaze upon Moroka, who acknowledged with a nod.

After reading the letter, Kwena returned it to Moroka, who perused its contents once more, then proceeded to tear it into fragments and ingested them.

"Why do you have to be dramatic? Burning the letter would have sufficed," quipped Kwena, to the amusement of Prince Maru and the princess.

"I cannot take any risk of this falling in the wrong hands," Prince Moroka responded gravely.

"Yes, but fire could have done the same thing," Kwena did opine, casting a glance towards Mapula, and the two exchanged smiles.

Prince Maru moved towards the cell of the princess, which was located nigh to her father's, and presented her with a book. "I know you have read this book before, but it was the only one I could get my hands on."

"Thank you, Maru. *War of the Kingdoms* is a most cherished book of mine," Princess Mapula responded with excitement.

"Did you know?" the princess said to Prince Maru.

"The book *War of the Kingdoms* chronicles the ancient Ashari era, before Basoso Tribe was divided, and also when the Ngori Tribe was but one kingdom.

This was prior to the Veka and the Shangas crossing the Lipalipa Sea."

"Of course, he knows that. You do know that, do you?" mocked Kwena, pointing at Maru.

"Let me finish," implored Mapula. "Before Ashari and Pagero were separated, the Ngori Tribe journeyed from the north and settled in the lands, which now belong to the Baloki, Shanga, and Veka tribes. However, when the Ngori Tribe arrived in the north, they were not solitary, nor were they the first men to arrive. They encountered the Khoro Tribe, an ancient nomadic group that lived in isolation, relying solely on hunting and gathering and maintaining a primitive way of life."

"Cousin, I know very well about the Khoro Tribe. Remember the time we went to the Khoro Forest and …" Prince Maru caught the death stare of the princess; they had promised to never speak of the events that transpired in that forest.

"Oh, what happened in the Khoro Forest?" Kwena enquired.

"Nothing," Maru responded suspiciously. "Mapula, you were just about to share what you know about the Khoro Tribe," Maru quickly redirected the conversation to avoid discussing their encounter.

"Well, you might know their history when they lived in the Molotli Mountains, but *War of the Kingdoms* records their early history," Princess Mapula said proudly.

"But ..."

"Hush, let me finish telling you the story," Mapula cut off her uncle, a bit irritated from the constant interruptions. "Their language had not progressed, but they could communicate amongst themselves. The Khoros were very diminutive, gaunt, with scanty fat in their bodies, sharp facial features, and coarse, cropped hair," she continued.

"Most of the land in the north of Ashari was greatly fertile. As such, the early Khoro Tribe, who are indigenous to the area, lived there. However, they had reoccupied the north a few summers prior to the invasion of the Ngori Tribe.

Tales speaks of a migration towards the south, taken by the Khoros in their attempt to escape the Fefre meteorite impact that brought forth death and destruction, laying waste to the majority of all living creatures on the continent.

"I guess we have the meteorite to thank for your father's evil friend," Kwena jested, a wry smirk touching his lips.

"There is greater good than evil brought forth by the meteorite," interjected Prince Moroka, who was busy writing a letter. "Princess, the wielder of power is the one who determines its path. 'Tis the sin of pride and the lure of greed that has corrupted mankind," he continued.

"I know, I know," Mapula replied with a nod of understanding.

"Now, where was I?" she mused aloud. "Ahh, I remember. Those who survived the calamity did inherit some magical abilities, brought forth by their exposure to the impact. These survivors did multiply and procreated a generation of Khoros that possessed mystical abilities," Mapula explained.

"I wish I had mystical abilities," Kwena interjected.

"Shh, Uncle Kwena, I am still telling the story," Mapula said to her uncle.

"After taking root in the semi-arid south, the Khoros did return to the north, strengthened with their newfound abilities. Their number grew to thousands, but alas, their inability to read and write meant that their history was poorly recorded. Thus, what is known of them today has been written from the perspective of the Basoso and Ngori scribes. Yet, from the cave drawings that have been found, it is known that the Khoros possessed powerful mystical abilities, bestowed upon them by the Fefre meteorite impact. Those who survived had discovered a way to harness the meteor's power, granting them a unique ability to commune with nature and tame wild beasts, which they used in battle," she continued.

"If I had that power, I would rule the world," Prince Maru interrupted.

"So would I, young prince. And my first order would be to feed your brother to lions," Kwena jested.

"There is more to life than ruling the world. Let me finish my story," said the princess.

"When the War of the Kingdoms erupted, the Basoso Tribe, having invaded the north, battled Ngori Tribe for land.

However, both tribes had a common enemy, the indigenous Khoro people. After both tribes' unsuccessful attempts to push the Khoros to the south, the Basoso and Ngori tribes united under the leadership of King Shaza I, who hailed from the Ngori Tribe..."

"Princess, I am certain Prince Maru cannot tarry any longer," Kwena interrupted Mapula.

"It is okay, uncle. I am waiting for Uncle Moroka to finish writing his letter," Prince Maru responded.

Mapula smiled and continued, "The war waged on for twelve long summers, and when the end finally came, the Khoros had been reduced to a mere few hundred. Although they had magic on their side, the cunning nature of the invading men proved to be too much for them. King Shaza I, having emerged victorious, ruled for a mere two summers ere being struck down by his own brother, Sholozi, who then ascended the throne.

King Sholozi, who was known as The Cruel, had a hobby of putting his enemies in lions' pits and watching them being devoured alive.

He was the last king of Ashari, for under his rule, the Basoso did rise up and decide they were an independent kingdom. At the same time, the Swarai Tribe also broke away from the Ngoris to form their own tribe under the leadership of King Moshwana."

"How many times have you read this book?" Kwena asked.

"Clearly a lot," Maru laughed.

"I am almost done," Mapula replied, rolling her eyes. "King Sholozi was obsessed with the magic of the Khoro people and sought to use it against his enemies. He decided to pursue the Khoro Tribe, who were migrating south to their former abode. The Basoso were now the sole rulers of the north, and the Swarais migrated towards the east, where they still dwell to this day."

"Cousin, thank you for the telling me the story, but I cannot stay any longer. I must depart before Legatlo returns," Prince Maru interrupted.

"I do ask your forgiveness, for I did get carried away. I cannot wait to peruse this book again," responded Princess Mapula, with excitement.

Prince Moroka, who was busy writing a letter, did heave a weary sigh. "Son, I bear a message of importance, which I may not entrust to a mere scrap of parchment. Go hence to the usual place and bid the man you met to come visit me on the morrow."

"Brother, what dire need compels you to put this man's life at risk?" enquired Kwena.

"I am trying to save our lives," Prince Moroka replied.

He then handed the letter he was writing to Prince Maru. "My boy, bear this to Kazi. He will know what course to take."

Trust In Me

"Our cause is just, and we shall emerge triumphant! The madness of Tlou has gone unchecked for too long, but today we shall reclaim what is rightfully ours. We do not fight solely for ourselves, but also for the generations that will sing songs of our valour in this war. We fight for our freedom and for the future of Soru!" exclaimed Palesa, in her regal armour, her voice swelling with pride and determination, as the soldiers cheered.

Earlier in the day, King Gauta, Palesa, Perega, Lefefe and Nonyane, representing Batana Kingdom, had convened for *lekgotla* with King Tlou, Gasane, Nare, Sedi and Leko representing Soru Kingdom, to negotiate the terms of their demands.

Neither party conceded, and it was agreed that the claim to the throne would be settled in the old-fashioned way, with the gods deciding the true heir.

"Any man who brings me Tlou's head shall be rewarded with his heart's desire!" declared King Gauta to his soldiers. "Today, we dance with death!" he cried out proudly, eliciting cheers from his army.

The clanging of metal and the thundering hooves of horses blended into a cacophony of war as the men charged forward. The first line of attack was led by Nonyane, proudly sporting the purple and black colours of the Batana Tribe. The soldiers in the front line carried large leather shields of the same colours, along with spears that stretched two-and-a-half metres long.

With a cry that echoed across the battlefield, Nonyane spurred his noble horse onward and did charge forth into the fray. Palesa watched from a distance, surrounded by the royal guards, while King Gauta was proudly with the fighting men, also surrounded by his royal guards.

As the Batana warriors charged valiantly behind their chariots, their blades glinting in the rain and their shields raised, a sudden gust of wind and rain swept through the battlefield, making it difficult for them to maintain their formation.

"It appears the gods favour us," said Gasane, witnessing the sudden rainfall upon the battlefield. Together with King Tlou, Leko, and Sedi, they watched from the safety of Thaba Ntsu.

Nonyana cried out, "Charge, do not break the line!" Yet his words were drowned out by the clanging of steel and the tumultuous roar of battle. He beheld the tenacity in his warriors' eyes, the courage that had brought them here. He inhaled deeply and then charged forth once more, this time with greater intent and command.

"We cannot allow them to breach our defences!" a thunderous voice bellowed from the Soru encampment. "We must hold the line, come what may. The first man to falter will see his entire family thrown off the highest cliff in Thaba Ntsu!" Nare shouted.

With his war hammer raised, Nonyane and the front line of the Batana army marched headlong into a trap. The Sorus had excavated a large pit, deep enough to swallow three hundred men. The pit was cleverly disguised with a covering of grass, sturdy enough to hold the weight of a hundred men. As fate would have it, nearly three hundred Batana soldiers charged forward, oblivious to the danger beneath their feet. The ground gave way, and they plummeted into the abyss, their screams filling the air as they were impaled on the spikes below. Nonyane glanced around in horror, the cries of his men echoing in his ears. Before he could fully grasp the catastrophe, a thunderous voice rang out, "Archers, release your arrows!" And the gloomy skies were illuminated with flaming arrows.

"Raise your shields!" Nonyana commanded, and the men who survived the calamity complied. The arrows rained down upon the soldiers trapped in the crevasse, and at least one hundred of them met their doom.

"Archers, fire!" Nare roared once more from the Soru camp.

Nonyane watched in horror as twice as many arrows as before soared heavenward, arcing towards his army. Desperation filled his voice as he shouted, "Lefefe!"

Leading the Batana mages, Lefefe stepped forward chanting an ancient incantation. With the rest of the mages, they raised their staffs, and the arrows suddenly ignited mid-air, bursting into flames and raining down as harmless cinders.

"Retreat!" Nonyana shouted, seeing that the ground might be laid with traps that awaited his men. The few surviving soldiers clambered out of the drenched pit and retreated to join in formation with the rest of the Batana army.

Noticing the retreating Batana army, Nare urged his men to attack. The Soru soldiers marched around the fallen Batana warriors.

"We must not rely solely on our might, for we are not mere brutes. No, we must be wise about this and use our enchantments to gain the upper hand," Lefefe said to Nonyane, who had rejoined the rest of the army alongside King Gauta.

With a wave of their staves and the recitation of a spell, Nonyane watched as the Batana mages caused the ground beneath the Soru soldiers to quake and crumble.

As the Soru soldiers stumble on their feet, he called out to his archers, "Archers!" A rain of arrows then fell on the Soru army.

Nonyana let slip a smile. "That shall give them pause," he remarked, looking at King Gauta.

"Aye," agreed Lefefe.

Meanwhile, King Tlou's face darkened as he realised the tide of battle had turned against his forces. They had sorely underestimated the potency of the Batana mages' magic.

"Order the archers to release arrows on my command," he barked to his guards. "We must stem the advance of the Batana army."

"Advance!" Nare roared to his troops.

The surviving soldiers surged forward to engage the Batana front line, who were standing behind their shields, with their spears ready.

Steel clashed against steel, spears pierced flesh, and the air was rent with the anguished screams of dying men.

Observing the fracas from a nearby hill, Palesa, Perega, and Legomo stood flanked by a hundred fully armed men.

Palesa wore a platinum crown and a suit of armour fashioned from black and purple plate, reinforced to safeguard her burgeoning belly.

"The battlefields are not kind to womenfolk, especially those ready to bring forth life into this world," Perega said, observing Palesa's face at the wailing of the men.

"Yet, he- here you stand, Perega," Legomo retorted. He held a deep mistrust of Perega and found his presence suspect.

Palesa emitted a sarcastic chuckle, acknowledging Perega's concern. "Perhaps you should join the brave men down on the battlefield," she replied.

"Princess, I am many things, but a warrior I am not," Perega responded.

"I- I must remind you once more that she is no mere princess, bu- but your queen, and you shall address her accordingly," Legomo interjected with his slight stutter.

Palesa remained silent, but her stillness conveyed her displeasure to Perega.

"M- my queen, our men are making great strides. Sho- should we break through their th- three lines of defence, we- we shall surely triumph," Legomo said.

Palesa felt exceedingly uncomfortable in her battle garb, and the contractions were causing her considerable discomfort.

Nonetheless, she could not allow the men to perceive her weakness.

They had all risked their lives for her, for her unborn son, for her kingdom's sovereignty. She must display strength and exhibit no fear. If she was to govern until her son reached maturity, these men must both respect and fear her.

As the battle raged on, she watched with a heavy heart. She knew that many lives would be lost, and that the tales of this war would be sung for years to come.

Suddenly, a loud noise caught her attention. It was the horn from the Batana army getting information for another attack.

"Can you set your eyes upon my father?" she enquired.

"Your Highness, your father stands behind the line of mages, where he is guarded with utmost care. He will be safe," Perega replied.

Palesa grew increasingly irate with Perega's response. "How many battles have you fought, Perega?" she asked.

"In truth, the past years have been peaceful, and I have scant experience in war," Perega confessed.

"Then how can you assure me that my father is well protected and will be safe?" she retorted. "Men do not march to war seeking protection. No, they know the risk of losing their lives, yet they come to fight for their cause nonetheless. If you are not prepared to die, perhaps you should have remained in Batana, with the womenfolk," she added, her tone sharp.

But before the exchange could escalate further, Legomo interjected, "Yo- Your Highness, let us not bi- bicker amongst ourselves. The battle is still un- underway, and we must stay vi- vigilant."

Palesa nodded, taking a deep breath to calm her frayed nerves. "You are right, Uncle. Let us focus on the task at hand."

Meanwhile, in the Soru camp, King Tlou stood atop a hill near the main entrance to Thaba Ntsu, with Leko, Sedi, Gasane, and fifty well-armed guards scattered in the hills around him. If the battle were to turn against them, King Tlou could retreat to Soru, and the narrow road would be blocked with boulders.

"I can see King Gauta from here on his golden horse. If we take him out, the entire army fall to its knees," said Leko, the half-sister of King Tlou.

Suddenly, Lehlo arrived, out of breath and covered in mud and blood. "Your Highness, our men are struggling to keep the Batana army at bay. They're advancing as we speak," he said, worry etched on his face.

King Tlou frowned. "Send a message to our archers to prepare to defend our position. We cannot let the Batana army advance any further."

Lehlo interjected, "Your Highness, we must change our strategy. Our arrows are no match for the dark mages, and thus we must face them with all our might on the field of battle."

Just then, a loud horn blared through the air, signalling another Batana army attack.

"Lehlo, tell Nare we need to break through Batana second line of defence and separate Gauta from his mages," declared King Tlou.

"Your Highness, your strength as a warrior is well known, and I am certain that fighting alongside your men would boost their morale. Would you consider joining the battle at some point?" Sedi suggested, choosing her words carefully.

Although the king was proud, he did not want to risk his own life. After all, if he falls, all his men fall. He knew Sedi was playing mind games with him, but he refused to be caught in her bluff. "Indeed, I will fight with my men," he replied.

Sedi then offered to prepare the king's horse, but before he could respond,

Leko cautioned against such a course of action, advising that their best strategy lay in fortifying their defences and remaining within the safety of the mountains.

However, the king was resolute in his decision, declaring, "Let history remember me as the king who fearlessly led Soru to victory by confronting our enemy on the battlefield. I shall not be remembered as the boy who cowered behind these mountains."

"Your Highness," Sedi interjected, "everyone here knows you are a fierce warrior. However, please reconsider calling back our men to the mountains. We lack the necessary number of mages to counter their magic, and we do not have enough men to mount an effective attack, unless Shaza has sent us reinforcements in this very moment."

The king's wrath was kindled by Sedi's opposition to his will. "Guard, take note," he thundered, "should Sedi dare to question my judgement again, give me her tongue."

The guard, a young man named Pulana, son of Pulakgulu, a trusted friend of the late King Shadu, received the order with a nod.

Sedi, realising her mistake, quickly sought to appease the king, offering her apologies for any offence she may have caused.

Mounted upon his horse, King Tlou radiated regal authority. He was garbed in the aqua-blue colours of Soru, with the emblem of his noble house prominently displayed, as he rode his horse to join his fighting men.

At a signal from the king, Nare cried out, "sons of Soru! ready on my command!" and with pride, watched as King Tlou led the charge down Molotli hills.

"First line, attack!" Nare shouted. The Soru warriors charged into the fray, colliding with the Batana front lines in a thunderous clash.

The once-serene river now turned a crimson hue as the battle raged on, transforming the once-green grass into a bleak black as the fallen warriors lay strewn across it. The moonlight behind the clouds cast an eerie red glow upon the battlefield, amplifying the intensity of the conflict between the two sides.

The battlefield was intense. Soru men fought with all their might until only aqua-blue colours, which were now stained in blood, were left standing, and the tired solders started shouting, "Tlou, Tlou, Tlou!"

King Tlou looked back towards Molotli Mountains, making sure that Sedi saw this spectacle.

What the Soru men did not know was that the Batana men they killed spilled some potions on the field, which gave the mages control over that land.

As the Soru men were celebrating their small victory, suddenly some of them began to bleed from their noses while others choked on their vomit.

Those who were not afflicted began to panic as some of their comrades started hallucinating and attacking one another.

It was a scene of chaos and destruction that left no man standing on the battlefield. The Batana mages' dark magic proved too strong for Soru.

King Tlou, surrounded by his army, retreated to the base of Thaba Ntsu, with his pride wounded by the short-lived victory. He was close enough to retreat into the hills, but also still within the battle grounds. The Batana army advanced forward, as they moved past the dead men.

"Hold your ground, men!" shouted Nare, who was still in the thick of the battlefield.

"Nare, I thought we are attacking?" shouted King Tlou, confused by Nare's tactic.

"My king, if we attack now, we are sending our men to be slaughtered. The dark magic they are channelling only works in places where their army has set foot," said Gasane, who was now on the battlefield with Nare and Tlou.

"What we need to do now is to make sure they do not advance any further," Nare responded.

Gasane was trying to use his own spells to counter the Batana mages. But powerful as he was, he was outnumbered.

"Sons of Soru, take your defence position!" Nare shouted.

The king did not like this strategy; he did not want Sedi to be right.

"Hold your ground!" Nare shouted again.

As the Batana army advanced, Nare shouted, "Archers now!"

The archers drew their arrows and shot at the Batana army.

The mages stepped forward and said their enchantments, which burnt up the arrows mid-air.

However, unbeknownst to the Batana mages, the arrows shot towards the mages were decoys, Soru archers had shot four arrows towards the back, sides, and front of the Batana mages and the two front lines.

These flaming arrows ignited the ground beneath them, which was coated with *Sefura*.

Within seconds, the field was engulfed in flames, and the sounds of men screaming in agony filled the air. *Sefura* was a very flammable oil, which burned until the object was consumed. This oil could only be made by mages who had studied the highest magic and specialised in rare potions, with the main ingredient only found on the eastern continent of Macara.

The Batana mages attempted to put out the fire, but their efforts were in vain. As they struggled, Nare signalled for the archers again, who launched a second wave of arrows, this time thrice as many as before. The Batana army was overwhelmed, and despite their best efforts, they couldn't defend themselves against the onslaught. The attack proved devastating for the Batana army, resulting in the loss of one-third of their troops, including six of their nine mages. The battlefield covered in *sefura* turned from the once-verdant field to ashes. A hush fell over the battlefield.

Princess Palesa, who was watching from a distance, could not stomach what she was witnessing. She started to throw up.

"My queen, the men have seen your bravery, however, I think we should retreat to your tent and regroup," Perega suggested.

"I will not leave my people. These men are dying because of me."

"M-My queen, I-I have to agree with Perega on this one. We are t-too close to the battlefield. Yo- you are the be- beacon of hope for these men. I- if you fall, this war i-is over," added Legomo.

Watching the clamorous battlefield and witnessing the cries of the wounded, Legomo's anxiety deepened with each passing moment as he realised that the tide of war has turned against them. His stutter, already a constant companion, worsened under the weight of his apprehension.

Palesa was hesitant, but she heeded the advice of her counsellors and retreated to their camp.

"Retreat, retreat!" Shouted Nonyana, who was wounded from the arrows.

"Men, attack," commanded King Tlou, seeing that the Batana men were retreating.

"No, my king, their enchantments are over the ground," cautioned Gasane.

"I want my glory. Archers," he declared, his voice booming across the battlefield. Soon after, a tempest of fire arrows rained down upon the fray.

"Your Highness, our own men are still out there. We risk injuring our own men with this tactic," Gasane cautioned.

"Perhaps you should join them then," retorted King Tlou, who had retreated to the safety of the mountain with Gasane. Sedi wished to speak out yet knew it best to hold her tongue.

"Ha!" exclaimed King Tlou, his grin spreading from ear to ear. "Victory is mine!"

Just as the Batana army, having suffered heavy losses, began to pull back, the sound of a horn echoed through the air, and the ground shook with the thundering of horses' hooves against the dark that was making way to the sunrise.

"Now we have them surrounded, for Shaza has sent aid," the king crowed triumphantly.

"Your Highness," Gasane, ever watchful, said urgently, "look closely at the emblem they bear. It is not Shaza's, but rather the rain and lightning of the Baloki Kingdom."

The Baloki army, a force of five thousand strong, stood resolute in their formation.

"Your Highness, I ask of you, listen unto my words. We cannot emerge victorious in this battle," Sedi cautioned, her voice filled with concern. "Please withhold our men from confronting the Rain Queen. We will not win against them on the battlefield," she continued, her tone weighted with apprehension.

"But we have the numbers," King Tlou, said proudly.

"My king, I have to agree with Sedi; our men have fought all night long. It is almost dawn. They are tired," Leko interjected.

"Aye, I also agree, Your Highness," Gasane echoed.

King Tlou pondered for a moment. "What course of action do you propose, then?" he thundered, his anger brewing like a tempest.

"Summon our men to retreat. Our strength lies concealed beyond the protective embrace of the mountains," Sedi advised, her voice imbued with the wisdom of strategy.

"And what of my glory?" the king retorted, his thirst for renown unabated.

"Your glory shall fade like a wisp of smoke, for when the Baloki unleash their fury, our men shall perish. Underestimate not the Baloki army," Sedi asserted, her words laced with conviction.

"Beloved king, should we withdraw. The Baloki army shall lay siege upon us, and history shall forever brand you as the king who turned his back," Nare interjected, his body adorned with wounds and smeared with the blood spilled in the battlefield.

The king cast a disdainful gaze upon Sedi, his dissatisfaction palpable. Then, he shifted his attention to Pulana. "Pulana, I told you that if Sedi spoke again, sever her tongue."

Pulana nodded to his king's command. "Guards, apprehend her," he ordered the guards that were surrounding Sedi.

Seeing the blaze within King Tlou's eyes, fully aware that his threat was no mere idleness, Sedi lunged forward with all her might. "Your Highness, I have served your father in many battles. I was loyal to him. By listening to my words, he lived as long as he did.

If you remove my tongue, you shall not taste victory in this war. Keep me in your service, and I pledge you victory by noonday, without the further spilling of our men's blood."

King Tlou raised his hand, commanding the guards to halt their advance. "My father is dead; maybe he should not have listened to your counsel. Please tell me, how do you propose to accomplish such a feat?" the king enquired.

"My king, the fields of battle are not fit for women," Nare asserted.

"Yet, the army that send shivers down your spine is composed of valiant women, yea, led by a girl no older than your daughter," Sedi countered, drawing near to the king, who seemed disconcerted. She whispered a something in his ear, whereupon his face changed. His ire gave way to curiosity. With a nod of assent to Sedi, she returned the gesture.

"Nare, tell our men to retreat. Seal the gates," the king commanded.

"But Your Highness …" Nare hesitated.

"If you dare challenge my command, it will be *your* tongue Pulana shall deliver unto me," the king sternly warned.

"Men, retreat!" Nare bellowed reluctantly.

The men heeded the call and withdrew to the mountain, while the treacherous path was blocked with mighty boulders.

"I have heard murmurs of men falling at the mere sight of the Baloki army, but to witness it firsthand, it is beyond belief," said Nonyana, addressing King Gauta.

"By the heavens, I abhor their presence, yet we find ourselves in dire need of their aid," King Gauta replied with frustration.

With regal grace, the king dismounted his horse to approach Princess Seroka, the commander of the Baloki army. As he prepared to tread forth, a messenger hastened towards him, whispering urgent news into his ear. The king's countenance displayed surprise.

"Are you certain?" the king asked the messenger.

"Aye," he nodded.

"Nonyane, make haste and greet the Rain Princess," were his final words before remounting his horse and vanishing towards the encampment, trailed by a host of his loyal men.

"We journeyed far and wide to offer our assistance, yet he could not deign to extend us a proper greeting," Seroka grumbled, her displeasure evident.

As the Baloki army loomed menacingly, their faces fierce, Princess Seroka mounted her dark stallion and rode to meet with Nonyane.

Meanwhile, Palesa and Perega and had retreated back to her tent.

"My queen, may I suggest you take off your armour so that you can get some relief," Perega suggested, seeing how uncomfortable Palesa was with her armour.

Palesa's handmaids came to her aid and helped her remove the heavy steel armour, leaving only her undergarments of purple and black. She felt a great sense of relief taking off her armour.

As Palesa washed her hands, her father entered the tent, covered in blood, with the smell on war around him.

"My daughter, I heard that you call for me with urgency," he said, putting down his shield next to the entrance.

"No, Father, I did not call for you. Who has spread such falsehoods?" Palesa replied.

"One of your guards came for me. What is the meaning of this?" the king demanded.

"I sent no messenger. Mosese, can you please ask my guards to come inside and explain," Palesa instructed her handmaid.

"The war is over, Your Highness," Perega said, as he limped toward Palesa.

The king and Palesa were confused by Perega's words.

"I long to return home," Perega added, his face heavy with sorrow.

Palesa was perplexed by Perega's words and sought to understand what he meant.

Two of the guards, who had been stationed outside Palesa's tent, entered as instructed by Palesa's handmaid.

"You are new. I have not seen your face afore" Palesa said with curiosity on her face, pointing a finger toward the guards.

The guards looked down in an attempt to conceal their faces, but their efforts proved futile. "Your face does seem familiar," she continued, drawing closer to them.

"Palesa, stop," Perega interjected, seizing her hand with a forceful grip.

"Perega, what manner of conduct is this?" Palesa enquired, suspicion etched upon her face.

"Someone tell me as to the nature of this affair," King Gauta, who remained deeply perplexed, interjected. He had stood near the door, in front of the guards.

"You are one of Tlou's men," Palesa recollected, her memory stirring.

"The name be Bonolo, and Prince Tlou sends his regards," the guard declared.

"Tlou's men! We have a trai–" King Gauta began to speak. As the king was about to turn and reach for his sword, a sudden and icy pain pierced through his back. "Palesa, run," he whispered before collapsing.

Palesa caught a fleeting glimpse of the gleaming blade's menacing tip before chaos erupted in the tent. One of her handmaidens attempted to escape the tent, only to be seized by the second guard, who swiftly slit her throat. Palesa stood frozen, her eyes fixated upon her beloved father's lifeless form. Tears streamed down her face as the realisation of what was happening dawned upon her.

"Why, Perega?" Palesa wailed, her voice laden with betrayal.

Clutching her belly, she approached Perega. "Wherefore, whatever price have they paid you, I shall double it. Let me leave. I do solemnly swear, by the mountain gods, I shall stop this war and return to Batana," she pleaded. "I will never set foot in Soru, I swear it," she continued. The heavy breathing of Mosese resonated from a distant corner of the tent.

"I did advise you against placing trust in me, Princess," Perega retorted, his face devoid of warmth or feeling. He drew his sharp dagger, and with measured pace, Perega advanced, swift as a striking serpent. The edge of the blade met Palesa's throat, and in the blink of an eye, she fell to the ground lifeless. Blood gushed from Palesa's neck, accompanied by the anguished cries of Mosese in the corner and the tumultuous cacophony of chaos that resounded from outside the tent's confines.

With a heavy heart and tear-stained eyes, Perega took hold of Palesa's hand and gently kissed it, his voice quivering with sorrow. "Forgive me, Princess," he whispered softly, the weight of regret heavy upon his soul as he knelt beside her lifeless body.

Appendix

Kingdoms And People of Ashari

Baloki Kingdom:
Gold and white; Lighting and clouds sigil

King Pula: The founding father of the Rain Queen line.

Prince Pulana: The first-born son of King Pula and the heir of the Baloki Kingdom. According to folklore legends, King Pula sacrificed him to the rain gods.

Queen Motapo I: The first Rain Queen of the Baloki Kingdom. Daughter of King Pula and Queen Mmapula. She died prematurely without an heir, and her sister became her successor.

Queen Motakia I: The second Rain Queen of the Baloki Kingdom. Second-born daughter of King Pula and his second wife, Queen Karabo.

Queen Motakia II: The third Rain Queen, who was murdered by her uncle, Prince Tlou.

Queen Motapo II: The fourth Rain Queen, who married her uncle and ascended the throne after the murder of her sister.

Queen Motapo III: The Rain Queen who ruled briefly but committed ritual suicide so that her twin sister could become the next queen.

Queen Motakia III: The Rain Queen who assumed the throne after the passing of her twin sister.

Queen Motapo IV: The daughter of Queen Motapo III, also known as the Queen of Peace. During her reign, there was peace in the kingdom. She is also the mother of Prince Noka the Ruler.

Prince Thupa: The youngest brother of Queen Motapo IV; father of Princess Thato and Princess Kgolo.

Prince Noka the Ruler: The only male heir to inherit the Baloki Throne, but he ruled only as a custodian.

Princess Thato: The oldest daughter of Prince Thupa and the first wife of Prince Noka the Ruler.

Princess Kgolo: The youngest daughter of Prince Thupa, the second wife of Prince Noka the Ruler, and the mother of Queen Motakia IV.

Queen Motakia IV: The first-born daughter of Prince Noka the Ruler and Princess Kgolo. The youngest Rain Queen in history.

Queen Motapo VII: The mother of the current Rain Queen.

Prince Mifako: The father of Queen Motakia VIII.

Queen Motakia VIII: Sister of Queen Motapo VIII and mother of Neo.

Queen Motapo VIII: The current reigning queen, previously named Princess Letsoba. She ascended the throne after her sister's death.

Prince Moroka: The great Baloki mage and father of Queen Motapo VIII's children.

Heir Princess Motakia IX: Seventeen summers old at the beginning of the book, the first-born daughter of Queen Motapo VIII and Prince Moroka.

Princess Seroka: Fifteen summers old at the beginning of the book, the second-born daughter of Queen Motapo VIII and Prince Moroka, nicknamed 'Flower Thorn'.

Prince Thebo: Third-born and only son of Queen Motapo VIII and Prince Moroka, training to be a mage. Thirteen summers old at the beginning of the book.

Princess Mapula: The youngest daughter of Queen Motapo VIII and Prince Moroka, twelve summers old at the beginning of the book.

Neo: The son of Queen Motakia VIII and the nephew of Queen Motapo VIII. Eighteen summers old at the beginning of the book.

Black Mamba: Queen Motapo VIII's most trusted advisor, presumably born in the Gauta Islands.

Kwena: Younger brother of Prince Moroka and Queen Karabo (King Shadu's late wife). Serves on the royal council-trade.

Morena Tlou: Oldest son of Morena Tladi, from the Lefa Clan, and sits on Queen Motapo VII's council.

Morena Tladi: Father of Morena Tlou, head of the Lefa Clan, and the richest man in Baloki.

Morena Seriti: A youth of nineteen summers, from the Metsi Clan, currently sits on the queen's advisory council.

Morena Sehlare: Father of Morena Seriti, presumed dead after being lost at sea. He was an advisor to Queen Motapo VIII and Queen Motakia XIII.

Morena Hlogo: Member of the council who oversees the royal finances.

Tlounyana: Eldest son of Morena Tlou, currently serving in the royal guard.

Kobo: Neo's secret friend and former advisor to Queen Motakia VIII, who was exiled from Baloki.

Mohale: Groom who was part of the Baloki entourage to Soru.

Sefefe: One of the royal guards in the entourage that travelled to Soru with Prince Moroka.

Folo: Head of the royal stables.

Selo: Baloki High Priest.

Leboa: The lady in charge of the noble ladies' training school.

Soru Kingdom:
Aqua blue; Mountain sigil

King Thabang: King Shadu's father.

King Shadu: The King of the Soru Kingdom and a very close companion of Morena Moroka.

Queen Karabo: The late sister of Morena Moroka and the first wife of King Shadu, who died during childbirth.

Prince Thubo: The first-born son of King Shadu and Queen Karabo. He was heir to the Soru Kingdom before his untimely death.

Princess/Queen Palesa: The daughter of King Gauta of the Batana Kingdom. The widow of Prince Thubo, fighting for the Soru throne.

Prince/King Tlou: The second-born son of King Shadu and Queen Karabo. He is seventeen summers old at the beginning of the book and served as the commander of the Soru army.

Princess Puo: King Shadu and Queen Karabo's oldest daughter.

Princess Lebo: King Shadu and Queen Karabo's youngest daughter.

Prince Maru: The youngest son of King Shadu and Queen Karabo, third in line to the throne. He is thirteen summers old at the beginning of the book.

Lera: The daughter of King Shadu and Leshoba.

Leshoba: Lera's mother, a commoner from the Gauta Islands. The second wife of King Shadu.

Leko: The daughter of King Shadu and Princess Funi. Leko later sits on King Tlou's council.

Princess Funi: The third wife of King Shadu from the Veka Tribe, and Leko's mother.

Khutso: The son of King Shadu and Princess Funi. Later appointed as King Tlou's cup bearer.

Kara: King Shadu's royal guard, who poisoned the king's wine at Prince Thubo's funeral.

Sedi: King Shadu's right-hand woman and later King Tlou's advisor.

Perega: Sits on King Shadu's council, in charge of money. Later served as Queen Palesa's right-hand man.

Gasane: The great Soru royal mage, who sits on the council.

Masega: The high priestess of the Soru Kingdom.

Nare: Second in command of the Soru army, sits on the council.

Pelo: King Tlou's guard.

Pulana: King Tlou's guard.

Pulakgulu: Pulana's father, who sat on King Shadu's council before his mysterious disappearance.

Lehlo: King Shadu and King Tlou's guard.

Bonolo: King Shadu and King Tlou's guard.

Peno: The musician who had his tongue removed by Prince Tlou.

Naka: The squire of Prince Thubo.

Bohlale: Prince Thubo's cup bearer.

Lukobo: Prince Thubo's groom.

Murule: Prince Thubo's spearman.

Batana Kingdom:
Purple and black; Raven sigil

King Gauta: Princess Palesa's father and king of the Batana Kingdom.

Prince Futhuma: The younger brother of King Gauta and heir to the Batana Kingdom.

Kolobe: Sits on the royal council.

Kolojwana: Kolobe's great-grandfather, a former farmer turned platinum miner. The second richest man in Ashari.

Lefefe: Batana royal mage, who also sits on the king's council.

Fika: Lefefe's apprentice.

Legomo: Hand of the King, with a stutter in his speech. Princess Palesa's uncle through her mother.

Morena Matsebe: Legomo's father.

Nonyane: Commander of the Batana army and loyalist of Prince/King Tlou.

Mosese: Princess Palesa's handmaid.

Veka Kingdom:
Red, blue, and silver; Ngoma ngoma drum sigil

King Masha: The first Veka king.

King Mikado: The current king of Veka Kingdom.

Prince Rendu: King Mikado oldest son, eighteen summers old.

Queen Naki: Prince Rendu's mother, married to King Mikado.

Musha: King Mikado advisor.

Thileli: King Mikado's righthand-man.

Mulafa: King Mikado's advisor who is colluding with Morena Seriti and Kubo to put Neo on the Baloki Throne.

Manaka: Mulafa's sister, who own a brothel.

Duvha: The harlot who works for Manaka.

Mulemba: The voice that called unto Neo.

Zuka Kingdom:
Brown, white, and black; Lion sigil

King Shaza I: First king of Ashari.

King Sholozi: Second King of Ashari.

King Shaza II: Current king of Zuka.

Swarai Kingdom:
Red and black; Spear sigil

King Moshwana: The first King of Swarai.

King Swalazi VI: Current king of Swarai.

Queen Bile: Fourteen winters old youngest sister of King Shaza, married to King Swalazi.

Ntombe: King Swalazi advisor.

Kazi: King Swalazi advisor and an ally to Baloki.

Legatlo: Prison guard in charge of the prison where Prince Moroka, Princess Mapula and Kwena are being held captive.

Terego: Swarai veteran royal guard.

*"So let your light shine before men, that they may see your good works, and glorify your Father who is in the heavens."

―――

*Matthew 5:16 From the Codex Sinaiticus English translation

Milton Keynes UK
Ingram Content Group UK Ltd.
UKHW011831210624
444498UK00001B/32

9 781738 551903